THE FRIENDSHIP

Connie Palmen

THE FRIENDSHIP

Translated from the Dutch by
Ina Rilke

HARVILL PRESS
LONDON

First published in the Netherlands by Prometheus, Amsterdam
with the title *De Vriendschap*, in 1995

First published in Great Britain in 2000
by The Harvill Press
2 Aztec Row
Berners Road
London N1 0PW

3 5 7 9 8 6 4 2

www.harvill.com

The hymn quoted on page 86 by W. J. Sparrow-Simpson, is taken from
The New English Hymnal, with acknowledgements to the publishers, Novello & Co.

Connie Palmen asserts the moral right to be
identified as the author of this work

A CIP catalogue record for this book
is available from the British Library

This translation is published with the financial assistance of the
Foundation for the Production and Translation of Dutch Literature

ISBN 1 86046 560 9

Designed and typeset in Sabon at
Libanus Press, Marlborough, Wiltshire

Printed and bound in Great Britain by Butler & Tanner Ltd
at Selwood Printing, Burgess Hill

Soup on the stove
is
like
a good friend at home
extra good soup
is
like a new family

ISCHA MEIJER
1943 – 1995

I

THINGS AND WORDS

I

THE SCHOOL YARD WAS BOUNDED BY A LOW BRICK
wall, and she stood leaning against it. It was an exceptionally
warm spring, a few weeks before the end of the summer term
of 1966, and we were frisky and excited by the good weather
and the prospect of the holidays. At a quarter to eleven one of
the girls in group six rang the bell for break, and when I ran
outside I saw her. She was wearing a black woollen winter coat
which came down to her ankles. The temperature was rising
twenty degrees Celsius.

She stood there in a way I had never seen anyone stand, with
an air of regal nonchalance: brash, proud, devil-may-care. The
playground was almost empty and she reigned over this emptiness. I stopped short because I wanted to look at her and also
because it suddenly struck me as childish to go and play games
with my classmates.

Actually, the low wall's where the soppy girls hang out. There are
always a few from groups five and six, and in our group Josien
Driessen's one of them.

No one would take it into their head to pick her to make up
a team for a game of touch ball, for example. With her on your
side you're bound to lose as she's got two left feet. She can't run
and she can't throw a decent ball, let alone a hard one. Sometimes

during Games you can't get out of taking her whether you want to or not, because if she's the last one left she'll automatically join the team with the last choice. So there's always a fifty per cent chance of being stuck with Josien, except when it's Margriet Suren's turn to pick a team, because then there's no way you won't be stuck with her. Margriet's aspiring to sainthood if you ask me, because she usually picks Josien right off, the thing is she's a complete drip, because if you aren't interested in winning there's no point playing the game, and anyway why go out of your way to pick a spoilsport?

Josien's one of the girls who always stand by the wall during break. No one else from our class stands there, except Diny van Helden, but she hangs around there with two girls from group five. She had to repeat last year, that's when she was put in with us, and she doesn't really belong yet. It's her own fault. She acts like we're all twenty years younger than her, she's always putting on airs. Her friends from group five, they all act so grown-up and snooty. The other day one of them was wearing nylon stockings instead of woolly tights like the rest of us. She looked the pits, besides I reckon this is what my mother means when she calls things tarty – a kid wearing nylons. Still, I do think it's a shame Mies Luyten's been so chummy with Diny lately, because Diny really is beneath her. Mies is very shy and I think it must be because she's so tall, it's not natural. I never know what to say to her, but she often lifts me up in the air and there's nothing I like more than being lifted up in the air. I myself am the shortest in my group, not that I mind being the shortest – it means the bigger girls can easily pick you up and swing you around and practically everyone at school is taller than me, so there's plenty of opportunity. Not everyone likes being jumped on, but Mies doesn't mind, ever. Not even when I take her by surprise and jump onto her back, or make a sudden dash for her from the front so she has no choice but to catch me when I leap up against her. It makes her laugh.

Mies truly is a nice person, I really mean it.

While I was eyeing her up and down from afar it occurred to me that the new girl didn't really belong by the brick wall, but that by posting herself there she had claimed that space as her own and had changed its meaning for good and all. So there was something languid about her stance, but it had nothing to do with the general soppiness of the wallflowers. What was no more than pretend-grown-upness in the others, all put on, was genuine with her.

She was already a woman and she had never been anything else, she'd been born a grown woman.

What she tried to hide under her long winter coat was in fact only emphasized: an enormous body, two metres round the middle, probably. From the smooth, almost sculptural fullness of this body rose a head atop a long slender neck circled by an upturned collar. Her face was long and angular, and crowned by a shiny jet-black bob with a bit of a wave to it.

She has the prettiest face I have ever seen.

She was sure to be in group six, to my reckoning, but if that was where she belonged what was she doing here? The school year was almost over and the group six girls were busy doing their entrance exams to secondary schools. In those days our village was expanding steadily with new housing estates, so there was nothing unusual about meeting strangers and children from families you hadn't known all your life. But the timing of her arrival was odd and hard to explain. With mounting excitement I imagined her being insolent and provocative, the sort of girl no one got on with, which would've been why she was sent packing from her previous schools. She'd be getting a last chance to mend her ways at our school, so she could prepare herself for her entrance exams.

I imagined all sorts of things, except that she might be in a lower group than the sixth and would be staying around for a while. She'd never had a best friend, I imagined, and I was overcome by a deep sense of regret, because she was so much older than me and so remote and because I'd seen her now and yet she'd disappear from my life so soon.

I decided not to get attached to her, although I didn't know quite how to go about this. But I was aware that this was exactly the kind of situation my mother had warned me about and that I'd better take her advice because I was in danger of making the same mistake all over again.

She had explained it to me after what happened with our Morris. One Wednesday afternoon, about a year before I first saw the new girl, my father turned up at home. As this was very unusual, I asked him what he was doing there. He explained that a new car would be delivered later that afternoon, a nice new Fiat.

"What about the old car?" I asked.

Trying hard to sound casual he said the old one was to be traded in and that the men from the garage would be coming for it later. I was shattered. I couldn't help noticing that my father was upset too, but that he should be capable of such craven infidelity to our Morris – that was the limit.

"Will it be gone for ever?" I asked, although I knew it would be.

"Yes," he said. "Sad, isn't it?" he offered, but I was already rushing out of the house. In the kitchen I ran past my mother, who put on her let's-be-sensible voice for my benefit, but I knew perfectly well this wasn't something she was going to sympathize with me about.

"It's a complete wreck you know," I heard her say. The fact is, nothing's sacred to my mother.

It was our first car, a grey-green Morris. It stood parked in front of the house. I opened the door and slid inside. Because I didn't know how to do it, how to say goodbye to a car, I kissed everything: grey leatherette upholstery, dashboard, steering wheel, gear lever.

"Thank you," I said. Thank you, thank you, thank you.

The back seat had been my brothers' and my domain and that was where I lay down full-length, so as to be close to the Morris and so it wouldn't be all lonely in these final hours. First I cried a bit, because I was bewildered and because the idea that something of value, something that had served you so well, could be got rid of, dumped, given up without so much as a by-your-leave, was too horrible to face. I had never experienced anything like this, and didn't know such things could happen in life. I thought I'd never be able to forgive my father and with that thought my misery only increased.

I fell asleep and don't know how long I lay in the car. Someone wrenched a door open and shouted. Waking up was horrible, because the next instant I remembered what was about to happen. In the distance I heard my mother, relieved and grumbling about having searched all over.

I wasn't at all the kind of child to hide away. On the contrary. By that age I was as clever at inventing ways of not being the kind of child to make people worry over as I was at acquiring pins for my collection; but this time I took it for granted that everybody would know I'd be in the Morris.

"Come along now," my father said quietly, reaching in to help me out. He grinned apologetically at the two strange men beside him, jangling their keys in a show of mild impatience.

Once outside the car a violent, uncontrollable shiver passed through my body. My father laid his hand on my forehead and glanced at my mother.

"You'd better take her inside," he said. "I think she's running a temperature."

The next day I didn't go to school. The thermometer read thirty-eight point five.

My mother was fed up. This was the second time already, she said in a low voice to my father that night in the kitchen. I was lying under a blanket on the sofa in the living room, but I could hear what they were saying.

"It's not normal," my mother says, "she needs to see the doctor." What my father says I can't quite make out, he's mumbling something soothing, no doubt. That I'll be fine.

"The same thing happened with that silly bird," I can hear my mother say.

My mother says things like "that silly bird" because she doesn't like animals, nor birds either, although they're not the same as ordinary pets in my opinion. Birds are less of a bother. They're very self-sufficient and all they need is some water and birdseed and they can live in cages, which is rather special, because any other animal in a cage looks out of place while most birds look all right in cages. My father likes birds. We have two canaries and they always start singing when he gets home from work. They know him.

I can see what she's getting at. It's the jackdaw my father brought home a few months ago. One of his workmates had got it from someone else to look after, but he'd had to get rid of it because it brought on an allergy. The jackdaw's name was Manus, and it was tame. They'd done something to its wings, so that although it could still flutter about a bit it could never fly up and away. My father had said that he had a little girl who'd be delighted with it and he had taken it home for me. That was unusual, a present just for me.

In our family everyone's treated the same.

No one gets singled out.

If one of us got a jackdaw, the others would have to have one too: it was an unwritten rule, but in this case it didn't apply. There was only one bird, and Manus was mine.

You can't share animals. They only recognize one person as their proper master.

In the garage my father built a makeshift open cage, in which he placed a dish of water and some of the canary's birdseed. He told me I was to feed the jackdaw, as that was the only way to get an animal to know who its master was. So as not to disappoint him I didn't let on that I was a bit scared as I wasn't used to handling animals and the jackdaw kept opening its beak wide, according to my father because it was hungry and maybe because it was scared too, but I thought it wanted to peck me so I snatched my hand away whenever it snapped its beak.

Before breakfast next morning I ran to the garage. It smelled of bird, which wasn't very nice. At first I couldn't find it anywhere, but when my eyes got used to the gloom I discovered it huddled in a corner, looking dazed. The birdseed hadn't been touched. There was no reaction to my whistling. I crouched down and took a good look at it. Its head hung on its breast and I could see that it was breathing heavily: the breast heaved up and down.

"If you don't eat, you'll die," I said. I remembered seeing a nature film in which people fed sick birds baby food, bits of bread soaked in milk, at least that's what it looked like. So I decided to try that too.

"Manus won't eat," I told my mother, and asked if I could have some bread and milk to feed my bird. She said fine. Carrying a saucer filled with neat little squares of sodden bread I returned to the garage, stuck a cube of bread on the end of a twig and held it out to Manus.

"Eat," I said.

The bird didn't react. I pressed the bread against its beak but the stuff just dangled there, looking messy and untidy: a very sorry sight. As it hadn't moved until then I dared to reach out my hand and touch it; I stroked its head with the tip of my forefinger.

It didn't protest, and that made me love it even more. It was a beautiful bird and from now on it would be my constant companion. Perched on my shoulder I'd take it wherever I went and even if it fluttered off a short distance away it would never go far. Flapping overhead it'd keep a close watch over me. Being a jackdaw it could easily talk with other birds and explain to them that it was mine. From now on all the other birds wanted to be with me too, but for me there could only be the first bird and the first was Manus, and they accepted that. But they did agree among themselves that every one of them would protect me wherever I was in the world, because I was the bird-woman and I understood their language. Sometimes whole flocks of them circled around my head, they all recognized me and followed me from the sky. Even in the playground. When I sat in class staring out of the window the low wall would be full of birds, all waiting until it was time to go home so they could follow me there. All the children knew they were my birds and they also realized that they were the reason I didn't need people – I belonged to the birds.

That night, at supper, my father remarked that the jackdaw might not pull through. It was sick. It had been ferried around too much, and birds didn't like that. My mouth went so dry that the food stuck in my throat. It wasn't the bird's fault I knew, because Manus hadn't been with us long enough, it was something else, something that had been there longer and may even have been there always.

"You mustn't go on so," said my mother.

The next morning she told me the jackdaw had died and that my father had buried it in the garden, before going off to work. So as to spare me the sad spectacle.

"And now get on with your breakfast," she said. "We're not going starve just because of a silly bird. There are worse things between heaven and earth. Save your tears for later, when you'll have more reason to shed them."

I couldn't swallow a mouthful.

"That's what you get with animals in the house," my mother said plaintively, and made me a cup of hot chocolate so I wouldn't go to school on an empty stomach.

"You can't do your lessons on an empty stomach," she concluded.

It was the morning after they came to collect the Morris and I'd been kept in bed that she explained about getting attached to things.

"You shouldn't get so attached," she said.

So what did I do wrong? She said that was why I got so upset when something broke, or got lost, or died.

"It really isn't worth all that grief," she said.

Then what *is* worth it? I asked myself, but I didn't ask her as I could guess. Family, children, your own flesh and blood, plenty of grief there, but at least it was proper grief.

She left me in a state of confusion. The word attachment stuck in my mind and although I understood what the word meant, I was still puzzled because I didn't know what I kept doing wrong. That's what I found so confusing. The enemy was invisible, because it was within. How could you grapple with something if it was inside you? It wasn't at all like not committing a sin, because when you sinned you knew you'd sinned, you always knew, you didn't need anyone to tell you. The Seven Deadly Sins were there on the first page of my exercise book, I'd given it the title Important Things, and I went over them regularly, so that now I knew them by heart and would never forget.

1. Pride
2. Covetousness
3. Lechery
4. Envy
5. Gluttony
6. Anger
7. Sloth

Attachment wasn't among them, but perhaps it belonged to one of the two sins I didn't understand properly, perhaps it had something to do with pride or lechery. The next time my mother came up to my room I'd ask her, I decided, and I did. Whether attachment had anything to do with pride or lechery, I asked when she came upstairs with a glass of orange juice.

"Whatever made you think that?" she asked, distraught, as if she'd got them mixed up herself.

"They're Deadly Sins," I said, and I couldn't understand why she didn't see what I meant right away.

"Oh, don't you worry about Deadly Sins," she said. "You get all het up about that kind of thing, it's not that important you know. It's not a sin to get attached to things, it's just a nuisance, a nuisance for you."

Her remark was more of a disappointment than a reassurance. If it's not all that important why make a fuss?

"I'm hungry," I said.

"Good," she said brightly, "you must be getting better."

She fished a jumper out of the wardrobe and held it out to me. We went downstairs together and she asked me what I'd like to eat.

Nothing pleases her more than being asked to fix you one your favourite dishes, that's what really cheers her up. Although her pleasure seems to evaporate when she's finished preparing the food and puts the plate in front of you and you start eating, but perhaps I'm imagining that part. According to my mother I'm always imagining things.

I was not in the least self-conscious when I was looking her over, because I had no idea I was staring. It wasn't until Karin Weerts came up and asked if I'd play hopscotch that I realized I was still rooted to the spot. I said I didn't feel like it and sauntered off to the wall. It felt like a defeat and a victory at the same time: the wall was the place I always avoided, as I'm neither soppy nor stuck-up. Going over to the wall and leaning against it made me feel embarrassed, but the embarassment was somehow special, as I was doing all this for her and was convinced she knew because she understood me from the moment she first saw me.

As usual Diny and her friends from group five were there. I decided to go up to her this once, as it would bring me closer to the new girl and I could get a better look at her.

"Stupid sums, weren't they?" I said, addressing Diny as I joined her group, and I leaned against the wall in such a way that I could observe the new girl from the corner of my left eye. Diny muttered something in grudging agreement and resumed her conversation with the others without paying any further attention to me. It took a while for me to pluck up enough courage to twist my head round and face the new girl. When I finally did so I looked her straight in the eye. As if she'd been waiting for this, she gave a mocking smile and held my eye commandingly. She didn't move. I blushed, but in spite of the blushing I couldn't turn away. If I had she'd despise me, I thought, and things would never work out between us.

She was testing me and I had to brazen it out. Defying the rush of blood telling me to run away or hide, I stared right back into a pair of wonderfully pale eyes which contrasted oddly with her dark complexion and black hair. We gazed at each other as if we were in a competition and so we were, it was a test. Just before the bell went for the end of break Diny asked if I knew the new girl. To reply to her question would have meant breaking off contact, I'd have to look away and that meant failing the test. She'd see this as losing out, same as I'd have done if she'd glanced away to answer some idiot's question. I turned to Diny and said I didn't know her, that I'd never seen her before. When I looked back to where she'd been standing she'd gone, and I couldn't make her out in the crowd streaming towards the double doors of the school.

Next morning she was standing in the same spot and in the same way, arms folded, one hip thrust forward and one leg lightly crossed in front of the other. She was wearing the same coat. I was relieved to see she was alone, that no one had joined her yet. I didn't dare look into her eyes and ignored her when I went past.

During break I played with the others and raced around madly until the bell went. She was never out of my thoughts, but I didn't look in her direction. Now and then, though, I laughed and whooped so loudly that everyone in the playground and far beyond was bound to hear.

Including her.

After a week I had found out two things: she was in group six and her name was Ara Callenbach. She and her family had moved south because of her father's job, but I'd heard people say it was a typical excuse to hide the fact they were gypsies always on the move, leaving behind homes in a total mess. The family was large and some said there were ten children and others said there were over a dozen. They were all swarthy types.

The new girl herself didn't give much away, because she only spoke when she had to. As soon as you spoke to her she'd look as if she didn't understand what you were saying, raise her eyebrows and keep her mouth shut. She lived in an ordinary terraced house, and when she spoke at all it was in proper Dutch. She didn't understand our dialect, or pretended not to. She was quite uppity. She was in the highest group, but wasn't sitting for any entrance exams yet because she was going to stay at our school for another year. It was the second or third time she'd repeated a year, she was fat and dim, she weighed a ton. She was very old, fourteen at least, and she had boobs and also the other stuff.

Not that I knew what the other stuff was, all I knew was that I had to pretend to know all about it, or else they wouldn't tell me any more about her.

How come they knew so much about her, if she never talked to anyone?

They knew.

I'd heard enough. I'd find out the truth from her. The main thing was that she was here to stay, she was living here in a proper house, and she wasn't likely to be going away for a while. We would be in the same classroom after the summer, because groups five and six were combined and our teacher was the Headmistress. I had plenty of time. I was certain that she would be my friend, that we belonged together, that she was like me. Everything I did from now on would count as for her or against her, and everything she did would count as for me or against me. That's how intense it was and that's how both of us wanted it to be.

That night I dreamed of Ara Callenbach for the first time.

2

POLLY GAVE ME THE PIP FROM THE MOMENT SHE turned up on the first page, but then I still had *Polly Takes a Trip, Polly Comes Home* and *Polly Finds Happiness* to get through.

By the time I'd got to the end of Polly there were plenty of other adventure series waiting for me, with no less charming, kind, pretty heroines experiencing the same unlikely adventures and playing the same boring pranks with their twittering friends, and all they did was make me sneer, that's what goody-goody drips I thought they were.

In our village there was no library as such. An extension to the priory served as cinema, disco, gym room, practice space for every activity requiring practice, and youth club. In one of the two main rooms where cut-outs were made, songs were sung, billiards and ping-pong were played and a little smooching went on once every three months, there were also three oak wall-cupboards. Every Saturday at noon the Headmistress would unlock the cupboard doors and for the next two hours her eagle eyes made sure the girls took their pick from the girls' cupboard and the boys from the boys' cupboard.

Grown-ups were already free to make their own choice in those days – that was no longer frowned upon.

So this was the library.

For ten cents each I could choose three books from the girls' cupboard. I could keep them for three weeks or else apply for an extra week and pay five cents more. I never needed the extra week.

On several occasions the Head hauled me away from the wrong cupboards – the boys' one and the grown-ups' one – and steered me back to the shelves intended for me. Had I really read them all, all those girls' books? No I had not. Repartee like "if you've read one you've read them all" didn't occur to me yet at the time, and even if it had I wouldn't have dared say it out loud to the Head.

The Head has authority. This is thanks to that oddly taunting smile of hers and to her unmarried status.

The only way I dared to show my displeasure was in a small yet persistent provocation on my part. Each week, after casting a statutory glance at the girls' cupboard, I would cross to the boys' cupboard. Sometimes I couldn't even read the titles on the spines I was so keyed up, and I'd stand there squirming until she mercifully ended our confrontation by waving me back with a patient, weary sigh to where I belonged. But in time she took my persistent contrariness to be a sign of serious protest. One Saturday she took me aside and gave me a dose of psychological medicine to which I was extremely responsive then and still am now: she appealed to me directly, acknowledged my problem and proposed terms of agreement.

I'm the kind of person who'll listen to reason. If I promise something you can be sure I'll keep my promise. Promises and agreements are sacred to me, and I'd never forgive myself if I let the other person down.

Flushed with a newfound sense of maturity I agreed to her terms. Every Saturday I'd be in the library at ten to twelve, at which time I'd select a book from the boys' cupboard subject to her approval. After that I was free to pick two other books from the girls' cupboard. And I wasn't to tell anyone, because all the other girls would want to stick their noses into the boys' cupboard too, and then there'd be a free-for-all and she didn't want that. Did I see what she was driving at? I felt half proud and half underhand as I nodded in assent.

As a rule it's better not to keep cupboards locked.

In the meantime my expectations of the forbidden books ran so high that, with hindsight, they couldn't have been met by any book. But I didn't know that yet.

The following Saturday morning I was already hovering around the building at eleven o'clock in anticipation of access to the boys' cupboard. The knot I felt in my stomach then strikes me as absurd now.

As with virtually every book I read as a child, I can't remember any particular thrill at making the acquaintance of Old Shatterhand and Winnetou. But the author, Karl May, did make a lasting impression, and it was thanks to him that I gained a certain insight into the eternal battle between cowboys and Indians as well as some notion of the role I might be expected to play in dramas of that nature. And that was to be of practical advantage to me.

I began to have an inkling at last of what the boys were getting at with their games and why I wasn't supposed to join the warrior braves in their combat with heartless cowboys or Red Indians from enemy tribes. If they let me play with them at all I'd have to stay behind in the wigwam and wait. As a squaw, of course.

So I could tend their wounds after battle.

I did this just once, from then on I knew what the word squaw signified: waiting around and being bored. While entire tribes went off scalping armed with clubs and axes and got every chance in the world to prove their mettle, I was stuck in a hut biding my time.

Boys' games are always about winning or losing.

With girls it's a question of who's best at pretending.

I wasn't interested in being good at pretending. I wanted to be a warrior brave and I wanted to go the whole hog until victory or defeat.

As I didn't know whether there might be any glory in tending the wounds of warriors, I accepted the role they assigned to me for this once and waited patiently for their return. But when they crawled into the hut, knackered and all sweaty, none of them had the guts to let a squaw lay a finger on them. There was something amiss here. Fundamentally amiss, I mean.

The boys are dauntless in battle, valiant too and unstoppable in their zeal, but they will not suffer their wounds to be tended. They can't even admit to having any. So that left me looking like a right idiot.

With a little effort you could easily conjure up the Wild West in someone's garden or in a field, but there was no room for girls then and there still isn't now. That's how it was in Karl May's stories, and things are no different today.

I'm always grateful for fresh insights, even if they are monstrous.

Obsessions, however, you are better off without.

What obsessions share with addiction, hysteria and fanaticism is that they are out to destroy insight.

Everyone has obsessions to a greater or lesser degree. Whether they're necessary for the survival of the species I don't know, but it does seem as if human beings have been lumbered with a certain deficiency which prevents them from seeing the whole truth about themselves.

This deficiency feeds on addiction. The more addictions you have the less you'll be able to acknowledge the truth about yourself. It's not a question of searching for the truth, it's learning to face up to it.

The most unbearable truth is the truth of death. No one really accepts that. I think the unbearable truth of death is the basis of all our lies.

I learned early on not to be surprised at deception and lies and to see them as armour. That they were armour against death didn't occur to me until later. It was also later, much later, when the lies and deceit started hurting more than I cared to admit, that I came up with the malicious idea that liars and deceivers are their own worst enemies, because each lie takes them further away from what they most esteem, most crave and strive for.

I know of no more truth-loving person than the liar.

Having read the bit about Old Shatterhand and Winnetou becoming blood brothers, that was what I longed for more than anything else: to be blood brothers with someone. From then on I always carried a needle around with me. I kept it in a small plastic case, which had previously contained the flints my father used in his lighter.

It was a holy instrument.

Blood brothers are not thick on the ground. You can't become blood brothers with just anyone in your class, because it's a bond for life and you have to think twice before giving your word, it's that important.

In order to find out how it felt to have your finger pricked on purpose I decided to try it out on myself first.

It is very difficult.

Pressing the needle gently against the skin didn't hurt, but neither did it achieve the desired result. Not even when I pressed harder. The skin of my fingertip was wonderfully tough, which I thought very loyal of it, although it didn't make things any less arduous. I broke out in a sweat. Clearly blood brotherhood was not something to be taken lightly. It had to hurt.

The operation wasn't successful until I betrayed my left hand

and pretended it was someone else's. The right hand was mine and that was the hand that had to do the work. I jabbed the needle firmly into the tip of the alien forefinger and when I saw there was a tiny hole in the skin I whispered quickly there there, dear finger, you're mine all right, I just had to do this as there was no other way. Next I squashed my finger until a glistening bead of blood appeared.

I felt proud. I was standing in the back garden. There was not a living soul except a row of freshly planted conifers. One of them was shorter than the rest and its branches were tipped with brown.

I would become blood brothers with this conifer. I pushed away all thoughts of inequality in the relationship – what could a conifer do for me if I was in mortal danger or if someone attacked me, after all? This drop of blood was intended for a higher purpose and it struck me as more sinful to stick my finger in my mouth and suck my own blood than to sacrifice it for someone else. A conifer was better than nothing. I thought it might do the poor sapling some good, in which case I'd have the most convincing proof of all that blood brotherhood actually worked.

The blood had already started to congeal, so I quickly smeared it over a spot in the stem where some resin had collected.

I whispered to the tree that we were now bonded together for ever, for better and for worse, and I promised to take good care of it.

Talking to the sad-looking little tree flooded me with a deep love, and I wanted to talk a lot more so as to prolong the sense of togetherness, but I couldn't think of any other solemn things to say. I resolved to pay special attention at the next church wedding I attended to get inspiration for future ceremonies of this nature, and I said goodbye to the conifer by clasping one of its branches and shaking hands with it.

Two weeks later it was dead.

Armed with a spade my father strode into the garden, with me at his heels. The spade turned up a sodden, mouldy clump of roots still wrapped in a thin piece of sacking.

"What on earth?" he asked no one in particular.

I had given my tree an extra bucket of water three times a day, and I couldn't make out why it had turned browner and browner until only a few twigs in the top were still the original shade of green. Without letting on that the conifer was my blood brother I told my father that it was me, that I'd been watering the tree now and then because it looked so forlorn.

"You've drowned it with your good intentions," my father said with a smile.

My father always looks on the bright side.

There was only one way to deal with my anguish: I had to draw the obvious conclusion, which I wrote down in my exercise book.

Trees are stupid.

They can't even walk or talk.

They don't have any blood.

They don't feel.

You can buy them in a shop and things you can buy can't love you.

So: blood brotherhood with a tree is worthless and a worthless bond doesn't count.

That evening I asked my father if it was very expensive to buy a conifer and I offered to pay for the tree in instalments out of my pocket money. Kids cost such a lot of money these days and I didn't want to cause my parents undue expense.

In the meagre collection of mostly well-thumbed books every new acquisition, even a slim paperback like this one, was immediately conspicuous. Eagerly I pulled the book out from among the others. It was brand-new and the spine cracked when I splayed the covers. It wasn't the name of the author or the title that filled me with wonder as I turned the book this way and that, sniffed at it and checked to see whether it was in fact a proper book full of sentences. It was the illustration on the cover. This was a proper book, sentence after sentence in print and I could barely believe my eyes.

The picture on the front was of a girl smiling, hardly more than a child, not much older than me. She was twelve and a southerner, the blurb said, and *Keep Smiling, Irmgard* was her first book. It was about herself, about her life in the sanatorium near us. Twelve years old, a girl, a southerner, it sounded so familiar. How could that familiarity, that sense of immediacy have anything to do with something as grand, magical and unreal as a book?

I read it in one sitting.

After that I wanted only one thing: TB.

For the first time since the Headmistress and I had made our arrangement I arrived at the library at the normal time and did not stray from the girls' cupboard. She eyed me with a mixture of surprise and amusement when I laid my three books on the table. The covers of all three displayed the perky features of a young girl with a mop of invariably unruly black curls. The picture alone made it quite clear that the heroine was a wild little gypsy girl.

The girl on the garishly coloured dust-jackets was not remotely like Ara Callenbach, but I couldn't think of any other way of staying close to her during the holidays apart from reading these books.

When I got half-way through the first book I'd had enough. I put it aside along with the other two. I could only bring myself to do this because I didn't really believe all the drivel I'd heard at school about Ara Callenbach and her family. It was just idle talk. My mother didn't believe it either. She said that's what always happens in a village, every newcomer gets talked about, she said, and the craziest stories do the rounds. Just to have something to gossip about. She herself thought they had to be quite well-off, otherwise they couldn't afford to live in one of those nice new houses on the outskirts of the village.

Being rich was far more interesting than having gypsy blood, really.

The less unusual things were the more fascinating I found them. People who try to be different and go out of their way to be interesting and unusual always turn out to be more predictable than people who don't seek attention and lead ordinary, everyday lives. Making an effort to be interesting makes people less interesting. Truly exceptional people seldom realize they're exceptional, and once it sinks in that they're different it usually takes them the rest of their lives to come to terms with it.

I'd rather see Ara Callenbach simply as the daughter of rich parents than as someone outlandish like a gypsy.

I never liked fairy tales either.

Somehow that had something to do with it.

Not knowing exactly where she lived, I often cycled through the new housing estates that summer in the hope and fear of coming across her.

No such luck.

The advantage was that my most elaborate fantasy about getting to know each other stayed intact. We'd meet again in the playground on the first day of term, and soon after that we'd be in the same classroom. That simple occasion had to be enough for us to be bonded together for the rest of our lives. From the moment we stepped into the classroom our fates would be sealed. She knew that and so did I. There was nothing we needed to do to make that happen and there was nothing we could do to stop it. That's the way it was. All the things I imagined about us no longer took place in class nor on the school premises but somewhere totally different, in some faraway, desolate place where the two of us would be utterly alone. As if I had a premonition then that whenever we'd be together there'd be no room for anyone else.

It was towards the end of the summer holidays when, one Sunday morning, my elder brother Willem and I went for a walk in the woods and I saw her. She was walking down the sandy lane, some fifty metres away. She was accompanied by a big dog on a leash. I was startled and felt my face flush with embarrassment. I didn't want my brother to notice so I spun round, ran back a little way, crouched down and raked my hands through the fallen leaves. I'd tell him I thought I'd spotted something, something shiny, but that I'd been mistaken. By the time I rejoined my brother and told him, she'd gone, but my embarrassment was still there. Not until I'd wiped my forehead with the back of my hand, said oops bending over always makes my face red, did it go away. My brother hadn't noticed a thing. He just thought it odd that I wanted to turn left at the sandy lane. We never turned left.

"I don't suppose we could have a dog, could we?" I asked my mother the next day, just in case. The least you could do was ask. People do change their minds sometimes and you wouldn't even know. But my mother hadn't changed hers, she said she had enough work on her hands already, just with us kids.

I went behind the garage, and from a heap of red bricks I picked out the best-looking one. I went into the garage and brushed it clean, cut a length of twine from the ball and tied it securely around the brick.

"Come along, Dog," I said, "we're going walkies."

From the yard I called to my mother that I was going for a walk – taking the dog, I added under my breath. The brick dragged over the pavement, but I was overjoyed and chattered away to my dog. About where we'd go and what I'd give him to eat when we got back.

Quarter of an hour later my arm started to ache from dragging the brick and I took my dog in my arms. He had just one failing and that was that he didn't pull me along, which I'd seen Ara Callenbach's dog do and which had made her look so pretty, hips thrust forward, back slightly arched, kept in balance by the large animal straining at the leash.

To find out what that felt like I had paused now and then to lift the brick and chuck it ahead of me a little way, but it didn't feel right and besides it didn't do the brick any good, because each time it hit the ground it got more chipped and I was left with less dog. That's no way to treat animals, I decided, and by way of consolation and penance I carried him all the way back home.

3

THE FIRST DAY OF TERM I SAW HER AGAIN, AND SOON
we were together in the same room. From the moment we stepped
into the classroom our fates were sealed. It went the way I had
imagined.

As things usually did.

For years this was indeed the hard-and-fast rule I would live by:
as soon as I left the confines of my parents' house things would
happen the way I wanted, if I really wanted them to. If something didn't happen the way I wanted, it only meant I hadn't
wanted it badly enough.

Out of doors things work out or they don't.

Out of doors is where I play games and have fun.

Not indoors.

Indoors I was powerless. Indoors I was at the mercy of a confound-
ing tangle of security and anxiety, loyalty and betrayal, upheaval
and tranquillity, care and neglect, cruelty and compassion, goodness and craziness. Indoors was where I ate and slept.

Indoors I'm either happy or miserable.

In my mind feeling helpless, dependent and vulnerable will
always be linked with love and happiness, always.

That link is impossible to break.

Every morning when I leave home my stomach aches with love. With each step I take to school the ache lessens and by the time I reach the playground it's gone.

Not today, though, the very first day I'll be in the same room as Ara Callenbach. Today my stomach's still knotted and the queasiness is still there.

It will be some years before I develop an ear for the wisdom of my body, which keeps reminding me it is there and keeps trying to tell me things that would stand me in good stead, if only I could understand what it is saying.

But I didn't understand then, not yet. I found it difficult to ally myself to my own body. I was stone deaf to the messages sent by my skin, heart and brains, by my liver, intestines, kidneys and by those nagging, griping organs in my female pelvis.

The classroom was crammed with desks and chairs. Group five was small, there were only twelve of us, but group six counted twenty girls. I only had eyes for Ara Callenbach and I ignored my classmates' cries for me to come and sit with them. I pretended not to hear.

Group five had to sit on the left half the room, group six on the right.

That's the hierarchy of the clock. Ever since we humans have visualized time as moving from left to right, not only before and after but also lower and higher, less and more, past and present all follow the rule of the clock. Everyone obeys it as if it's nature's way.

I don't think anything's nature's way.

I often practise thinking against the rule of the clock.

Ara Callenbach strode to the desk at the end of the third row and I trailed after her as if it was the most natural thing in the world. She made a lot of noise as she walked. She put her feet down heavily and bumped against the desks as she made her way to the back. The other girls watched her with indignation, but I was proud of the racket she was making.

She's a bit clumsy.

The third row was the row that both divided and joined groups five and six. I sat down next to her. She ignored me. She seemed to take it for granted that I should sit there.

Our teacher didn't, though.

As a teacher she was new to me, but because she was the Head she knew everything there was to know about every pupil in the school. She hadn't been in the room five minutes, surveying the class, before she signalled me to come over.

"I think you and Mies had better change places," she said.

Mies sat near the front.

She knows about me, she knows I'm disruptive. That's what they tell my father and mother on parents' evening: I'm a nice girl, but disruptive. They say I'm a wild child, bursting with energy, that I'm headstrong and that it'd be better if I paid more attention instead of fooling around in class. They say I don't do anything I don't fancy doing and that I'd get better marks for arithmetic, geography, history and nature study if I tried harder. As it is, all I get good marks for is writing and grammar.

Sighing loudly I moved to the second desk in the second row, sat down and then twisted round to look at Ara Callenbach.

There wasn't really anything out of the ordinary about the part of her above the desk. Her shoulders were fairly narrow in proportion to the rest, and her waist was a bit thick but still you'd say she was sturdy rather than fat. Somehow everything around her seemed just that bit too small and too tight, even the air, but that was more to do with the way I saw her, I supposed. From what you could see of her above her desk you'd never have thought the rest of her was so outsize.

29

She glanced round sullenly. It was a couple of seconds before she noticed that I was trying to catch her eye. When our eyes met I smiled and she raised an eyebrow.

That was all.

I thought it was plenty.

First our teacher would call the register for group five, then for group six. When your name was called you stood up. She read out the names in full, so Margriet answered to Margaretha while Katrien, Diny and I unfortunately had the same first name, formally that is, but once you were standing she'd give you a nod and say the name by which everyone knew you.

I'm at the beginning of the alphabet so my turn comes early on, which is good as I find this sort of thing very nerve-racking. Perhaps it's because I'm too eager to stand up and hear my name spoken out loud and listen to whatever our teacher may have to say. We do have a sort of bond, she and I, so I expect her to say something special.

A moment later it was all over.

"Well Kit," she said, "all kitted out for the new term are we?"

It wasn't very original, but I beamed as I replied: "Yes, Miss."

I couldn't wait for her to finish reading out the names of all my classmates. When she started on group six I leaned over sideways to get a good look at Ara Callenbach. In her own cumbersome way our teacher set about giving a little speech and then I knew it was her turn. She said things about her being the first real newcomer in class, and that we ought to do our best to make her feel one of us as quickly as possible.

I hope no one's paying attention, because I want to be the only one to make a fuss of her.

"Barbara Callenbach," she said.

It almost didn't fit in my head, I was so used to the name I'd been saying to myself over and over again. There was a stir in the classroom. Some girls sniggered and repeated her name: Barbara, Barbara. And I also heard mutterings of thick and fat and elephant.

Ara Callenbach jerked her chair back and drew herself up to her full height. There she stood, straight-backed, chin up. Her hips were wider than the desk in front of her.

"Ara," the Head said, glancing down her list, "welcome to our class."

The class was restless. Everyone was whispering to their neighbour, about her, about Ara. A sharp look from the Head was enough to restore silence.

Hopefully Ara has noticed that I've kept quiet and haven't been whispering to anyone, that I'm perched on the edge of my chair ready to fly at anyone who goes too far and says something really nasty.

They haven't done anything yet. It's just the way they always behave, the other girls. Their reaction's quite normal, for them. Because it's Ara it's obvious there'll be some commotion, as Ara's that special.

I reckon she thinks it's perfectly normal, that like me she's proud of the stir she's causing. It doesn't occur to me that she might feel ashamed. I can see the connection between blushing and being naked and feeling ashamed, but not between those things and feeling proud.

That's the kind of mistake beginners make.

Ara hasn't noticed that I didn't side with the others, and pride does go with shame after all.

Before break we had ten minutes during which we could read or draw. I decided to make a drawing for Ara. I wrote our names on a sheet of paper, in fancy letters. Her name at the top: Barbara Callenbach and mine at the bottom: Catherina Buts. My first attempt was not a success as her name was too long and didn't fit on the page, and the next time I just thickened our initials, because that was what was special in my eyes.

I've discovered something that thrills me and makes me glad: a wink from Fate confirming what I thought all along. Both of us are deceiving the world with our ordinary names, but for the register we have the same initials, except they're the other way round.

I've drawn two crossed arrows linking the B's and the C's and a ring of flowers around our names, carefully avoiding every hint of a heart-shape.

I'm sure she thinks hearts are sissy and sentimental, same as I do.

Out of sheer habit I race to the door when the bell rings for morning break. I discover too late that Ara's taking her time, letting everyone else go first.

In the corridor there are two rows of coat-pegs. One is bare. The other one, by our classroom, has a single coat hanging from it.

It's Ara's long black winter coat.

Long isn't even in fashion.

I lingered in the corridor, not straying too far from her coat. She slowed down when she saw me, then leaned in the doorway giving me a steady, unsmiling look. But I smiled at her. I smiled broadly and showed her the folded sheet of paper I'd been holding behind my back.

I was so nervous I forgot to speak correct Dutch and told her in our dialect that I'd made her a drawing. The speed with which I translated my words was my apology. In the same breath I said it again: "I've made you a drawing."

"Ah," she said, curling up the left corner of her mouth.

She went to her coat-peg and pulled on her coat with a wide, exaggerated gesture and only then did she look at me again. She seemed slightly peeved, as if I had caught her out and had seen something I shouldn't have.

My mother gave me the same look on occasions when I saw her popping something into her mouth, or flopping into an armchair. I didn't understand that look either.

What was it that I wasn't supposed to see?

She was at least two heads taller than me. Maybe two-and-a-half.

"Let's have a look at it then," she said.

"It's for you," I said, "You can have it. Don't look at it now."

Although I couldn't wait for her to see my drawing, I was suddenly overcome with embarrassment, terrified she'd think it silly – a drawing of our names linked together. It wasn't even a proper drawing. I could do much better than that. She gave me a quizzical look, and slipped the paper into her coat pocket without unfolding it. She turned round, strode across the corridor and outside without a backward glance. There was nothing for it but to follow her across the playground and stand next to her when she posted herself by the wall the way she'd done the very first day.

4

SHE DIDN'T SAY A LOT. EVERY BREAK TIME I TAGGED after her and soon afterwards I was jostling her and lolling against her thigh. She smelled nice. Sometimes I would launch myself at her and leap into her arms. I would clamp my calves around her waist and the backs of my knees on her wide hips. It was a good fit. If I had nothing to say I would swivel round until my full weight rested on one of her hips, I would rest my cheek in the curve of her shoulder and stay like that quietly for a quarter of an hour on end. I would be resting from all the things that tired me out without me knowing why. She supported me with one arm, that's how strong she was.

"You don't weigh a thing," she said, but of course that's not true, everyone weighs something.

When my grip slackened and my body slid down she would hoist me up again, gently and lingeringly as if she didn't want to disturb me. Now and then she would run her hand through my hair and then I would long for her hand to stay there, it felt so good. Sometimes it was too long before she stroked my head again. Then I'd take her hand, guide it to my head and stare up at her.

"Beast," she would say, smiling as she ruffled my hair with her fingers.

Snuggling up to her with my face buried in her neck and my back to the playground, I pictured her cool stare sweeping over the others while she, like me, felt invincible.

She wouldn't let anyone else get as close to her, I knew that for a fact without feeling particularly proud about it. I took it for granted, it was part of the logic of our bond.

Playing ball, hopscotch and tig were irresistible to me. While playing with the others I kept glancing at her to see if she was looking.

She was.

Acting normal was impossible. I was noisy and frantic, my play was rough, fierce, fanatical. Not to win, but because I knew of no other way to enjoy a game. When I returned to her side, tired and perspiring, she would ignore me for the first few minutes and hold her arms folded. Not until I had prised one of her hands loose from the clenched fist and put the limp captured hand on the top of my head and stood there waiting without looking up, would she unbend, give a little sigh and stroke my hair to let me know that all was forgiven, that I could look her in the eye again.

She always got back at me when she thought I was being disloyal. Which was pretty often. I never let this stop me from playing ball, hopscotch and grandmother's footsteps if I felt like it. I couldn't see the harm in it. I belonged with her anyway.

She didn't join in when we had a reading lesson. Dutch lessons were for the most part given to groups five and six together, except for the difficult things like clause analysis and parts of the dictation, which only the girls in group six had to do, but we all had the same reading book. Only Ara had a different one.

She had trouble reading and writing. On Wednesdays, when everyone else had the afternoon off, Ara stayed behind for an extra hour's lesson with our teacher, using special textbooks. Our teacher had sent for these books specially and it was also our teacher who said that Ara's difficulty had nothing to do with being stupid but that it was something in her head which made the words come out wrong. It wasn't that she was ill or anything, but still it was something in the brain. Quite a lot of people had it, and it was difficult to cure. She had good eyesight, yet it was a sort of blindness inside her head.

That's just like our teacher, she finds out about things. Our teacher knows a lot about children, also the modern stuff. In the course of the school year she takes each pupil aside during an afternoon and then she talks to you for ages, about things like what you want to be when you're grown up and if there's anything worrying you.

I'm already looking forward to it, to that talk with our teacher and all the things she'll say about me.

But she singled Ara out on the very first day, because Ara's case is serious. She's told her she can't imagine why no one ever bothered to pay some extra attention to her at her previous schools, that they just left her to struggle on with her reading and writing, not realizing she doesn't make ordinary mistakes like other pupils, but that it's something in her head which muddles her. She's told her she's not lazy and not stupid either. She's promised to coach her.

I envied Ara for having something mysterious in her head which entitled her to extra help from our teacher. I'd have liked some extra help too, but I couldn't think what for. At the same time I felt as proud of Ara as if I'd had her strangeness myself and I thought it proved how special she was, her having a funny brain which produced words of its own accord. So I didn't really mind that she had something no one else had, not even me.

Most of all Ara was relieved. She was glad she wasn't stupid.

I deeply regretted that our teacher had got in ahead of me, because I could've told her that myself and then I'd have been the one to make her happy.

Of course someone who can't read and write properly must be a bit dim, but only in a certain way, and if you look and talk like Ara then it has to be something different, then you're not just dim.

"I'll help you with your language lessons if you like," I'd said and she'd said all right, but when I began to discover how odd she was with words I didn't know whether I really wanted her ever to change.

Nor did Ara.

Perhaps it was just that I was so fazed by her view of things and words and that she quite enjoyed having that effect on me, but I couldn't help noticing that Ara wasn't too sure about wanting to improve her language either.

"It's as if she's trying to take away my secret," she said after her extra lesson one day.

"Which secret?"

"The exciting part," she said, "that the words outside can trip me up and take me by surprise at any moment in the day."

She hated it but it was also exciting. She said that sometimes a word could stay out of sight for a whole day.

"Then I want to say: 'The flowers are blooming' but what comes out is 'the blooming'. The rest has disappeared into a black hole. I know it's got to be somewhere and so I start looking for it, in books and magazines. It can take ages before I find a picture of what I wanted to say in the first place and even then I have to look to make sure that the word that goes with the picture is there too."

"How wonderfully odd," I said.

So she had to hunt and hunting is exciting.

Hunting for something which is unknown to you but which you

know can only be one thing, the only right answer to a question, the only solution to a problem, the one single thing that fits – that's more than exciting, it's a need, even though a chosen one. It is the need inspired by crossword puzzles, the enticement of the cryptogram, of the little squares waiting to be filled in correctly. This craving for uniqueness, for one-and-onlyness is, to my mind, the wellspring of addiction and obsession.

When she talked about how she was with words I had the strange sensation of hearing things which were utterly unknown to me while reminding me of the kind of longing I had, too. Ara seemed to be trying to get somewhere from the opposite direction, or the other way round, I couldn't quite tell. Eager for some more of this weird disjointedness, I would go on questioning her about her thing with words and each time I would exult in the contrariness of it all, which I didn't understand but which I knew was important, for it would have a bearing on how my life would develop.

I listened to her and was dismayed when she fell silent. Afterwards I would mull over all she had said.

After God, happiness and death, Ara became my most favourite subject for pondering.

What she had in common with God, happiness and death was they seemed to be problems requiring solution, while it was obvious from the start that there was no solution.

God, happiness and death and Ara were both hard and pleasant subjects to think about, that's what it was.

She preferred listening to talking. That's what she said: preferred. She liked the word prefer and especially the way it was written, with the p at the beginning and the f in the middle. It looked nice on the page, too.

There were things she invented her own words for. It could

happen that the words that already existed for those things had been neatly stored in her brain, but that they came out distorted. Then she would invent new ones.

"That word doesn't agree with me," she would say.

About other words she would say: "I don't agree with it," or: "I don't think this word goes very well with that thing."

She thought "glass" was a terrible word for glass and also that all words with the letters gh were disqualified from being used at all, except perhaps for the exclamation "ugh", because that's exactly what it sounded like.

"Because 'ugh' is really yucky, don't you think?" But how could I hold the same opinion if my head was geared so differently?

For a long time her parents had thought there was something wrong with her, as she didn't talk when she was little. Not until she was about four years old did she say her first words.

"I am Ara," she had said.

She herself maintained that it had taken so long because the pronunciation of her own name had been simply too difficult.

"I don't like those b's," she said, "they just slow things down. They're not right for me."

She'd begin these explanations with an expression of moody defiance, her eyes fixed warily on mine, as if to warn me she'd clamp her mouth shut at the slightest reaction that wasn't to her liking.

Not that there was any chance of me reacting in the wrong way, so enthralled was I by what she was saying. I was filled with compassion for an Ara I could not picture as a little girl, but who I saw before me in a different way, as the Ara of now, battling to master the elusive words.

I wondered whether she'd been fat when she was little, but didn't dare ask.

"Someone ordinary won't do for our Kit, as usual," my mother said the first time I brought Ara home. All the girls in my class had been to our house, she said, I'd had them one by one, I'd played with them for a while, nice girls all of them, ordinary girls, from ordinary families like us. And not one of them had lasted, not one of them had been good enough for me. So what was the matter with me? Why did I always want something different than other girls? Take that nice Katrien, surely she was good company? Nicely dressed, fresh-faced, well-mannered, decent parents, she'd have loved to have been my friend, just like all the others, and even then they'd be beneath me, even then I'd lose interest. Why I hadn't found a good friend after all that effort she couldn't understand. Why did I have to get involved with someone who was so different? It wasn't her fault, of course, the way she looked – that was bad enough – but what did I see in someone like that?

"Like what?"

"So different," said my mother, "so hefty and sullen and mature. She doesn't strike me as a very nice girl, I must say."

Hefty, sullen, mature – this was an excellent description of Ara and I thought it clever of my mother to think of words that fitted her so well.

"She *is* nice," I said, "she's a really nice girl."

She said it was beyond her, all of it. Of course it was all right for us to choose our own friends, Papa and she would never interfere, as we knew perfectly well, never. We could do as we pleased, it was our choice and ours alone, but why did I have to pick a girl like Ara? She could talk her head off, she could offer advice for all she was worth not that anyone listened, it was useless, like talking to a brick wall, we went our own sweet way. Well, I'd find out in my own good time. She wondered how long I'd stick with this one.

I listened meekly, I knew what she meant. I wasn't at all bothered by my mother's bluntness, that was pure concern on her part, concern for our happiness. Besides, all this was typical of Ara.

Ara gives offence and I'm proud of that.

I liked the surprise and irritation her presence always aroused, the uneasiness she spread around. I liked it that she was clumsy and gawky and that I had to follow her around to repair the havoc she caused as best I could. She seemed to be blind to everything that intimidated me. Where I stepped cautiously and whispered she stamped and shouted; where I grinned, smiled, nodded and bowed, she drew herself up and looked daggers.

It's incredible. Each time I'm amazed to see how she manages not to be spun into the delicate invisible web of rules and regulations which I can't help noticing as soon as I come into a room full of people and which summons blind obedience from me.

I thought it was courage and integrity on her part and that it was cowardice and dishonesty on mine.

I thought she did not adapt, and not adapting was something I regarded as a personal choice.

She caused the tumult that I soothed, she broke rules I obeyed, she conquered spaces in which I tried to be invisible, in which I wanted to vanish into thin air.

Sometimes I have the feeling I haven't got a body of my own and that she counts for two, that her body is my body too and takes up my space in the world and makes everything all right that I'm scared of.

I couldn't explain to anyone, not even to myself, but from the moment I saw Ara I had felt allied with her, as if she somehow encompassed my body with hers.

That makes her a double body, leaving me to exist only in my thoughts.

Whenever we went out together we were offensive, and we

would inspire a sort of belligerence in others wherever we went. It was logical and because we knew it, the hostility we aroused only made us stronger.

Since I started writing in my exercise book I've reserved the middle pages for this purpose. I've almost finished the left page, except under the heading FRIEND, that part's still blank.

I don't like a messy exercise book. Just one crossed-out word ruins the whole book, I find, and then I'd rather throw it away and start again in a brand-new clean one in which I copy everything from the old one first, because working in an exercise book with old corrections in it is no fun. Exercise books must be quite expensive, as my mother complains sometimes that I use up so many and nowadays I think a bit longer before writing something down. She says I should just start on a new page, that you don't see the crossed-out words on the other pages anyway. What you can't see isn't there, my mother thinks, but I know it's there all right, and that only makes it worse. Once I've made a mistake and crossed it out, the sight of it nags on and on in my brain and when I next open the exercise book the first thing I do is turn to that messed-up page. By which time I have lost all desire to write.

On the right-hand page I've already written down the same headings as on the left, but for the rest it's still empty.

Luckily I've had my own fountain pen since I started group four, a Diplomat, which I fill with pale blue ink from my father's ink bottle. Thank goodness he always buys the same colour and the same brand, because different colours of ink in my exercise book – I can't stand that either.

Before checking my list of personal details I had to see whether I'd grown any taller since last time. There were faint pencil marks on the wallpaper by the door, indicating my height. I stood with my back to the wall, held a pencil across my head and made a small mark. That's how tall I am. The new line was barely higher than the old one. I didn't grow very fast.

NAME: Catherina Maria Buts (Kit)
STREET: Bosjesweg 7
AGE: 10
HAIR: blonde
EYES: green
HEIGHT: 1.38 metres.
WEIGHT: 26 kilos.
MOTHER: Henriette Christina Maria Buts-van Walen (Jet)
FATHER: Wilhelmus Petrus Maria Buts (Wim)
BROTHERS: Willem (age 14)
Peter (age 13)
Christian (age 3)

I wanted to fill in the space following FRIEND very neatly and so I tried out my pen first on another piece of paper, to make sure the nib was nice and inky and wouldn't make one of those useless dents. Next I wrote down her name.

I was dismayed to discover that there wasn't much I could fill in on the right-hand page. I didn't know Ara's names, nor how tall she was, nor her weight, nor the names of her parents and how many brother and sisters she had, let alone all their names.

I filled in what I knew:

NAME: Ara
STREET: Willem de Zwijgerlaan 11
AGE: 13
HAIR: jet-black
EYES: pale grey
FRIEND: Kit Buts

*

43

Jet-black was a very fine description, I thought. At least I had those insipid books about gypsy girls to thank for that, because all of them had jet-black hair and hazel eyes. Perhaps the colour of Ara's eyes was hazel too, but I didn't know exactly what hazel meant and to be on the safe side I used an ordinary word to describe their actual colour.

5

ARA HAS ONLY ONE FIRST NAME: BARBARA. SHE'S 1 METRE 61 tall, she's got six sisters and no brothers, and she won't tell me how much she weighs.

It's disastrous, and I don't get it.

"But now I can't finish filling you in," I said indignantly.

"I don't trust you," she said.

That shocked me deeply.

My first visit to Ara's home filled me with amazement. It had taken her a long time to ask me over, without mentioning why she wasn't keen. I had nagged endlessly about going to her house, why didn't I come and play this afternoon, say, but she kept making excuses. It was more fun in my house, she said, and that was that.

It *is* fun in our house, everybody thinks so. My mother keeps plenty of goodies in the cupboard and we have ordinary red and yellow lemonade but also Coca-Cola in family-size bottles, not those swing-stoppered bottles but ones with caps you flip off with a bottle opener. Hardly anyone has Coca-Cola, but my mother says only the best will do for her children and my father works very hard to afford it all. When people stop by my mother never lets on she's miserable or has been crying with worry about us. According to my father my mother didn't get enough love when she was little and that's where all that sadness comes from. She wants us to have a better life than she had and we do have a wonderful life I keep telling her, we get our hearts' desire and we're allowed to do all sorts of things and never have to help with cleaning or anything.

"Take no notice of me," my mother says, "just you enjoy your telly."

When it's hot my mother even makes ice cream and when it's cold she gives us hot chocolate and biscuits. She doesn't mind people dunking their biscuit into the chocolate, which is odd, because surely it's bad manners. I don't like the boys in our family doing it either, because then they make slurping noises and if anything's rude it must be that.

Making noises when you eat is utterly revolting I think. I keep telling the boys not to, that it's rude to slurp or smack your lips or blow on your food or slouch over your plate. Mashing up your food is disgusting too and an insult to our mother, as if you're saying that the taste isn't very good on its own and that you'd rather disguise it by mashing it up with apple sauce, for example, just so you can get it down more easily.

The boys are rather picky about their food, all three of them, they'll go off into a sulk if we have ordinary sausages for supper, but I like everything and although that isn't completely true I'd never let my mother notice, never, because I feel sorry for her when people don't like her food after all the trouble she's taken. Our Willem and little Chris do listen when I show them how to eat decently, but Makkie gives me angry looks and smacks his lips extra loud.

His nickname is Makkie and he's a difficult lad. It's hard to bring him up properly. He can be really scary when he glowers at you and he's quick to lose his temper, so you have to know how to handle him, but I love him a lot.

46

I love all my brothers the same: very very much.

I also love my father just as much as my mother and I can't stand the idea that I might possibly love the one just a teeny bit more than the other, that really hurts, deep in my heart.

You wouldn't think so, but compared to my father and Willem, Makkie is a naturally civilized eater. He holds his knife and fork in a special way, different from us, more elegantly – no problem there – but what's so awful about Makkie is that he has no consideration and starts eating before everyone else is sitting at table, nor does he ever look if there's enough left for the others when he takes a second helping. It's specially hurtful for my mother, as I see it, because it's a challenge to conjure up a different meal for a whole family day in day out and if Makkie doesn't even wait till she's sitting down it's like not appreciating her effort, as if all she's good for is cooking, as if she herself doesn't count at all. The boys hardly ever say her food tastes good, which is so gross I think. That's why I tell her with practically every mouthful how delicious it is and thank goodness when my father eats with us on Sundays he often comments on the wonderful job Mama's done.

"Yes Mama, I think so too," I say loudly and look hard at the boys, but they're too dim to notice.

Actually my mother seems to get less upset about the food business than I do. She says I shouldn't go on about it.

"Just let them enjoy their food in peace," she says.

By the time a meal is over I often have a stomach ache from the aggravation, that's how wound up I get at the sight of all those horrible munching jaws while the boys just stare stupidly at their plates and go on munching and never say a word, let alone something nice.

It was a Wednesday afternoon in November and within an hour of getting home from school I was bored. It was gusty outside and now and then it rained. Willem was reading a book, Makkie was in the garage working on his perpetual-motion machine and little Chris was asleep. We'd had our dinner – pancakes, as we often had on Wednesdays, and pancakes are very quickly eaten.

Ever since Willem and Makkie started going to school in town we have a hot meal in the evenings, except on Wednesdays when they have the afternoon off and sometimes we have two hot meals that day, especially if the weather's cold. Then my mother makes pea soup and what we used to do is eat the pea soup first out of deep plates and then turn our plates over for my mother to lay those small round pancakes on top. Very odd, come to think of it. Nowadays we eat the pancakes in the afternoon, because they're a bit like hot bread, my mother says, and in the evening we have the soup.

Ara's extra lesson lasted until one o'clock and if I hurried I could catch her as she left school. I told my mother I was going to fetch her and that we might come here afterwards.

"Always here," said my mother.

The school looked deserted. I was afraid that Ara had already gone and that made me very miserable. Less than an hour and a half ago I'd been mucking about inside and outside the school building heedless and carefree, but now it seemed like forbidden territory, a place that was none of my business and I didn't dare go past the low wall into the playground. Thrusting my hands deep in my pockets I stayed on the street side of the wall and gawped at the windows of our classroom. I saw no one.

My school reports sometimes say I'm impatient, but I suspect that's because of the needlework mistress, that she's been saying things to my own teacher and it could also be because of art and PE, although personally I think I'm a very patient person. I can spend yonks on a drawing until it's exactly the way I'd pictured it in my head, and when I've got a good book to read I'm miles away and can't put it down for hours.

That I have no patience for needlework isn't because I'm impatient, it's because I loathe needlework, while PE only gives me the jitters when we have to get in line and wait until it's our turn and I'm stuck behind one of those twits who just stands there for ages squirming in a girlish sort of way before she dares to vault over the horse.

Arithmetic is too simple for words, especially if you do it the way you're supposed to, and with my method I'm finished in no time at all. I get all my answers only more or less right, but that's good enough for me, because after doing our sums we're allowed to read our own library books and I'd much rather do that.

I can't imagine why you have to learn things you can't for the life of you see the point of, things you wouldn't ever bother with of your own accord – no one's been able to explain to me why that is. Knitting, crochet and embroidery, I hate it all, so I don't want to learn how it's done because I'll never do it of my own free will, never. The boys don't have to do that stuff, because of course when they're grown up they'll be doing a sight more exciting things than knitting, so why should I be forced to do it?

Sometimes, after a needlework class, I smuggle my knitting home with me, because it's got so bad that I'm sunk. I knit much too tightly and far too much. I keep thinking I've dropped stitches and then I add stitches like mad and get so wound up that my hands get terribly sweaty, which makes the knitting all grotty. My mother sighs when I come to her yet again with a grubby scrap of textile because it's extra work for her and she's busy enough as it is, so then I'm glad when she breaks into a smile at my clumsy efforts at fabricating what is eventually supposed to turn into something utterly boring like a tea cosy. Out of sheer relief I try to make her laugh some more by imitating our needlework mistress, how she goes on in that posh accent of hers about the advantages of using a teapot-warmer-cosy-thing and how delighted our mothers will be when presented with such a wonderful gift crafted by their own diligent daughters. And that makes my mother laugh. Then she pulls and tugs at my knitting to unravel it down to the first row and knits a triangle in loose, supple stitches.

She doesn't think much of that needlework woman either, because she's so full of herself, acting as if she owns the place just because she gives the odd hour of something hopeless like needlework or knitting. And my mother really isn't so keen on stupid things like tea cosies. We don't even drink tea in our house, none of us like it. We only have tea when we've got the runs and then we drink it down holding our noses, as if it were medicine, because it's good for us.

"Tea constipates," says my mother.

I had so looked forward to fetching Ara from school that I could hardly imagine she had gone home already and that I might have missed her. I never had that kind of bad luck when I was out of doors. I had left the house at seven minutes to one and had covered the distance to school in less than five minutes because I'd come running and when I ran I didn't have to watch the cracks.

Normally I do watch them, I avoid stepping on the lines between the paving stones and when I do so by mistake I have to go back four and start again, because if I don't something terrible will happen to my brothers or me that very same day. If it was only me at risk I wouldn't be bothered as much, but I can't bear the thought of my brothers getting hurt through a fault of mine.

Sometimes I imagine things like that, at night, about one of the boys having an accident because of me having stepped on a crack this morning and about him dying in a little room in the hospital and how overcome with grief my parents will be and that especially my mother will never get over it and won't want to go on living at all.

She doesn't think life's so great as it is.

It's very difficult to shake off unpleasant thoughts, especially at night. It's as if your thoughts are held back by the dark so they can't possibly get out of your head when you've finished thinking them and so they stay in your head getting noisier and noisier and that always makes me sweat. The only solution I can think of is to climb out of bed and pray on my knees. In our house we don't have to get on our knees to pray before we go to sleep at night because my mother thinks that's being too strict with young children, but I reckon being strict can be good for a child, especially one like me, because if your sins are forgiven just like that, without your repenting or making up for them, then it's all much too easy and doesn't mean a thing.

Willem and Makkie already had a watch, but I hadn't got mine yet because we don't get our first watch until we've done our Confirmation and that doesn't happen until you're in group six.

I didn't know what the time was.

Trusting that I was two minutes early and knowing that our teacher was very punctual with lessons, I waited patiently and thought about how I might spend the afternoon with Ara.

She came outside before I'd had any bright ideas. She saw me and waved. Only then did I dare set foot in the playground and I ran towards her. "That's nice!" she said.

I jumped for joy and whooped because I could never predict whether Ara was going to approve of something or not, so I was thrilled at having made the right decision.

We walked down the pavement together, me walking normally because when I'm with someone it doesn't count, and Ara saying nothing. With her I was good at saying nothing, so I kept my mouth shut too. But there are different kinds of silence and when we got near to our house I sensed that something was troubling her and that she was preparing herself to tell me what it was.

"After my extra lesson I'm supposed to go home first," she said.

"Shall I come with you?" I asked.

She stopped and turned to me with a frown. I tried to look as nonchalant as possible, so as not to let on how excited I was at the prospect of going to her house at last, because it was my excitement that she distrusted and if she saw it written on her face she'd stop me from going with her. She'd suspect me of having planned all this, that it wasn't for her sake that I'd gone to meet her but that I was just making an underhand attempt to get into her house.

"Kit," she said, in a quizzical sort of tone.

"Yes?"

"You are a wicked beast," she said and then I knew that this time at last Ara Callenbach would suffer me to accompany her to the house where she lived.

Cool as a cucumber I told Ara I'd run and tell my mother and raced to the back door of our house. I called out to my mother that we were going to Ara's house first and my voice cracked from nervousness, but also from pride, because my mother had said once or twice that we'd never get to see the inside of Ara's house, and anyway, what could you expect from people who were well-to-do like they were, penny-pinchers every one of them who'd think twice before opening their doors to the children of strangers and offering them all sorts of goodies, because if you added it all up, if you totted up all the money we got through each month, then it really was a tidy sum, and all of it had to come from our father's hard-earned income, he worked his fingers to the bone to provide for us. There was nothing wrong in that, she wasn't complaining, everyone was welcome in our home, so long as it made us happy, that was all she and my father cared about, but it wouldn't do us any harm to dwell on that from time to time, we shouldn't take it all for granted and there weren't many parents as indulgent as they were, come to that.

On the way there Ara didn't say a word. To make her see that my visiting her house was no big deal and needn't last very long either – because of course that wasn't what I was after at all – I started talking about all the things we'd do once we got back to my house. I told her I'd thought of a new word game for us to play, that I'd gone to meet her specially so I could tell her about it and we could try playing it. You had to write down the names of everyone in your family, including second names if they had them, and then you had to use the letters of these names to make as many new names as you could. I'd thought all this out a few days ago, and it would be good practice for her.

I was making the whole thing up as I went along, but I was doing it to reassure Ara and to put her in a better mood, because if she kept up this sullenness when we got to her house her father and mother might think she didn't really want me tagging after her and that it wasn't her idea at all. That wouldn't be a good start. It would be better if she showed those people that she really was my friend even though I was younger and shorter, that such unusual friendships did exist, just look at us. I got so worked up that I was rabbiting on, because besides dying with curiosity I also felt a bit apprehensive and shy, the way I always feel upon entering a strange place or going to meet people I've never seen before.

Ara was as moody and silent as before and I began to think I was getting my just deserts. I was being punished for my duplicity, she could see right through me and was therefore fully justified in ignoring me completely and doing nothing whatsoever to make my entry into her house the slightest bit easier, it was all my fault. She knew what I was up to.

By the time we arrived at her house I'd already told myself ten times over that I could simply wait for her outside, but Ara went ahead of me down the narrow path beside their house and didn't look round once so there was nothing for it but to follow her meekly.

At the back of the house there was a garden, a sizeable portion of which was taken up by a steel cage with a roomy dog kennel made of brick. As Ara approached a dog crawled out of the kennel, sprung up against the metal bars and began to bark loudly. At last Ara beamed. She talked to the dog.

"Brutus! Good doggy," she said.

She opened the door of the cage and patted the dog which had jumped up against her and now rested its front paws on her shoulders.

I stayed outside the cage and watched. Ara and the dog were a good match, I thought.

"You can stroke him if you like," said Ara. "He's very gentle."

I didn't dare to and told her so.

When she'd given the dog some food Ara opened the door to what turned out to be the kitchen, a big spanking-new kitchen, with white cupboards and shiny white tiles on the walls and floor. It looked as if no one had ever cooked in this kitchen, it was so clean and so lacking in the things you cook with, the pots and pans and canisters with herbs and bins containing flour and vermicelli. There wasn't a towel-rack either, as there was in our house and in other people's houses, with a sort of little curtain embroidered with a motto like Home Sweet Home. Everyone had those.

But what made the kitchen so completely unreal was not the absence of kitchen utensils: what was most conspicuously lacking was the smell of food. The place smelled of paint.

Ara took a step sideways, opened the door of the cupboard under the sink near the door, crouched down and took out something I couldn't identify at once.

"Here," she said, "put these on over your shoes."

She reached me a pair of shapeless slippers, made of pieces of shammy leather gathered at the top with elastic. She didn't look at me. It was beginning to dawn on me why Ara had been reluctant to take me to her house.

"Feels nice," I said.

Now she did look at me, not smiling but with a soft expression on her face.

It can really make you happy when Ara looks at you that way, and that's how I felt. I wasn't in the least worried about what might be in store for me next, because just one of those looks was enough to keep me going for a month or more.

I suppose it's a natural thing in your head that when you meet a new girl and you haven't ever seen that girl's parents before, that you expect those parents to resemble their child or at least to be as short or tall and more or less as fat or thin and to have hair of the same colour, for instance.

I couldn't imagine the woman I saw being Ara's mother.

Ara had opened the door more carefully than she usually opened doors, she had looked inside before going in and had nodded for me to follow her into the living room. She pushed the door wide open and the first thing I saw was a pool of wood, a glossy expanse of bare floorboards. The first steps I took gave me an odd feeling, as if I'd drown in the shine. The slippers made a squelching noise, but I was lucky to have them because without the slippers I wouldn't have had a grip on the wood at all.

Ara said hello to two young women sitting at a table hunched over their books. They eyed me with faint interest.

"This is Kit," said Ara.

The two young women got up. I shot Ara a questioning look and felt the old rush of heat rising to my face. She grinned and gave me a poke in the back. Red-faced I walked towards them and when the one nearest to me held out her hand I realized that I was supposed to shake it.

We never did that in our house.

Both of the young women said their names, but I didn't catch them.

"Is Mother in the front?" Ara inquired.

Mother as the name to call your mother struck me as odd. We used the word when we talked about "our mother", because our mother was what she was, it was a sort of vocation I suppose, and we'd say things like: our mother cooks delicious food, but her real name was Ma or Mama, that's what she was called by us.

The living room was L-shaped and the "front" presumably meant the part we couldn't see from where we were. Shuffling in our slippers we crossed to the other side of the room and then I saw the woman who I couldn't believe was Ara's mother.

I'd been surprised that the two young women sitting at the table had ordinary-looking bodies, quite different from Ara's, but still they had enough in common with Ara to be her sisters, say. Both of them had long hair, but it was the same sort of hair as Ara's, jet-black and wavy. They were slim and tall, they looked grown-up and attractive, but their faces weren't as pretty as Ara's.

Nor could they have been, seeing as Ara has the prettiest face in the whole world.

"Mother, I'm home," Ara said.

She was speaking to a thin fair-haired woman of at least fifty who, upon rising from her chair, proved to be only slightly taller than Ara and for the rest utterly unlike her. Ever since my own mother had another baby when I was seven – our Christian – I'd known that babies spent some time inside their mothers and that I'd done so too. It was quite unthinkable that Ara should have been inside this slight, narrow, fair-haired woman before she came out of her body. It couldn't fit.

They exchanged kisses on the cheek.

This mother cupped Ara's face in her two hands.

This mother patted Ara and then even stroked her cheek.

I was inclined to keep my eyes glued to the floor, because I felt I was witnessing something that wasn't intended for my eyes, something secret, but I couldn't help looking at them, it was such a wonderful sight.

I had never seen so much love in real life.

"This is Kit," Ara said, stepping aside so I stood face to face with her mother. We shook hands.

"Nice meeting you," she said in a mildly questioning tone.

I didn't know what to do next.

"Yes," I said.

Ara must be overjoyed to have the kind of mother who cupped your face in her hands and stroked your cheek.

"Goodness me," she said, "you poor thing to have hands that perspire so. And that at your age. Any problems with indigestion?"

What was I supposed to say to that?

I didn't know having hands that perspire was something to be ashamed of and I'd read something about indigestion in the

Encyclopaedia of Medicine, but what that had to do with perspiring I had no idea.

"Please, Mother," Ara said.

"Shall I make you a nice cup of tea?" her mother asked.

Ara made me go first up the stairs. There was no need for tea, she'd told her mother. She was going to show me her room and then we'd go to my house and do some writing exercises.

My head was brimming with questions, about the piano which stood in the living room downstairs and about all those shelves crammed with books, where her father was and where all the other sisters were and when Ara would get something to eat.

At the top of the stairs I waited for her, because I could see a corridor with at least five doors and I didn't know which one led to Ara's room. She went to one of the furthest doors and opened it. I followed her inside and found myself in a large airy room with twin beds and also a big wardrobe and several tables and chairs. And there was still room left to walk about in. What impressed me most was that there was a wash-basin on one of the walls.

"Can you get water from the tap all the way up here?"

"Of course," she said.

We didn't have running water upstairs and I couldn't imagine how you could make water stream upwards.

They also had a bathroom upstairs, Ara said, and a lavatory. She was enjoying my amazement and drew me into the corridor.

"This is my favourite room," she said, showing me the bathroom. I'd never seen a proper bathroom before and hers was absolutely brilliant. I was reminded of church, but didn't know why. Suddenly I was filled with longing to be back in my own house.

"Aren't you going to have anything to eat?" I asked Ara.

She said no and gave me a stern look. I pretended not to notice.

"When do you have a hot meal?"

"Half past six."

"Do you all have it together?"

"How d'you mean?"

"With your father and your sisters?"

"The ones that live here, yes," she said.

I stared at her uncomprehendingly. She said her two elder sisters lived away from home, that they went to school in another town.

Of course I asked what her sisters were called, where they lived, what sort of schools they went to, when they would be coming home, if they had boyfriends and if they still had their own rooms in this house, with beds in which they could sleep, but Ara didn't like being interrogated, that always annoyed her.

I suggested it was time to go and she agreed. Going down the stairs I realized that I hadn't taken a proper look at Ara's room and that I already found it impossible to recall whether there'd been any pictures on the walls.

In the hall downstairs there was the front door and the door to the living room, and also a chest of drawers. Ara pulled her slippers off, waited for me to do likewise and then put them away in one of the drawers. I wondered what they did when they invited people, whether they'd have to put those slippers on over their shoes, too. What if a lady came wearing high heels, that would be quite impossible as stiletto heels did much more damage to floors than our sensible shoes with rubber soles.

Ara opened the door to the living room, but didn't go in. From the doorway we could see her mother. She was reading a magazine and wore glasses.

"Mother, we're going to Kit's house," said Ara.

"Have you had some fruit, and a drink of milk?"

"Later."

"It was nice meeting you, Kit," said Ara's mother.

"Yes," I said feebly.

There had to be a more satisfactory response to this sort of remark, I was certain.

She told me about not trusting me when we were up in my room. My mother had got us glasses of fizzy lemonade and Ara had eaten two of the leftover pancakes, which can taste very good even when they're cold because my mother puts raisins in and apples and she makes them with flour that has to rise first, so that the air stays in the batter, even when they've cooled off.

I'd never seen Ara eat anything before and she hung back when my mother offered her the pancakes, but my mother said she should go ahead, that there was nothing she liked more than having people finish her food, she found that really pleasing.

"In that case yes please Mrs Buts," Ara said and my mother laid two pancakes on a plate and got out the sifter especially for Ara's benefit. She filled it with lumpy sugar and then shook the fine powder over the pancakes until they were snowy white.

Other kids call my mother "Auntie Jet", but Ara says "Mrs Buts", and I'm so relieved she's being so polite because with Ara you never know when she'll go all sullen and embarrass you. Her calling my mother Mrs Buts shows she's properly brought up and well-mannered.

I kept hoping Ara would mention how delicious the pancakes were, because all things considered it was very nice of my mother to offer them and get out the clean sifter all over again and I can't stand it when my mother doesn't get the appreciation she deserves, not even if it's Ara. Eventually Ara did say they're delicious Mrs Buts, she said it twice and I beamed at my mother to show her that Ara was a nice girl after all and not half as sulky as she'd thought.

Resting my chin on my arms I sat facing Ara at the kitchen table watching her eat. I had never imagined anyone could open and close their jaws with such grace, but I saw Ara do it. She chewed magnificently, with small regular movements of the jaw and delicate flicks of her tongue to remove the white powder from her lips.

Chewing is something you do unconsciously, without thinking about it, I always thought, but now I'm sure you can only chew so daintily if you've been taught.

My room was small, but it was all my own. Ara and I were sitting side by side on the bed and I had pulled my exercise book out from under the mattress to show her the middle pages. She inspected them and frowned, which I thought was a disappointing reaction to a revelation of such importance. I told her I still had to finish filling in her page, that it didn't really count yet. Grudgingly she told me she had only one Christian name and that her height was 1 metre 61. Then she went all quiet.

"I don't want this," she burst out, "I don't want stuff about me being written down."

"Why not?" I asked, taken aback.

First she said she just didn't like the idea. I protested that the exercise book was secret and I'd never show it to a soul, and that she should tell me all about herself or I wouldn't be able to fill in her space.

That's when she said: "I don't trust you."

6

"YOU'RE FRIENDS WITH EVERYBODY" ARA HAD SAID, and also that she loved animals more than people. Animals you could trust completely, they didn't lie and they never betrayed you and were ever faithful.

At first I was shocked, then I felt sad and when she said that about animals I got angry.

Loving an animal is dead easy, I find, because they don't know evil, and that's why they can't do good either. They can't really think for themselves and even if they desperately wanted to they couldn't lie, because you've got to be able to think to do that, and they only get attached to whoever gives them their food and drink, not because that person is good or anything, an animal can't know that. They even love you when you kick them and treat them badly, I've seen it with my own eyes, because our neighbour has a dog and he's dumb, my mother thinks so too.

She says I shouldn't be too hard on the people next door because that's the way country folk used to be, they had other things to worry about than improving their minds, after all in those days a farmer worked day and night and didn't have time to bother about clean clothes and not being smelly. As it is our neighbours are quite old and they don't have any children, just some chickens and that dog. The dog's so pathetic, our neighbour never strokes it, he just swears at it the whole time and even kicks it.

But the dog doesn't mind, it follows our neighbour everywhere just the same. He's never without that dog at his heels, with its head on one side gazing up at its master. That's because of the food it gets, my father's explained about that. Every animal listens to the person who feeds it and no one else.

Animals are dead stupid. You might as well take a brick and pretend it's a dog, that amounts to practically the same thing.

I told Ara all this and also that I thought it was thick to love animals more than humans. Humanity is the world's greatest good, I said.

I was indignant. I couldn't see how Ara could be so cruel as to say she didn't trust me, just because other girls wanted to play with me and I got along with everyone. Maybe she didn't really mean it, I thought, maybe it had something to do with my birthday, which I had celebrated the week before.

Everyone wants to come to my birthday party and for weeks before the event I keep getting notes from girls I've been less chummy with lately. They write me these notes inviting me over to their houses in the afternoon to play, all just to curry favour of course, and Diny actually gave me a drawing with those soppy little hearts all over it, but then she's the soppiest of them all and I wouldn't dream of inviting her to my birthday party, not in a million years. Each year I'm allowed to invite eight girls and there's always a bunch who don't count and who I needn't be bothered about. Like Diny and Josien, as I don't particularly like them anyway. What it boils down to is having the opportunity to dish out terrible punishment by not inviting someone.

Being left out is just about the worst thing that can happen to you.

I can't understand why God didn't make leaving people out a Deadly Sin – it's beyond me, that is.

I made Katrien cry her eyes out once, and she's not even one of the crybabies. It was when we were in group three and I hadn't asked her to my party, just to get back at her for something I can't even remember. On the day itself they all sang Happy Birthday to me in class just before morning break, and that's when it happened, Katrien crying her eyes out. I felt a bit guilty about that but I was cross too, because she was sort of spoiling my birthday with her sobbing. So in the end I invited her after all, and really you can tell much better by someone's gratitude after-wards how much it hurt them to be left out than by all that sobbing, and she was so grateful that she kept twirling around me, which made me all nervy again. I now felt good and kind-hearted all right, but I spent the rest of the morning worrying about it being too much of a bother for my mother, having this extra girl at my party.

There's no escape from your sins, you always pay for them.

Naturally Ara had been the first person I invited to my eleventh birthday, but she didn't want to come.

"I'll celebrate your birthday here with you," she'd said, and that she didn't fancy being stuck with the girls from group five. I could see her point. It might be sensible too, as whenever Ara and me get together we ignore everyone else and when it's you giving the party you're supposed to take notice of everyone, it's only good manners.

After she had said she didn't trust me it occurred to me that she might be annoyed by how eager the others were to come to my party and to what depths of hypocrisy they were prepared to sink for the sake of getting invited.

But if that was how she felt it was pretty daft, as it wasn't my fault. Everyone wanted to be friends with me, it was something in me and it had always been like that. What was important in life was not *who* liked me, but who *I* liked – I was quite sure of that. And I got on all right with people, but that was all. I didn't care what other people thought about me, as I didn't think they had particularly interesting thoughts anyway. They were a bit like the textbooks we had at school. They always gave me the odd feeling I'd read them before and practically knew them off by heart, as if I could have written them myself if someone else hadn't beaten me to it.

I told her there was no harm in being friendly, and that there was a world of difference between just being friendly and being friends. I told her she was my best friend, that I wasn't best friends with anyone else and never had been.

"I don't care a hoot about the others," I said.

She was not easily persuaded. She couldn't understand why I'd chosen her of all people, seeing as the others were just as nice or even nicer. And cleverer and prettier.

I told her she was the nicest person I'd ever met and I thought she was the prettiest girl I'd ever seen in my whole life and in a very special way she was also the cleverest girl I knew.

"Really and truly," I said.

She smiled.

It seemed a good time to make the proposal to her, though I was scared she'd think it too childish, which was why I'd dismissed it from my thoughts all this time. But Ara demanded serious proof and I couldn't think of anything more serious than blood.

I made the proposal.

She said all right.

Sheer joy kept me awake that night. I crept out of bed as quietly as possible, groped my way to the table and snapped the light on after draping my vest over the lampshade. I fished my exercise book out from under my mattress, got out the needle we'd used that afternoon and an old-fashioned pen I sometimes used for drawing. I was beginning to get used to it. The tip of my right forefinger was still hurting, so I started on my left thumb. To write down everything I wanted to say I needed blood from all the fingers of my left hand, but after a while it was all there on the bottom line of the middle page of my exercise book: On this day, November 14th, 1967, B.C. and C.B. became blood brothers.

Back in bed I remembered there were a whole lot more sentences that I'd have liked to add if I'd had more blood and more space. In a blur of phrases like: till death do us part, for ever after, eternally united, never-ending alliance, friendship for life, I fell asleep.

The next day I went to school extra early and, as I had so fervently hoped, Ara had left home early, too. She was leaning against the wall. We were both a bit shy and didn't mention our bond. I nudged my head into her side and lolled against her. She put her arm around me, rocked me gently to and fro and then rubbed her right forefinger over my nose.

It was a pity I was so taken aback that I shrank from her touch, but then I'm not used to people touching my face.

She remained utterly calm, that's the way she is.

I expect she's used to it because her mother strokes her and also because she's good with animals. Animals go all nervy and funny too sometimes and she'd said that about me a couple of times, that I could be just like a nervous animal and also that I was a bit funny about touching.

She waited patiently until I'd quietened down and my head was back to normal, then she actually tried again. This time I was prepared and I let her stroke my nose and I began to enjoy it more and more. At the first shrill of the bell I stuck my right forefinger in the air. She held the tip of her forefinger against mine and when I twisted my head round to look up at her I could see she was every bit as happy as I was.

No one could understand what it was about, it was our first secret code, and during all those years Ara and I pressed our fore-fingers together and then linked them whenever we met, by way of greeting. Only we knew what our gesture signified.

Our teacher discovered one of my secrets when I was called in to have that interview. It was on a Friday and in a way it was a good thing you got a note for your parents the day before, as in our house we have home-made chips every Friday and since the boys and I love chips my mother makes sure they're ready by five o'clock – at least that's when she sets the first bowl on the table. We can polish off four of those bowls easily, and if there are other children there my mother has to make even more.

The record is twelve bowls, but that's because our Willem's birthday was on a Friday and my mother made chips for all his friends as well. It was great fun, but I was a bit cross too, because that Nissen boy really is a creep and I couldn't stand him eating our chips. He helped himself to an awful lot of them too. I looked daggers at him, but the selfish pig didn't notice a thing, he's got such a thick skin. He must've reached puberty, I thought to myself.

Puberty is a sort of swear word for us.

We hate everything to do with it.

The note was a stencilled form and the Head had only filled in two lines in her own hand: the names of my parents and the date of the next parents' evening. Dear Mr and Mrs Buts it said, I would be kept at school until five o'clock on Friday because the Head would be having a private talk with me and she'd appreciate a follow-up interview with the parents about their daughter's future on such and such a date.

The bit about "their daughter" pierced my heart.

I hoped my parents would be equally moved.

So that Thursday afternoon I told my mother she should keep some chips for me the next day and she promised she'd see to it the boys didn't eat them all. The trouble about knowing about the appointment beforehand, though, was that I couldn't get to sleep that night and woke up much too early the next morning. School outings, birthdays, St Nicholas, Christmas, Easter, travelling fairs, carnival, my First Communion and my school swimming test, they're the kind of things I always lose sleep over.

The Head started off in a friendly enough tone, about all the books I'd read and that I was good at grammar, all that was just fine. She also liked the way I was with the other pupils: helpful, willing, kind, except with Josien, that is. I teased her too much and teasing wasn't the kind of behaviour she expected of a nice girl like me. Of course I was still far too playful and noisy in class, we'd discussed that before and the purpose of our talk was not to rub it in but rather to try and establish the reason for my restlessness, to hear what I had to say about it. Was I bored? Did I enjoy playing more than doing lessons?

She had a question to ask me, she said, it was about my sums, why they were sometimes all wrong and sometimes all right. Didn't I understand them? Were they too hard? Was I simply lazy on some days and not on others? As soon as we were doing a proper test, for marks, I made few mistakes, but with ordinary exercises it could happen that I didn't get a single answer right. What could be the reason for this? And what about those problems?

Problems were the hardest sums of all really, but I nearly always got them right. Could I please explain to her how this came about, because once she understood the reason we might be able to do something about it, she and I. To be quite frank, things were getting out of hand. Right now she had no idea which type of senior school would be best for me. I was bright enough for grammar school, she thought, but just being bright was not enough. It was necessary to be serious about things. Pupils had to have the right attitude, to be prepared to make sacrifices in order to learn, and it was my attitude that wasn't right.

She had brought along the arithmetic textbook. She handed me a pencil and sheet of paper and showed me a long addition sum. She told me to do the sum and say out loud what I thought at each stage, as if it was an ordinary exercise. She seemed genuinely interested in my explanations, and I was in two minds about what to do: I could see she was pursuing a strategy and would be hurt if I was dishonest and kept my secret to myself, as she'd think her strategy had failed and that I was insensitive to her kindness and concern, but if I told her how I did my sums I'd disappoint her too, because I was careless and that was also kind of insulting, like saying she wasn't worth making an effort for.

Stammering with mortification I revealed to her how I did my sums. I kept saying I only did them that way when it wasn't really important, that I did do my best and worked out all my sums on paper when it mattered, for a test, say, as I thought with ordinary exercises it wasn't so bad if you didn't work out your sums on paper but did them in your head, making sort of calculated guesses by adding up the hundreds first and then looking to see whether the tens were high or low numbers and adding or subtracting a few hundred from the outcome accordingly.

The expression on the Head's face isn't one of anger, it's more like surprise and even amusement, which is a relief because we'd all do anything to please her and make her smile. She's brilliant when she's laughs so much she gets tears in her eyes, her face changes completely. Her life can't be much fun, because school's everything to her and she's got no one to love. What's so stupid of me is that I can't seem to stop playing the fool and then she goes all frosty and forbidding. It's hard to tell how much she can take.

I tell her problems are different, because sums don't really make you think and that's why they're boring. I enjoy having to think things out, that's what I like best, and that's why problems are fun as they're more to do with language than sums, which you can do in your sleep. You've got to read the question carefully, and then you find it's not just adding or subtracting but that the words are the sum and the sum has a meaning, like how long it takes to get from A to B, for instance, that's great fun, and it's worthwhile, too.

I like words, I explain, but not plain numbers, because without words numbers don't mean a thing and just the sight of them gives me the creeps. And history's a bit like that too, I say quickly, to get it off my chest. What those heroic stories mean when you do a test is just dates, dates don't mean a thing on their own and even make you forget the story. The Battle of Nieuwpoort can get completely overshadowed by a date like 1600 because you get so worked up about having to remember 1600 being Nieuwpoort that you forget what the battle was actually about.

"Kit, Kit," she sighed, "what am I going to do with you?"

That seemed pretty obvious to me: she could punish me more often for starters, because that was bound to teach me to try harder in the end.

Then she asked if I knew what I wanted to be when I grew up, but I didn't, I hadn't really thought about it. I couldn't imagine any job being right for someone like me, as all I wanted was to play, read, write or just think my own thoughts. My mother imagined I might make a good nurse, because I always cared for her when she was poorly and I knew a lot about diseases, too. I'd look them up in the *Encyclopaedia of Medicine*, and then my mother would be reassured when I told her she couldn't possibly have cancer, for if you had cancer you wouldn't be in such pain, that her stomach pains simply meant her intestines were hyperactive, and you didn't die from that. Or if she had a headache and thought it was a brain tumour, then I'd spring the question on her in the middle of the day whether she'd ever gone temporarily blind, as I knew she never had, and she'd say no and I'd say that proved it couldn't possibly be a tumour, because if it was you'd be struck blind for minutes on end, it was common knowledge, everyone knew about brain tumours affecting your vision.

"A nurse perhaps," I tell the Head just for something to say, because having to spend the rest of my life nursing people doesn't bear thinking about, after all nursing your mother isn't the same as nursing a stranger, not by a long chalk, and I'm not keen on sick people anyway. When my mother's poorly it's got nothing to do with the kind of illness that requires staying in bed, I'm quite sure about that. My mother's troubles come from something else.

"Or nursery-school teacher," I hasten to add, for the Head has kept silent, "because I'm good at playing with my little brother and at teaching him things."

That's true, but the reason I spend so much time with Chris has more to do with making things easier for my mother than with doing what I like. What's really brilliant about Chris is when he hugs me tight with his little arms round my neck, I adore it when he does that and then I love him so very very much and want to hold on to him for ever so that nothing bad will ever happen to him in his entire life. That's what I like best about Chris. For the rest there's not much you can do with toddlers, you can't play proper games with them or anything because of the unfair competition. I prefer playing with my big brothers, they play exciting games that challenge you to out-best your best and you get all sweaty.

When you get all sweaty you know the game's serious, that it isn't just a load of rubbish.

The Head says that, whatever profession I might go in for, nursing or nursery education, I'll still have to stay on at school and I won't get any qualifications unless I'm willing to study subjects that don't appeal to me much or that I reckon aren't worth the bother.

I nod.

I think to myself that there's no point in getting good marks in subjects you really dislike, that no one can expect that from you. How can you be proud of getting a nine for arithmetic if you hate arithmetic? It's deceitful, getting such a high mark: it'd be far more honest to get a six, because a low mark like that tells everyone you hate arithmetic and can't be bothered with it.

I couldn't say what it was but I'd had the feeling a couple of times lately and now I had it again, this odd sensation in my stomach. I got it from this sort of conversation. It was as if the Head and my mother and nearly all the other grown-ups I knew thought exactly opposite to the way I thought about things. It reminded me of how I felt when Ara told me about her words and things would start spinning round the wrong way in my head so that I'd feel dizzy.

The Head began to rearrange her possessions in front of her and I took that to mean the meeting was over. All the nerviness fell away, my only concern now was that we'd have to leave her study together and what could I say during those final minutes walking down the corridor and across the playground. But these thoughts were premature, because the Head had been keeping an important topic for the very last. Her expression darkened suddenly, and before she'd even opened her mouth I realized what she was going to talk about. I felt my face redden, she noticed my discomfort and hesitated. I think she re-phrased her comments and didn't say exactly what she'd intended to say.

It was perfectly all right to go around with the girls in group six, she said, and it wasn't unusual, when groups five and six shared the same classroom, for the younger girls to be close with the older ones, but it was better to be best friends with girls your own age. In any case it didn't do to ignore them the way I did.

And Ara certainly was older, which wasn't surprising as she'd spent those extra years at school. She couldn't very well forbid me to spend time with her, she said, but during break I was to play with the others as well, not loll against Ara all the time, it really looked rather silly. It wasn't right, my parents wouldn't like it either and she was sure that if I stopped to think about it I'd see what she meant.

The Head wasn't finding it easy to tell me all these things, I could see that, and it raised my spirits. The red faded from my face and instead of cowering with hunched shoulders I straightened my back and met her eyes.

I looked at her steadily as if I had no idea what she was going on about.

Ara and me, we were nobody else's business.

"Any chips left?" I cried, panting because I'd come running all the way from school so I wouldn't need to watch the cracks.

"Chips aplenty," my mother called from the scullery where she stood guarding a blackened blistery pan with sizzling fat. She looked hot and tired so I slowed down and didn't run straight through to the kitchen, that would seem ungrateful. I waited for her to tip the chips into the bowl and sprinkle salt on top. Tossing the contents around, she carried the bowl to the table, and I trailed after her nattering on about how fantastic she was to make us all those chips, none of the other mothers did nice things like make chips for their children every Friday.

Makkie was sitting in my place at the kitchen table.

The boys didn't care where they sat, they used to flop down anywhere, but everyone knew I had my fixed place: on the long side, at the end.

"You're in my place, Peter," I said. I called him Peter because I didn't want to upset my mother by calling him Makkie, as she disapproved of that sometimes.

"Why don't you just sit here," my mother said with a sigh, "and let Makkie get on with his supper?"

The table was laid at one end. I sat down in a sulk and threw furious looks at Makkie, but he took no notice and only raised his eyes eagerly to welcome the new bowl of hot chips that had come to replace the previous one.

"Me first," I said, "I haven't had any yet."

My mother lifted the first bowl to take it away; there were a couple of chips left in the bottom which she scattered on my plate, saying I might as well start with these, at least they'd had time to cool off, and she went off to the scullery with the empty bowl. In passing she said: "What did the Headmistress have to say?"

I followed her with my eyes to decide whether she wanted a proper answer to her question or not.

The chips were less tasty than usual because I wasn't sitting in my own place, and I told Makkie he ought to think of other people for a change and not take such huge helpings all the time, that he'd left hardly anything for Chris, who was only small and needed food if he was to grow. Without glancing in my direction he raked some chips together on his plate with his fingers and dropped them on Chris's plate.

"There, you can eat them all up," I told Chris.

"I'm full," he said.

*

After the second bowl my mother repeated the same question.

"Nothing much," I said, "just that I'm noisy and that I should work harder at my sums."

"What did I tell you!" she said.

"She said I might go on to grammar school if I get my sums right."

"Oh well," said my mother, "no need for a girl to be a mathematician, eh?"

I could see her point.

I glanced at her gratefully. In my enthusiasm I announced that there was a new kind of sausage in the shops, for when we had chips. That was the sort of news my mother liked to hear, because it offered her an opportunity to please us and that always cheered her up. The new sausage was a *fricandel*, I said, and it was supposed to be quite delicious, even boys thought so. I thought it wiser not to say that my knowledge about fricandels had come from Ara and hoped desperately it wasn't one of her invented words, but that you were supposed to say it like that: fricandel.

"What's it called?" my mother asked.

"Fricandel," I said.

If we thought we'd like that, she'd see if she could get us some in the shops, in town maybe. In the meantime she was heating my frankfurters. The boys had croquettes with their chips, but I preferred frankfurters and so my mother put a saucepan on the boil especially for me, with four long frankfurters in it, which were all mine if I was hungry enough, but most of the time I ate only one. The rest would be eaten by the others.

"Don't you like frankfurters any more?" she asked as she deposited one on my plate, her face flushed from the heat.

That night I was violently sick. I'd eaten three whole frankfurters.

7

WE WERE ONLY ALLOWED TO WEAR TROUSERS TO school on rare occasions, which I thought was a great pity and also stupid. Rare occasions were for instance when the temperature sank to ten degrees below freezing point, and that's when the stupidity of it really hit you, because you'd be wearing a skirt over your long trousers and that made you look like an imbecile.

Imbecile is a word I got from our Willem, of course, he must've learnt it at his grammar school because they learn all sorts of difficult words there, and languages too. Nowadays when he wants to get at Makkie he'll say things like moron, imbecile, cretin, egoist, hypocrite. I don't know exactly what those words mean, but I'm sure they aren't things you want to be. Those new words haven't been able to oust puberty from first place, puberty is still our worst term of abuse, the boys go spare when you say they must've reached puberty. They never tease me about puberty or call me the other names. They just get at me for being oversensitive and a crybaby.

And I do cry easily.

Sometimes I feel weepy all day and I don't even know why, because I'm terribly happy, really.

My mother says it'll show in my face if I don't watch out.

*

Ara wore different clothes from ours, very nice ones that weren't trendy and yet she never looked like an imbecile. She wore skirts and dresses, sometimes reaching down below her knees and made of brightly patterned material. Her mother sewed them for her, she told me.

According to my mother Mrs Callenbach made those skirts from fancy materials, she told me their names but I couldn't remember them. Ara herself referred to one of her jumpers as her cashmisery jumper. It was bright red, very striking and suited her perfectly. It was made of super-soft wool, which I couldn't resist touching all the time. She'd leave her coat hanging open during break specially for me, so I could rub my cheeks against her jumper, which I really enjoyed and so did Ara. That way her cashmisery jumper became something we shared. Whatever the weather, hot or cold, Ara never went out without her coat, but in the mornings I could tell by the look on her face if she was wearing the red jumper. Ara could tell you all sorts of things with her face, she had all sorts of expressions on tap, and she'd have a special cheeky look when she was wearing the jumper. She'd cock her head, turn her eyes up and smile without parting her lips so that dimples came out in her cheeks. If she wanted to be extra funny she'd keep that look while she unbuttoned her coat slowly and then flung it open to show me what she had on underneath. The first time she did that I couldn't stop laughing and even had another fit of the giggles later in class, and so I got ticked off, because when our teacher asked what's so funny and would I share the joke with her and the rest of the class, of course I didn't say anything.

They just want to be different, my mother declared, after she'd seen Ara's mother at the supermarket wearing a funny-looking hat, and that on an ordinary weekday. Mrs Callenbach had introduced herself as Marlies Callenbach, and had invited my mother for a cup of tea some time.

"She even shook hands with me," my mother said with a contemptuous smile. That wasn't fair of her, I thought, she was only trying to be friendly.

"Yes," I said, "that's their way. That's what you do when you meet someone for the first time."

My mother says Ara's mother's hoity-toity, but that's because she speaks correct Dutch, not our dialect.

My mother doesn't like showy clothes, but I'm not bothered as Ara's family really are rather special and so it's only natural for it to show in the way they dress.

That's why Ara's so proud, I expect, it must be the way she's brought up, as I can't imagine why else you'd feel proud of yourself. You can be proud of something you've done, like a drawing, because of the effort you put into it, and you can also be proud about not committing a sin because you stopped to think.

Feeling proud never lasts very long with me, so I think it's pretty special when people are proud by nature.

Meeting Ara's father gave me an inkling of what their pride was about.

After my first visit I felt less in awe and I'd call at Ara's often and unannounced. I never knew how Ara's mother was going to react, whether she'd be stand-offish or show an exaggerated interest in every aspect of my life, but I didn't mind. I just told myself that I wasn't married to her after all and anyway I'd never let something like that come between me and Ara.

The Head hadn't been able to come between us, my mother hadn't and Ara's mother wouldn't either.

The man I saw when I came in through the back door a week

after my first visit to Ara's house was unmistakably her father. He was a big man with grey curly hair, but you could see it had been black. He was very handsome and didn't look like someone who works in an office, because he was burly and wore baggy trousers and a sweater and that's not the kind of clothes you expect someone to wear for the office. Ara had told me that he was an engineer and that he often worked late. Both statements intrigued me, because being an engineer sounded impressive and working late had the magic ring of a profession I hadn't a clue about.

Ara's father shook hands with me and said he supposed I was Kit Buts, the one who was so good at writing, and I said yes because Kit Buts is my name and I said not really because you're not supposed to lap up praise or people'll think you're too full of yourself. It made me happy to realize they'd been talking about me at Ara's house in my absence and that they had a favourable opinion about me, like being good at writing.

It got even better when Ara's father eyed me again, and said: "Well well, Kit, so you're my lovely little girl's friend?"

Two things flashed across my mind: that our friendship was being acknowledged and that Ara's father was proud of his daughter and said she was lovely in front of her. My father wouldn't dream of saying anything like that, about a daughter of his being lovely.

That wasn't the way we did things in our family. In fact we were told to look up to our betters and take their example, as they were bound to be cleverer than us in some way or other. We were modest and for all I knew it was right to be modest.

Ara's mother sometimes makes me feel rather dowdy when I turn up at her house in my grey pleated skirt because she can give you such a critical look, but Ara never mentions my clothes except to say something nice. She'll give me a really warm look and say:

"Kit, how very pretty that blue blouse looks on you."

When she says things like that I want to wear the blouse or whatever it is for a whole week, but my mother won't let me as she wants our clothes to be clean and fresh every day. She has an awful lot of laundry, but she never complains. I think she enjoys doing the washing and seeing the clean clothes flapping in the wind.

Ara has something nice to say whenever I'm wearing a new skirt or jumper. Most kids aren't like that, they'll just try to take you down a peg or two by pretending not to notice when you're wearing something brand-new. Girls can be so cruel that way, my mother says so too. My mother says you're better off having ten boys than one girl, and I can imagine why, as I think girls are a lot less fun than boys too.

Before our Chris was born I prayed in church for weeks and weeks for the baby to be a boy and I pressed my knees extra hard against the wood so it would really hurt and God would know I was serious, as another girl would drive my mother round the bend, what with girls being such a handful. When the baby was due we went to stay with our grandparents. My mother had to go to hospital. I was filled with remorse and thought I'd been praying all wrong, that I'd been bad and horribly selfish.

I had to think of some way of making amends, but I could hardly persuade God to undo my previous prayers just by shoving my knees hard against the wood. We had a very pious aunt who'd become a nun and gone into a convent, and every Good Friday she'd put a dried pea in each of her shoes so every step she took for the rest of the day would make her suffer.

I decided that would be a suitable penance. I asked my grandmother for two dried peas and put one in each shoe. After taking ten steps I decided God would never demand such suffering from a girl who was only eleven years old. A pea in both shoes was too bad, it was simply impossible to walk that way. One pea would have to do. It wasn't as if I'd committed a terrible sin. I'd meant well after all, it was only to spare my mother the trouble of another girl like me.

That day I staggered to school. Each step I took with my left foot made me cringe and so I tried to ignore the cracks between the paving stones, but I couldn't. Once you get started on that kind of thing you can't ever stop. And I reflected that my prayers might well come to nothing if I started cutting corners sneakily in other ways too. I only needed to go back four paving stones, and for the rest of the way I prayed that it didn't make the slightest difference whether it was a girl or a boy, just so long as my mother didn't die in childbirth.

Having me nearly killed her too.

I don't know if I hurt her a lot when I was coming out of her, but she caught pneumonia the day I was born. It was the coldest day of the year, she told me, and it was early in the morning. My father hadn't known how he'd ever manage to keep the room warm enough. All the neighbours had lent us their hot-water bottles to prevent my mother from freezing, and me too once I'd arrived. But it wasn't enough and my mother caught a chill anyway when she was having me. She ran a high fever, and the doctor was afraid she'd die and so they got the priest to come. She couldn't breastfeed me, and that upset her badly. She was so poorly they postponed my baptism and then her main worry was that something dreadful might happen to me before I'd been baptized and given a name.

Until you have a name and until you're a child of God, the devil can come and get you.

My mother was delirious, my father told me, and so they baptized me without her. After that she got well again.

Dozens of times I begged my mother to tell the story of my birth from start to finish. It was a harrowing tale, but also very moving. Harrowing because my mother'd had such a difficult time with me that whenever she told me about it I wished as hard as I could that I could do my birth all over again, I'd pick a sunny day in May when it wasn't too cold and not too hot to have me, and that I could start from scratch and come out of her without anyone getting ill at all. Best of all was when I came to realize how very much she had loved me, so much that she was delirious for days for fear of losing me.

Even so, she has to put up with a lot more bother from me than from all three boys together, she says sometimes. But that's mainly because the boys never cry, because they aren't so touchy, and also because boys aren't catty or critical all the time, they don't find fault with everything the way I do and they don't keep complaining about getting short shrift.

For instance I always think my mother's given the boys a bigger helping of meat than me, even if she hasn't, but if I think she has I can't swallow another mouthful because my throat goes all tight.

What I do like, though, is when my mother jokes with the neighbours about not having three boys but four and that I'm the worst of the lot. I'm very daring and so I have a lot of accidents. I've had a gash in my head four times already and once I fought so hard with some boy or other that I was knocked out. One of my front teeth even got chipped.

After school I used to change into trousers straight away and I'd try to get hold of one of the boys' jumpers, because they were more comfortable than girls' jumpers. Girls' jumpers always had something itchy about them, they tended to get caught on things and you could never pull them on over your head because they always put a little zip in for girls or horrid little buttons in impossible places, so you always needed help getting dressed. But if you hated having people fingering you and helping you to get your clothes on like I did then you were stuck. You'd stand there for two hours squirming around to get your jumper on properly which would put you in a bad temper for the rest of the day.

I also preferred the boys' shirts to my own blouses. Their shirts were made of coarser material, in which the scent of washing powder lingered longer than in the thin blouses you could almost see through which were considered smart for a girl.

The boys are more easy-going than me, even Makkie who's a difficult lad after all. The boys don't mind when I borrow their clothes, but I can't stand it when they take something of mine. I can't stand it when one of the boys puts on one of my T-shirts – pathetic, really.

And I don't let anyone in my room, but I go into theirs whenever I like, they don't mind. On the other hand I do keep my room clean myself, except for the sheets, that is, my mother does those and I wouldn't like to take that away from her because I know she likes doing the laundry. But for the rest I do everything myself and when I'm in a good mood, which I usually am, I make the boys' beds too in the morning, which takes some work off my mother's hands.

She's never asked me to do this and that's when I like doing things for her best. Being asked to do something usually makes me stroppy: say I've just decided to do her a favour and wash the dishes and then she goes and asks me to do it. By that time it's the last thing I feel like doing and I think things like: why don't the boys lift a finger and I say so too, so that instead of doing her a favour I make her unhappy, because we always get into an argument and then she goes all pathetic and says all right never you mind, I'll do it all myself, my children are useless, everyone in this house takes me for granted – that stuff. Then I feel like hanging myself from the tallest tree in the village, that's how desperately sorry I feel about being so mean and not going ahead and doing what she asked me to do without whingeing.

I'm the one who quarrels with her most. The boys tend to shut up, they just go a bit pale when they're angry. The boys are really good, deep down. All three of them.

My mother won't let me wear whatever I like, there are some clothes she considers too boyish.

"Now and then I forget I've even got a daughter," she'll say and that means I've gone too far, because if you've got just the one girl then you do want her to be a proper girl, even if you prefer boys. It's just that I can't always tell when she wants me to be a proper girl and when she doesn't. My mother's not clear on that point, so it's always a bit of a gamble.

When I did my First Holy Communion my mother bought me the most expensive clothes in the shop. Years later she could still remember exactly what my dress looked like and she'd tell me blissfully about the material it was made of, the name of which I've forgotten. Dressed to the nines, I looked like a little bride of Christ and that's exactly how I felt, because I was also wearing brand-new underclothes with fancy edging on both vest and knickers. Wearing special underclothes makes you feel special on the outside too, as if everyone can tell what you've got on underneath.

I wore a little crown too, which was very light but which I kept worrying about because it had to be fixed on my head with hairgrips. My hair is fine and straight, so nothing stays in it for long, not hair grips either, they just slide down. The day before the event my mother took me to the hairdresser. There wasn't very much she could do with my hair either as I wear it short and it's so fine, so she just put some clips in to make it wavy. My mother was in stitches at the salon, because I always act all funny when I'm fussed over.

And I looked dead stupid, sitting there with all those clips in my hair, no wonder I pulled faces and when I caught my mother laughing at the sight of me I pulled some more and couldn't stop. Whenever I notice my mother thinks I'm funny there's no stopping me, I go completely over the top.

The next morning the waves had vanished from my hair, which I thought a pity for my father and mother because it'd cost extra money and my father had said wavy hair suited me. The puffy-eyed look I had because I hadn't slept a wink disappeared after an hour or so, much to my relief. Once I was wearing all my gear I looked truly girlish.

It was beautiful weather the day of my First Holy Communion. Everyone was wearing new clothes and we all went to church together. I kept thinking I was about to swallow a bit of Christ. We'd rehearsed a couple of times, but we'd used imitation sacred hosts and that's hardly the same is it.

You're not supposed to chew the wafer, because of course it wouldn't be right to chew on the body of Christ. All I remembered about the practice wafers was that they got stuck to the roof of your mouth and I wondered if the real thing would get just as stuck, which was torture because then you had to fight the urge to wriggle it loose with the tip of your tongue. And you could hardly call that a suitable way of treating the body of Christ either.

The little white crochet purse dangling from my wrist held my commemorative prayer cards, all the children had those, except the ones from poor families. I was delighted with mine, neatly printed with my own name.

To remember the First H. Communion of Catherina Buts, Sunday 12 May 1963, it said, and then came a twelve-line poem, which I had learned by heart, for God.

All for Jesus! All for Jesus!
This our song shall ever be;
For we have no hope nor Saviour
If we have no hope in thee.

All for Jesus! Thou wilt give us
Strength to serve thee hour by hour;
None can move us from thy presence
While we trust thy love and power.

All for Jesus! At thine altar
Thou dost give us sweet content;
There dear Saviour we receive thee
In thy holy sacrament.

Every time it said Jesus I thought God, because I knew He was the Son of course, but still They were One, that was what I'd been taught. I just hoped that it was really true and that Jesus wasn't walking around up there all on his own insisting that you should love Him for His own sake, because I was more into God than into Jesus, but if they were One then it couldn't be bad of me, then Jesus was part of God from the start and had no reason to feel left out.

My cards had a picture of Our Blessed Lady with a caption printed in italics: *Through Mary unto Jesus.*

That was my mother's idea.

She's crazy about the Holy Virgin.

We had visitors all day and I got a whole lot of presents. The best one was my aunt Christine's, she'd bought me a pair of yellow dungarees. I couldn't wait to put them on and asked my mother if that was all right.

My mother said it was.

That's the way my parents are, they nearly always let us have our way, so long as it makes us happy. As I see it, my mother felt I'd spent enough time being a proper girl.

There was one shirt, it was our Willem's, which was the most comfortable shirt I'd ever worn in my entire life, but it was typically the kind of shirt my mother thought too boyish. Perhaps I did get a bit too ratty about things like that, it was just that it was hard giving up something you were so fond of, especially if you couldn't see what the fuss was about.

It was a shirt with different coloured stripes lying thick on the fabric like ribbing. It had a welt of black elastic along the bottom which made it billow out so it felt very roomy. There was a little zip by the collar, but it was conveniently placed in the front at the neck and you could leave it open if you wanted, which made you look like a cowboy. At least that's how I felt when I wore it: sturdy and strong, and that feeling would make me so happy that I'd start whistling. Although I made it very clear to my mother how much I loved that shirt, she didn't give in. I couldn't see what was wrong about me wearing it and so I smuggled it out of the house now and then after school. Then I'd leave the jumper I'd been wearing under a bush and put on Willem's shirt.

I didn't do this often, because I knew my mother would be upset if she found out.

You always suffer for your sins, and every time I did it I had bad dreams at night, about the jumper I'd left under the bush getting stolen.

Having bad dreams is a nuisance because I wake everyone up with my screaming, but sleepwalking is worse still.

I've been sleepwalking for a year now and my mother's already seen the doctor about it. The first time my parents found me wandering about in the corridor upstairs in the middle of the night they shook me awake, but that was so gruesome it made me vomit there and then. But my mother spoke to the doctor about it and they don't wake me up nowadays, they just let me get on with it and then try to steer me gently back to my bed.

What I do is chatter non-stop, apparently, about the boys and about school and about all sorts of things, but my mother won't always tell me what I've been saying without me even knowing.

Sometimes when I wake up in the morning I have vague memories of what drove me out of bed in the night and then I hope and pray I didn't go into my parents' bedroom to tell them all about it, or at least that my speech was so garbled that they couldn't possibly have made out what I was saying, because if they knew what I worry about most of all I'd feel terribly ashamed and besides it'd only make life even worse for my mother, because if she finds out I get so worried about her then she'll only worry even more about me and that's the last thing I want – people worrying about me.

It's pretty weird though to be doing things you don't know anything about. How can you ever keep a secret properly.

I made a whole scene about the shirt once when I was fast asleep.

"There you were standing stock still at the foot of our bed," my mother told me, "and you were going on about shirts and jumpers, it was all mixed up. And you gabbled on and on," she continued, with an expression of concern, "it was almost impossible to believe that you were actually asleep."

She asked me what on earth was the matter with me, after all, the boys didn't have this trouble.

How could I know, if I wasn't really there myself.

One day the shirt was gone.

I cried the whole afternoon.

That's the kind of thing that makes my mother say one girl's worse than ten boys.

8

I HAD TURNED ELEVEN AND TWELVE, BOTH TIMES without Ara coming to my birthday party. She preferred being just the two of us, without all the others crowding around, she said, and I took that to mean she loved me.

I was beginning to understand Ara's pride better and also that pride can be a burden, especially if people stick that label on you without your asking.

Pride was a sort of family trait in Ara's house, something that made her father talk about weird things like being A Callenbach and that A Callenbach would behave in such and such a way.

"What does he mean, being a Callenbach?" I asked Ara later on. "Surely he doesn't mean you're special because your name happens to be Callenbach, you're only special because it's in your nature, same as you don't do bad things because they're wrong and not because you belong to some family or other?"

Ara said crossly that she was glad her father was proud of her and that people ought to be proud of themselves or they'd just get bossed around. She didn't mind at all when her father told her to wear this or that skirt because she looked pretty in it. She really liked pleasing him with things like that.

"But isn't it terribly old-fashioned," I ventured, "to be treated like a girl?"

"But I *am* a girl," she said and glared at me in an attempt to squash me with her logic.

She succeeded. I didn't know what to say to that. I was certain I meant something quite different, something the two of us disagreed about, but I couldn't figure out exactly what it was and why I was so indignant.

In the spring of 1967 it dawned on our group that the pupils in the next group were leaving school at the end of term.

Some days there'd be just a few school leavers in the classroom, the rest would be elsewhere sitting for their entrance exams. More than half the girls in group six were going on to do domestic science, the rest were going to the comprehensive. Only one girl would be going to grammar school.

Thanks to our Head's extra lessons Ara had ended up among the girls doing their entrance exams, which I thought was wonderful because there was a secondary school in our village and it was a relief to know she wouldn't be going to school far away.

I prefer to have everyone around all the time.

My brothers, too. Both of them go to school in town, Willem goes to the grammar school and Makkie to the other one, and I've been to town often enough myself to know it isn't at all far, not more than five kilometres or so, and yet every morning I feel as if the pair of them are setting off for another world, a world far removed from the place I know from going shopping there with my mother once in a while. It's like they're embarking on a voyage never to return, and they don't come home at lunchtime, which is why my mother makes them sandwiches every morning, which she puts in plastic boxes along with something extra like a bar of chocolate or a roll of mints.

In the mornings she makes sandwiches for my father, too, but we don't see her doing that, because my father goes off to work at an unearthly hour when we're still asleep. So I only get to see his lunch box when he brings it back empty. Sometimes there's half a sandwich left and then my mother complains, because my father's skinny enough as it is, what with having to work so hard for our sakes.

The sandwiches my father eats are different from ours, and sometimes I eat one of the leftover halves he brings home. I imagine it'll help me understand him better, and besides he'll see that I love him, because if you eat someone's food even if you don't think it tastes particularly good, then that's a sure sign you love them.

My father's sandwiches are a touch old-fashioned, I must admit. He'll eat sandwiches made of one slice of white bread with a layer of rashers and a slice of rye-bread on top. That doesn't sound too old-fashioned, but what gets me is when there's butter and even treacle under the top slice.

My mother still gets her treacle from my grandmother, who makes it herself from sugar beets. All my father's brothers and sisters get their treacle from their mother, too, it's the only treacle they like. The stuff you buy in the shops is made from apples and my father doesn't approve of that one bit, nothing but factory fodder, he says.

Things like refusing to have treacle unless it's made by your mother strike a chord in me. So I always offer to go and fetch the treacle at Grandma's house, even if the neighbourhood she lives in isn't safe for a girl these days.

It's much harder to please my father than my mother, because my father usually isn't there and when he is he's content to have all of us gathered around him, that'll do him just fine, he says.

If I can make him happy fetching treacle from Grandma's then I'm glad to do so, even if I have to pedal like mad when I go past Uncle Stan's house. I'd do anything for my father, out of sheer gratitude.

My grandparents live on the edge of the woods nearby. I always go there by bike, because when there are lots of trees around it's easier to picture my bike as a horse. I've tied two strings to the handlebars, they're the reins for me to steer it with. My horse's name is Fury and when we career down the slope towards my grandparents' house I lift my feet from the pedals and give Fury a little kick in the side, which makes it very realistic indeed. After dismounting I pat its flanks and wipe the sweat away with the flat of my hand.

It happened in my last year at primary school. I was on the point of galloping down the slope. Uncle Stan lives at the top of the hill – not that he's my real uncle, we call him Uncle Stan because he drops by at our house now and then and my father visits him too. I think my father must feel sorry for Uncle Stan, living in that big house all alone like that and no wife to look after him, because it's not as if he's a good conversationalist, Uncle Stan's not that bright, quite the opposite in fact.

That's typical of my father, full of compassion, he is, which is why everyone always turns to him when they need help. My father's almost a saint, he's that charitable. And so he stops by to see Uncle Stan every now and then, just to pass the time of day and bring him a cake my mother's baked specially for him, because that's the kind of treat a man on his own never gets, she says. That's why I didn't hesitate when I saw Uncle Stan in his yard, beckoning me to come inside.

I hitched Fury to the gatepost, crossed the yard, and stepped into the poky dark kitchen. That's when Uncle Stan grabbed me. He didn't say a word. He was leaning against the sink, pulled me towards him and held me tight against his lower body. I was rigid with fear and shame and something else, too, a feeling of importance and excitement, which until then I'd only had when I'd spent a particularly long time pondering something, such as what is was like to die. That was odd, because the last thing I could possibly do from the moment he grabbed me was think. My head spun. I didn't know what to do.

He held me fast with his left arm, lifted my skirt with his right hand and slid his fat fingers under the leg of my knickers. And he began to stroke me.

It feels good to be stroked there, but it's forbidden.

I didn't come to my senses until he started thrusting his hips while he bent over me, his mouth making squeaky sounds in my ear, the kind of sounds people make when they're trying to get a strange cat to come close. You purse your lips and suck the air in.

Then I was flooded with rage. I started wrenching myself free and gave his shins a couple of half-hearted kicks, far too half-hearted if you ask me, but I didn't dare kick hard. It wasn't until the throb of a tractor in the distance made him raise his head that I was able to break away and run outside, calling over my shoulder that I'd tell my Grandma, but I was certain I wouldn't.

I didn't tell a soul.

It would upset my father, I thought, because it would show he'd been deceived about the goodness of other people, and my mother too, for having baked all those delicious cakes for somebody who turned out to be the very last person to deserve a treat.

I decided not to let the event distress me too much, so I wouldn't be frustrated later on. It hadn't been that bad, he was only human after all. Those farmers stuck in their farms all on their own, they did dirty things with the animals too to get satisfaction, everyone knew that. It was just human nature, you couldn't really blame them, they were just primitive and backward. Thick as two planks, they were. There was no way you could get through to those brutish, red-faced, ugly, gross fatheads with their pea-sized brains.

It's best to take a different angle, by comparing your worst experiences with the sinking of the *Titanic*, for example. The

Titanic didn't go down because of one thing that had gone wrong, but because thousands of things had gone wrong already, which they didn't know about, so the ice was just the last straw.

As soon as the boys left for school in the morning I'd miss them terribly, even when I'd just quarrelled with them. My mother said that would change once I was at senior school myself, but I wasn't so sure, because missing someone is such a weird feeling.

I get it in the evening sometimes when the boys are out. Say I want to be alone so I go upstairs, and then I can't even enjoy the peace and quiet of my own room because I'm so aware that they aren't downstairs in the living room watching telly. As soon as Willem or Makkie leave the house, to go to a friend's house or the youth club to play billiards for instance, being by myself in my room is a completely different feeling.

It reminds me of the way I missed Ara when she went to secondary school, but it wasn't quite the same. At primary school I got along fine without her, and didn't miss her in class or in the playground. I didn't miss her till school was over and I'd gone home and had a snack.

At those times I had only one desire, to be with Ara. Not to do anything in particular, just being with her made everything all right.

Ara's mother wouldn't let me see her until five o'clock because she had to get her homework done first, but sometimes I couldn't wait and would come knocking on their back door at half past four.

Ara was given heaps of homework at her new school and her mother was very strict about it. She'd scowl at me when I arrived early and asked her where Ara was.

Of course I knew where Ara was, she was up in her room, but I couldn't think of how else to wangle my way upstairs before time so as to spend a precious extra half hour with Ara. Her mother would tell me, not very kindly, that Ara was in her room doing her homework and then I'd have to grovel shamelessly to persuade her to let me in.

Ara herself is dead keen on learning, too, and she was thrilled to bits about passing the entrance exam and even jumped for joy, which isn't her style at all, though she looks really sweet with her big body going up and down.

She's thrilled but she also feels insecure. She keeps saying she won't be clever enough for her new school, that they must've made a mistake marking her exam papers and that somebody'll turn up any moment to tell her about the mistake and that she's failed after all. I've told her a thousand times that her marks average out at over seven out of ten, that of course she'll be bright enough, and that she's a million times brighter than the whole senior school with all the teachers in it. To build up her confidence some more I told her she'd soon be miles ahead of me at writing, because she reads stacks of books nowadays and besides her father is strict about language and knows exactly what's correct Dutch and what isn't.

If I had a father like Ara's I'd be a constant bundle of nerves, because he's always making remarks about speaking correctly. Sometimes I don't even dare open my mouth in his presence, because before I know it I've said something ungrammatical and then he'll correct me. For instance I'll say we don't never stay at home on Sundays, because that's the way we talk round here, and then he'll say ah, so you spend all your Sundays at home do you, and then I feel so humiliated I want to die there and then. He can tell when I feel that way, everyone can, because I turn beetroot red when I'm embarrassed. But somehow he can't resist correcting me, which gets on my nerves and that's why I don't admire him, because surely grown-ups should have it in them to be kind, so as not to hurt someone's feelings, however much they disapprove of sloppy grammar.

It's odd, but when you don't admire someone you can't stand it when that person's full of himself.

Every day at five Ara took Brutus for a walk and I'd go with them. We always took the same route, the shortest way to the wood where I'd first seen her with her dog. The wood was the best she'd ever seen, she said, with those lovely fens as old as time, the kind of place you could tell was untouched by humans.

We called it: The Land of Fen.

It was Ara's name, as everyone else referred to the wood by the name of its owner, Herstael, a proper baron, blind now and in a wheelchair, who in the old days could walk all the way into Belgium without leaving his own vast estate, my mother said.

I had never thought of the wood as a beautiful place and I still didn't. Ara did. Ara loved nature and liked to air her knowledge of it. She reeled off the names of all the trees and plants, and sometimes she'd lift her nose to sniff the breeze and say there must be some mint growing nearby or some such thing, because she could smell it. She was perceptive, not only about nature but in general, also about how you felt and whether or not you were in a good mood.

As it was, the wood didn't interest me overmuch. It wasn't the wood I cared about, it was the Land of Fen, our land, which she and I had claimed as our own by giving it a name and where we roamed every day, just the two of us and the dog.

In the beginning I used to take my own dog along too, so as to have something to hold, but my dog couldn't compare with a real live dog. I decided that all living creatures, like dogs, would from now on be Ara's speciality, not mine, just as the wood and all her knowledge about it had to remain her concern, and that for the rest of my life I'd be the kind of person who can't name a single plant. That's what Ara was good at and that's what I needed her for.

It's important not to bear a grudge when someone else, someone you love dearly, shines at something you're hopeless at. I try to be like that with our boys too.

With Willem it's a bit complicated deciding what you're going to let him be better at than you, because our Willem's a genius.

Every report Willem's had from the time he first went to school has been excellent. Any low marks he ever gets, seven out of ten, say, are for PE or craft, easy stuff you needn't be brainy for at any rate, but in all the other subjects he gets such high marks they make you dizzy.

So our Willem's incredibly brainy, everyone says so. You can tell from his face, too, I think, because he's paler than other boys and he isn't disruptive like me. The Principal of the boys' primary spoke to my parents about him when he was only nine, it was already that obvious he was brainy. He suggested moving our Willem up into the next group, but my mother wasn't having it. Not that she wasn't proud of our Willem, it was just that his birthday was at a favourable time, she said, which was why he was always one of the youngest lads, he'd only lose all his friends if they moved him up, and how would he cope being among boys who were that much older than him. My mother knows what's best for our Willem. He's very sensitive and he's hopeless at fighting.

"If only Willem was more like you and you more like Willem," she'd say sometimes, but it's too late for a reshuffle now and besides there's no point in wishing impossible things.

When it's your own brother, someone you love dearly, it's not hard to let him be the best in his field and to stop trying to compete, because that makes it less awful for him to be no good at other things, such as fighting. But as our Willem is good in all his subjects, it's not easy to figure out which one you're going to set aside for him to be best in and that's why I call him the scholar, which means, to all intents and purposes, that he knows a good deal more than other people. So when someone asks me what the capital of Russia is, for instance, then I shut up even if I know the answer's Moscow, I leave it up to Willem to say it so everyone will know our Willem's the one with all the answers, whatever the question.

With our Makkie it's a lot easier, because he isn't very good at reading and writing at all, but he is good at inventing. He's good at sums, which they call maths at his new school, and he gets high marks for that. He has other lessons at his school, too, like science and chemistry. Those are his favourite subjects.

Willem gets pretty good marks for those subjects too, but he's not as good as Makkie at inventing things. Willem is all thumbs, but Makkie is very technically-minded and he can construct anything once he sets his mind to it. Makkie helps my father fix the car, for instance, and he wants a moped as soon as he's old enough and it's legal. So I've assigned everything to do with electricity to Makkie. When a lamp goes phut in my room I always pretend to be scared to replace the bulb so as to have an excuse to ask Makkie to do it for me, so he'll know we all reckon he's the technical expert in the family. And I tell our Chris he's a super-huggy monkey and that he gives the best hugs in the world, because there isn't much else he's any good at yet.

Personally I'm not good at anything in particular. All I'm good at is the easy stuff, like art and drama, and writing of course. Our teacher always likes my compositions and that just shows, doesn't it, because writing compositions is what I like doing best of all and you even get marks for it, which you don't get for drama and the mark you get for art is a laugh anyway. But with writing you can't shine in the same way, because it's more of a private affair and not much use to anyone else.

On the day of my twelfth birthday Ara dropped by to see me before going to school. She gave me the most wonderful present I had ever had: a diary with a linen cover and a lock. On the fly-leaf she'd written: "To My Beloved Friend Kit from Ara" and I must confess it was the "beloved friend" bit that did it. It was as if Ara had given me a part of her, because you only wrote the words My Beloved Friend if you felt you'd be together for ever and ever.

For the first time that day I felt what it was like to be twelve. I stood on the brink of the yawning abyss that was my life stretching ahead of me, and I realized that from then on I'd really be getting older and day by day I'd get closer to an age that suited me better than any age I'd been until then.

II
FOOD AND DRINK

I

THE DAY I BECAME A WOMAN WE HAD CHIPS FOR supper. So it must have been a Friday. It sounds quite beautiful and moving, becoming a woman, but it was a purely physical experience and not at all what I'd expected. My Confirmation had more style.

I was hunched over my first helping of chips when the ache that had been nagging in my lower abdomen for days launched an all-out attack. I'd never felt like this before. A ferocious spasm made me groan and I let the chips in my fingers fall back onto the plate. My father and the boys were startled, but not my mother. I couldn't swallow another morsel, which is unusual as I'm the sort of person who finishes their food by scraping the plate.

The boys are much fussier with food than I am, especially our Chris. He even finds ordinary sandwiches an ordeal and has to wash down each bite with plenty of milk and fizzy drink. At mealtimes he often drives my mother to despair, because just the sight of a spoonful of greens is enough to make him gag sometimes. My mother invented and cooked dozens of exotic dishes specially for him, all to no avail.

I'll eat anything. My mother says at least I do her table justice, and although I know it's not a lot, that's exactly how I want her to feel about me. It takes so little to make her happy.

"I've got a terrible tummy ache," I told my mother apologetically.

"I think our Kit's got appendicitis or something," my father remarked to my mother.

"I don't think so," she said.

Now I'm nearly twenty the feeling that life isn't moving fast enough comes over me more and more often. Things aren't progressing. To be honest, I'm a bit disappointed. Things I used to think would mark a turning point in life seem to slip by with remarkably little effect. Even that longed-for day I was able to scrawl in my exercise book with capital letters that I'd become a woman at last like all the other girls, did not mark the beginning of a new era. The secret expectation that this would turn me into a grown-up by a stroke of magic was unfulfilled.

The following morning I was still sixteen years old, but now I had cramps. One day later the prospect of being stuck with this recurrent discomfort for the rest of my life dawned on me in gory detail and I decided my mother was right and Ara was wrong.

My mother had told me repeatedly there was no point in looking forward to it the way I did and that I could thank the Lord for having been spared so long. Once it started I'd get down on my knees and beg for a few more years' respite, but by then it'd be too late, for my fate as a woman would be sealed and all the years stretching ahead of me would follow the same rhythm set by monthly courses of blood and pain.

I didn't believe a word of it.

My mother's outlook on life was ever gloomy.

On the Friday of my metamorphosis I went to bed feeling weak, ill and elated. Down inside me things were going according to plan, it seemed, and I'd finally joined the ranks of all the other real women on the planet. After several hours of cramp-induced writhing I felt I'd got the message, and as far as I was concerned I could do without for the next couple of years.

My mother had put a packet of her sanitary towels on my bedside table with a downcast look, saying I had inherited that horrendous pain from her, more's the pity. She had suffered from it all her life.

"How does it feel?" my mother asked.

"Knives, daggers, war in my stomach."

She nodded.

The second day she asked me casually if I realized I'd have to be careful now, with boys. She was doing the dishes and bent her head even lower over the basin of washing-up as she spoke.

"'Course," I said peevishly and stalked out. The link between the bleeding and having to be careful wasn't clear to me in every detail, but your mother was the last person you'd turn to for information on that score. She'd die of embarrassment. I'd have to look it up in the *Little Red Book for Schoolchildren*, it told you about all sorts of unspeakable stuff. It was the most fascinating book I'd ever read and I was sure I wasn't supposed to have it. I kept it hidden under my mattress, along with my four secret exercise books. The little red book had led me to discover that I was able to bring on a quite delicious feeling all by myself if I wanted, anywhere and without any help from anyone or anything.

Not bannisters either.

It wasn't until years later that I saw the connection between the delicious sensation the book had told me about and one of the most pleasurable pastimes I'd had since I was ten. Sometimes Makkie would join in. We'd sit astride the bannisters and hoist ourselves upwards with our arms while our legs made frog-like swimming movements. When we reached the top of the bannisters we'd get off, race down the ten steps and start again. I went up and down until I was exhausted and the mounting delicious sensation between my legs was suddenly gone. All this clambering made us red in the face. I'd asked him if he liked doing it as much as I did and he'd said yes.

Without our ever having discussed it we'd halt our pitching as soon as someone came into the corridor, and let ourselves slide down backwards. Sliding down bannisters was wrong because it wore out the paint, but it wasn't a sin. We didn't know whether we were being sinful or not, but it was better to be on the safe side.

Ara suffered visibly too, but she had the satisfaction of feeling connected with nature, she said. It was only her insides being purified every month. She bore her cramps valiantly and even enjoyed them in a way because each stab of pain told her that her body was O.K. and in proper working order.

"I quite like the pain," she said. "At least my body gives clear signals."

Those were the only seven days a month she had no guilty feelings indulging her enormous appetite. It went with the pain, she said, and besides the desire to eat was more natural then than during the rest of the month.

"Pain makes you hungry," she maintained.

"Not a pain in the stomach, though," I'd told her, now that I was qualified to discuss the subject. She had to be making a mistake, I said, as it was obvious that the link she was making between pain and feeling hungry didn't apply to everyone, because in my case the pain stopped the hunger altogether and sometimes I could barely eat for three whole days. I survived on the endless mugs of hot chocolate my mother made me.

At first my comments excited Ara's irritation, and she grumbled that she supposed it was different for different women as some women obviously got hungrier than others – all her sisters got hungry when they had their periods, too.

"Oh well," I said, fearful as usual that she'd get into one of her moods and wouldn't speak to me for days, but in my head I continued our conversation and told her you just get cross because you've been kidding yourself and because yet another illusion has been shattered and you're left with no excuse for stuffing yourself during one week a month.

There's no point in making excuses for addiction, it's the motives that count. Excuses are invented to avoid feeling remorse and guilt, but digging down for your true motives brings you right to the core of your guilt and there, in that remote place shrouded in the darkness of ignorance, pain and denial, lies your sole opportunity of transforming your guilt into knowing. Knowledge is bearable, guilt isn't.

Most people believe that half-baked saying *What the eye doesn't see the heart doesn't grieve over*, and that it applies to them too, but that's not the way it works. What you don't see about another person you simply don't see and as long as you don't you can't grieve over it either, that much is obvious, but in a sense you can always see inside yourself. Which stands to reason, since you're the only one leading your life all on your own and can consequently be expected to know a thing or two. It's in you that every second of your life is vested, who else? That's the interesting thing about people, at least some people – that they're a fountain of knowledge about one life: their own.

It all hinges on the way you know yourself, that's essential. Some people know nothing about themselves. They can't get at the only true knowledge and history there is, because they keep it hidden away in that dark place.

Guilt is knowledge about yourself which you've stowed away in the wrong file, where it ceases to be knowledge of doing wrong and becomes a wordless blob you can't sort out and deal with, so you just get fat, or grumpy, or listless.

Knowledge belongs in the mind, where else? I couldn't imagine where words could reside other than in the mind. They're like the mind and the soul in a way, and like other abstract properties you know are yours even though they're invisible and virtually impossible to talk about.

That's the way I see it.

And so it can happen that all the things which you ought to know about yourself, but which are unspeakable in your mind, conspire to take on a visible and troublesome form, like several kilos of extra weight on your body or some other nuisance, some burden you carry around without knowing why it's been inflicted on you, while everyone else can tell something's wrong because you make the same stupid mistakes over and over again.

"Excuses won't get you anywhere, it's the motives that count. No one admits to being guilty these days," I mumbled, wanting to have the last word.

Ara turned to face me, fixed me with one her fierce looks and raised her left eyebrow. I knew I had better shut up.

I could go rabbiting on like that in my head for hours, it's one of my most favourite pastimes. Everything in life looks for a form in which to express itself, that's what I think, and I'm nearly twenty and can't imagine anything more satisfying than deciphering all those forms of expression, reducing them to the lightest and weightiest of common denominators: words. That's what makes me feel happy and free: putting things into words purely for the sake of it.

At times I worry about my future, because I have no idea how things can possibly work out if your greatest joy is thinking and then putting your thoughts into words.

Sometimes I feel it's such a shame that I'm finding it increasingly difficult to say what I think and that I get embarrassed about talking too much. My voice falters more and more often nowadays and always at the most awkward moments.

The conversations I carried on in my head became longer and my exercise books fuller.

Ara was the only person I felt truly at ease with when I went off the deep end, because she was the only one who ever asked me what I thought and also made it very plain she enjoyed listening to what I had to say.

During the cold winter weather we would spend whole afternoons and evenings secluded in her room or mine. We would draw the curtains, light candles, drink Coca-Cola and eat crisps.

In the summer we would go off to the Land of Fen, our secret place deep in the marshes, a tiny island which could only be reached by leaping across streams and pools. We both had gumboots, but she wore them under wide batik skirts and I wore them over tight jeans. No one could find us in the Land of Fen, so we could plan our futures to our hearts' content. Ara would sit leaning against the trunk of a fallen tree while I lay with my head on one of her generous thighs and talked or kept silent, that depended on the moment. Ara would stroke my head.

From the age of ten these were the only times in my youth when I felt utterly serene. I had yet to discover other ways of feeling at peace besides resting my head in Ara's lap when we were completely alone and there was no one else around for miles. Even when I was at home reading, curled up in an armchair, I was always aware of other people in the house, of my mother in the kitchen, of little Chris playing with his toys, and of my absent father and brothers, who were somehow there too, bound up as they were with all the objects which filled the house and whose sole purpose was to remind me of their existence.

Like everyone who thinks they've got a whole life ahead of them, I thought I'd eventually find ways to feel just as serene as I felt with Ara, that our friendship was a foretaste of what it would be like later on with a lover, that I would put up with and indeed delight in the same closeness.

At that time I didn't know yet that it was a once-in-a-lifetime experience and that it would never be the same with anyone else as it was then, during those hours, with Ara.

Ara and I couldn't imagine not being together. I told her there was no one who could make my body as calm as she could and she said she wanted to live in my words for ever.

Which was just as well.

They were intended for her most of the time anyway.

Ara could recall what I said word for word. At some point she'd decide it was the right time to remind me of some comment I'd made about her. She'd lean forward, assess me with an earnest, level look and say did I remember what I'd said on such and such a day, when we were in my room and I was wearing that blouse and those pants and we were eating those new chips, the ones with the paprika flavour, and that I'd told her she was making a mistake, that she was wrong to connect pain with hunger and that her stomach-ache was not a motive but an excuse for the hunger and that no one admitted to being guilty these days. She'd ask me to explain it to her once more and she'd always say my name in full.

Catherina.

She'd do her utmost to prevent me from looking away, to

make me take note of how eager she was to hear my answer. Her expression would show that I could tell her everything, that I needn't be ashamed to say anything, and at the same time she'd have that fleeting look I knew so well, the one she always had when she discovered she'd lost her grasp of a word: her eyes would show vexation, indignation and panic at her own bewilderment.

"So why do I eat such a lot, Catherina?" she'd ask.

I always answered her questions.

By and large it's fair to say that you can become a woman, make love, lose your virginity, go to bed with someone for the first time – which in my case, typically, had nothing to do with losing my virginity – without turning into a new, more mature, wiser or stronger person. In fact, nothing happens. You walk on air for a couple of days because you think you'll be different from now on, but the glow is spread by illusion, not reality. No change worth mentioning takes place.

I keep asking myself how you go about becoming an adult.

I dearly want to be one.

When I was twelve people of twenty struck me as a sight older and wiser than I feel right now. They tended to have fiancés, to be on the brink of marriage, and marriage is just about the last thing on my mind. Holding hands when you go for a walk with a boy is a let-down too. I thought it would be bliss, but it's dead boring. I feel a right prat when a boy holds my hand and wants to go out in the street so everyone can see, but boys always want to do that. It's quite a hassle persuading the boy you're going out with that you'd prefer to walk alone, not holding hands, and that you don't want to kiss in the café and you don't want to in the street either during the day – that obviously leaves little scope for cuddling, which suits me fine as after the first week or two I get bored with all that kissing.

I don't know what it is about kissing, but for me it always feels as if it ought to lead somewhere, as if that's the true purpose of kissing, but a kiss can last a quarter of an hour and still lead nowhere, which is why I think it's so terribly boring. It's like eating, in a way, except you don't get any nourishment, so why bother.

As soon as you switch off the boys always start whingeing that you don't really love them, and they're right of course, but then I'm so stupid as to deny it vehemently, which only makes them want to kiss me again and caress me and hold me in their arms until I just can't take it any more, then I go all stiff like a corpse at the slightest glance or touch. I never know when it's going to happen, but it keeps happening and it always takes me by surprise. Suddenly my stomach will lurch at a whiff of someone's clothes or of his lips after a kiss, and then I can't even bear to look at the person for another moment, so huge and so flagrant is my revulsion.

Every time this happens it means I'll give the boyfriend the push within a week. Telling them it's over is a nuisance, because some boys go all pale with grief and then there's always the risk that I'll feel so sorry for them that I'll plod on for another week, during which time I behave so coldly that they can't help seeing there's no point in going on and that no amount of talking things over is going to help. And the boys I fall in love with are always pretty much the same type: pale-faced, good-looking boys with narrow hips, never acting the cowboy or Marlon Brando but boys who model themselves on some manic-depressive blues singer who's known a lot of suffering and whose only means of expression is singing mournful songs about heartless parents, tragic love affairs and too much booze. They all play the guitar, write poems in English, talk about having the blues and they don't ride motorbikes. In other words, the type of boy with feelings.

Until now six weeks has been my absolute record. I can never stick it for longer. Each time I resolve to give it a rest for a while, because I'm not that keen on being part of a twosome anyway, but after a month or two I always fall in love again and then I think it's the real thing and don't let up until I've got whoever it is I've fallen for. I keep forgetting that, if you think about it, falling in love is the best part, that things can only go downhill after that, and that the conquest of your beloved simply means forfeiting what you held dearest. You can realize all this ten times over, but it doesn't help. Each time you fall in love you head straight towards the destruction of that love.

In my opinion love only works when you succeed in satisfying your heart's desire without forfeiting the desire itself.

It seldom works.

Except with Ara.

Since I became a woman love has become one of the topics I like thinking about most, like God, happiness, Ara and death. I reckon I must be a bit funny in the love sector, because other girls seem to be much keener to make sacrifices for boys than me.

As I had a big mouth I got elected class leader year after year at secondary school: you were supposed to keep the class register and help other pupils with problems to do with school, but eighty per cent of the problems I got on my plate were about love, especially from the girls. This taught me that most girls don't want to dump whoever they're going out with as soon as possible, like me, but that they want to hold onto them for ever and that they'll do anything to achieve that. I was horrified when one girl confided in me that she was scared she was pregnant. That meant she'd done it with a boy. And she was even younger than me, only fourteen or so.

On the whole, though, the love problems weren't particularly interesting as they were always the same. Either one person wanted someone else but didn't know how to get them, or someone had been dumped by someone else and wanted to commit suicide.

Puberty can be a time of harrowing drama.

Actually what surprised me most was that my classmates could be so unashamedly pubescent in their behaviour, that they hadn't a clue they were dutifully running the gamut of adolescent states they were told to expect in those awful teenage books they read. It was hard to find anyone not tormented by impossible parents or by acne, anyone not rebelling against the whole world and not devastated by love.

Puberty was not an issue in our house.

No one was devastated by love, either.

My mother told us we shouldn't expect too much of love and that it was better not to rush things, that there was plenty of time later to get yourself tied hand and foot and that we should enjoy our freedom as long as we possibly could.

And we did.

My elder brothers were in their twenties by then and still didn't have steady girlfriends. You'd think my mother was pleased about that, but she wasn't. She often complained about it being a bit odd that neither of our boys had found themselves a nice girl yet and that all my brothers' friends were spoken for already.

"Why do my children have to be so different?" she said.

When Willem and Makkie came home at the weekend and dropped their bags with dirty laundry in the scullery, she said it was no wonder our boys couldn't find themselves a girl, the way they looked, what with their long straggly hair and those torn grimy jeans. My own hair reached down past my shoulders by then and I reminded my mother that I wore my hair long too, after all, and that it's much more obvious when boys are hippies than girls and that my brothers had to dress that way in town, at their university, or else they'd be considered odd and would be left out and that she'd be a hundred times sorrier if her boys were looked down on by others.

"I suppose you're right," my mother said.

My mother's an easy person to talk to. In the end she always sees reason.

She wondered from whom we had inherited our interest in reading and studying, because it could hardly come from our father and not from her either. Since they got married neither of them had held another book besides a missal, not that they didn't like books, mind you. She used to like reading when she was a girl, and would have loved to have continued her education like her sisters and brothers, but where would she ever have found the time, what with so many children to look after.

"You're better off without them," she told me, "they just give you grief."

It's true. I've seen it for myself.

They worry about me, too, but less than about the boys.

"Our Kit's no trouble at all," my mother says and my father agrees and says I'm our little ray of sunshine in the house. And it's a good thing I am, too, because if you have a family with one member who finds life very heavy-going indeed, then there should be another member of the family who's light-hearted and carefree, to keep things in balance.

My mother thinks girls are better at managing their lives than boys. A man needs a woman, but a woman can do perfectly well without a man.

Where we live you can tell this is true from the faces of the men and women who've lost their partners. The men look forlorn and dishevelled within a month while the widows perk up and plunge into a new life of their own.

*

It wasn't her idea, my mother said, for her children to be clever and go to university. Other people had a far easier time with their children, who were ordinary and learned a trade and wore respectable clothes and earned proper wages, at least those children were some comfort to their parents, they didn't spring all those surprises on them. We got funny ideas from burying our noses in books all the time, from reading about all sorts of things that were beyond ordinary folk.

I was sorry for her and for my father.

This is a shit century for parents.

There had been a war when they were young and one winter they'd almost starved, they hadn't had much of a childhood themselves and only wanted what was best for us so we'd do well for ourselves in life, and then all of a sudden it turns out that being good parents is impossible in the twentieth century. They didn't need Freud to tell them that.

"Us parents, no matter what we do it's never right, we always get the blame anyway." That was how my mother summed up a parent's lot.

I decided to continue living at home with them for a while, to find myself a steady boyfriend, to get a proper diploma for their sake and to try wearing a tight skirt.

Which is why I'm at the teachers' training college now and why I'm going out with Matthias. I tried the tight skirt but found it impossible to walk in so I now stick to a pleated skirt on Sundays, even though pleats are hardly the latest thing.

2

I'VE GOT THE HANG OF THE COURSE NOW, BUT NOT yet of love. It's beginning to dawn on me which subjects are right for me, and the only disadvantage of teachers' training is that I'm still forced to learn such a load of cobblers, which I think is a waste of the space in my head. What I really like is education theory and psychology, as well as one of the teachers we have for those subjects. The psychology instructor's name is Verkruysse and he looks the way you'd imagine a psychologist to look if you'd never seen one before.

Verkruysse is our year's student counsellor. The first thing he said to me was how intriguing it was that a young lady, at the ripe and moreover highly attractive age of nineteen, with excellent exam results and a dossier that would make Freud's mouth water, should decide to enter the portals of this praiseworthy yet widely disdained institution.

I explained my reasons as best I could.

In the tone of his response – "Well, you've got quite a long way to go, Buts" – I could detect no trace of his initial cynicism, and that made me blush. He made it even worse by coming up close to me and saying things about modesty being a virtue and that at least I'd be ready to embark on the serious work in two years' time.

On the one hand it's really nice when someone has high expectations of you, but on the other it's absolutely infuriating. I haven't a clue what I'll be doing in two years' time. And besides, just because someone's kind and encouraging for once that's no reason to go and fall in love with them straight away.

It's got something to do with hormones, no doubt.

However loath you are to act the adolescent, your hyper-active hormones always seem to get in the way.

The explanation I offered wasn't even mine. I said I had to learn how to study, and that was literally what Barten, our teacher of Dutch, had told me some years before.

Barten had joined the staff of the secondary school in our village when I was repeating the second year. Ara had already moved up to the next form and the only time I had spent on anything resembling homework until then was when I helped Ara with her foreign languages. They were trickier for her than maths, science or chemistry, because she had to hear a word before she could use it. She had trouble figuring out what a word sounded like from the spelling.

"I have to get to know all the words personally before I say and write them," she said. "Words I've never dealt with before scare me, they're out of reach."

I had told her she must have a gigantic memory, bigger than anyone else's, as all the words she knew were safely stored away in her head and the only person I knew who was like that was our Willem, but he didn't need to learn the words because of his photographic memory: seeing a word once was enough to remember it for the rest of his life.

Ara liked being compared to our Willem and said she only felt clever when I was around, telling her all these things. I was so pleased about this that I rattled on, saying I wished I could sit next to her for ever, wherever she was, in class and anywhere else, till kingdom come, so I could whisper the words she didn't know in her ear and help her to master a few more each day for her to store away in her head.

She gave me an earnest look and said she'd like that, but that it wouldn't work out that way, not with us.

"Why not?" I asked, frightened and curious.

"One day you'll go away," she said with conviction.

The first essay I handed in to Barten got me nine and a half out of ten, and he asked would I read it out in class. I said no, because I had written it for him alone.

Could we have a chat after class, he said, and so for the next fifty minutes I didn't hear a word of what was being said, so excited was I at the prospect of being alone with him and, with any luck, getting to hear what he thought was so good about my essay.

He had given us three titles to choose from: "Your Own Room", "Nobody Understands Me", and "Partir c'est Mourir un Peu". I had chosen the last title, interpreting it in such a way that it could serve as the heading of one of my favourite fantasies, about what it was like to part with all my loved ones and venture on the road to ultimate death.

It was a very complicated fantasy, in which I was indeed required to travel great distances in the mind, all the way from my bedroom to the Land of Fen and then further and further, until I arrived at the Great Nothing where I could picture vividly being quite alone and eventually vanishing altogether. I could never think the vanishing thought to its conclusion as I was afraid I'd go mad. So I had ended my essay by saying you can only think a little about dying while you're alive, because if you imagined it all you'd lose your mind. Essays had to fit the title, I thought.

Barten waited patiently for everyone to leave the classroom and then asked Mieke Theunissen, who'd been hanging around my desk for ages in the hope of overhearing what he had to say, to please shut the door behind her. Then we were alone. I was so nervous and shy I was afraid I wouldn't be able to utter a single word and the next moment I prayed desperately that the conversation would not be about my essay. I was ashamed of having written it and wondered what on earth could have made me expect anything of Barten.

The teacher's desk stood on a low platform. Barten stepped down and crossed to a desk in the front row. He drew back a chair and motioned me to sit on the chair next to his.

In my view teachers were attractive for being teachers, but Barten was truly handsome to boot. Young, slim, tall, he had straight hair and a slight stoop, which gave him a tormented air. He was wreathed in the sweet aroma of pipe tobacco. I suspected he wrote poems in his spare time, which he didn't show to anyone. Not even to his own wife.

The lines in his face were gentle and kindly without being weak, but the most striking feature was his eyes. They were very unusual, and I'd only seen such eyes once before: Hendrik's.

They're the sort of eyes they call deep-set, I believe. They have something Chinesey about them, because you can't see the eyelid itself, all you can see is a neat little fold of skin marking off at least half of the iris. If the skin between eyebrow and iris is taut and the line goes down a bit at the corners as well, then it's as if you can tell that person is weighed down with knowledge.

Barten had eyes like that and so did Hendrik.

From the time I was twelve years old I was allowed to attend the summer camps organized by the girls' club, and during my third year there I met Hendrik. He was a youth worker, involved with maladjusted children. That summer of 1970 he and a friend were working as volunteers at the farm we would be taken to visit, all shrieking thirteen of us, from time to time.

The first thing I noticed about him was those eyes.

I didn't fall in love until later, after he had bandaged my hands.

Our days at summer camp were filled with games and expeditions from morning till night. As dusk was falling on the third day we were divided into groups. Each group was given a mission to carry out within a certain time. The group of four girls I was in was instructed to get hold of a copy of that day's newspaper. The farm was on the outskirts of a village and the nearest house was a few hundred metres away. We set off at a trot and on the freshly gritted path leading to the farm I stumbled, and tried to break my fall with outstretched hands. I called out to the other girls to go ahead, that I'd wait for them to come back here, and I scrambled to my feet. My palms stung, they were badly scraped, covered in blood, bristling with sharp grit.

Hendrik was truly concerned. He led me into the kitchen, got out the first-aid kit and took my hands in his. One by one he plucked the tiny stones out of the palms of my hands with tweezers, gently and with great concentration.

It took a very long time.

Not long enough for me.

For the next few days I tagged after him everywhere.

That's how I caught him with that boy.

I wasn't even shocked. My little red book had told me about this kind of thing, that it was quite normal and nothing to worry about. It said that at least twenty per cent of all people felt that way, which I had found impossible to credit as it meant they had to be living in our village and going to the same school as us, and I'd never seen one.

Hendrik and the other boy got rather a fright and Hendrik asked if I minded seeing them together like that. I didn't mind, as it happened, although I did think they looked pretty stupid.

"Oh no," I said, "not at all."

Hendrik came to me, picked me up and carried me into the kitchen. As he had done every day since my fall, he unwrapped the bandages and cleaned the wounds in my palms by swabbing them with iodine. He always asked if it hurt. This time he smiled a lot more than usual and when he was done he gave me a meaningful look and kissed me softly on the lips. We had a secret, that much was clear.

As it was, Barten came right out and said what he had thought when he read my essay. He had thought it was impossible that someone who could write such a good essay would have to be repeating the year.

Startled by the turn our conversation was taking I said it was only natural I hadn't moved up, as I never did any homework and I never revised for tests.

I was mildly disappointed that our conversation didn't touch upon my reflections on death and that he didn't ask me what I thought about life. Meanwhile I was wondering what writing a good essay had to do with how good you were at other subjects, but I didn't dare ask Barten to explain the connection. He wanted to know why I neglected my homework and didn't revise for tests.

"Lazy, stupid?" I offered.

"Nonsense, Kit," he said, "this is not the work of a lazy or stupid pupil. Do you find school boring, by any chance?"

I couldn't decide whether or not to give him a straight answer. It had to be deeply insulting for a teacher to be told how utterly bored you get during lessons. That would be like saying it's a rotten school and the teachers a bunch of boring old fogies, and he might pass that on to the Principal and then I'd be kept at school on Saturday morning for punishment.

"Sometimes," I said.

I hastened to add that it wasn't the school's fault or the teachers', that grammar and essay-writing were brilliant, it was just that I got bored easily, and I'd already read all the textbooks they gave you in the second year as I used to help Ara with her homework, so I thought I already knew them and didn't need to pay attention, but by the time a test came up I'd forgotten such a lot that I couldn't answer the questions properly.

"Ara, is that Barbara Callenbach?"

"Yes," I said, "she's my friend."

With mounting enthusiasm I told him about how special she was and how special her way with words and how I couldn't wait to start my third year because Ara had been learning such interesting things, in biology class it was, with Miss Mares, something about being able to predict whether a child will be born with blue eyes or brown.

"Genetics," said Barten. "So biology isn't one of the subjects you dislike?"

"Yes it is," I said. "Drawing the bits of plants is all right, but learning their names is mega-boring. I got a five for biology, but genetics, that sounds more fun."

"What else do you like?"

"PE, art, literature, projects, the school magazine and RE," I said, "just the easy stuff, I suppose."

"But you could learn how to learn, Kit," Barten concluded.

The next day he handed me a folder, smiling and saying it wasn't to show off that he was giving me this to read, it was just that he had confidence in me. The folder contained the dissertation he'd written in his final year at college, back in 1964.

He'd made a note, he said, of the parts that were important for me. There was no need to read the rest. If there was anything I didn't understand I was to ask him and when I'd had a look at it I was to let him know, then we would talk about it.

"Don't be put off by the title," he said as he left.

At school I didn't tell a soul, not even Ara, but as soon as I got home I boasted to my mother that Barten, our new Dutch teacher – he was great, the best teacher in the whole school – that at least he took an interest in me and that I'd got his dissertation here in this pink folder, which I wasn't to show anyone else, no one at all, and that he wanted me to read it so I could learn from it and that I was going straight to my room to get started.

Normally I'd come downstairs at least half an hour before supper and hover around my mother in the kitchen, watching her cleaning the vegetables and stirring the soup, and sniffing that wonderful aroma of meat sizzling as it touches the hot butter in the pan.

I was always hungry.

Lying on my stomach on my bed I inhaled the smell of the yellowed, neatly typed sheets of paper. I started on the first page and not for a moment did I feel hungry. Even when my mother called from the bottom of the stairs that supper was ready my stomach didn't jump and I could barely tear myself away from Barten's dissertation to go downstairs.

"It must be pretty gripping, what you've got in that folder," my mother said, "for it to keep you out of the kitchen."

"Yes," I said.

"What's it called?"

"*Troublemakers*," I replied, "but it's not what you think."

It wasn't what I thought, either. I couldn't for the life of me imagine having anything in common with the children Barten described. Each chapter ended with a little story about one of the pupils Barten had worked with when he was doing his teaching practice at a school for children with learning difficulties. Case histories was what he called them and they were all titled with a girl's name or a boy's. Usually a boy's. His research was about kids who caused a rumpus in class because they were bored, but according to Barten they weren't bored because they thought the lessons were too hard but because they were too easy. Some of those kids pretended to be thicker than they were, just because they were scared of being rejected by their classmates or by their family.

I wasn't bothered about that at all. Personally I never stopped to think about whether lessons were difficult or easy; most of the time they were boring and I couldn't see any point in doing them. Who cares whether you know what latitude Belgrade's on or what cross-fertilization means? A dreadful waste, I thought, to make room in my head for such trivialities, and I came across no mention in *Troublemakers* of children worrying about not having sufficient head-space.

Perhaps I'd get there later. I hadn't even reached Chapters Four and Five, which Barten had singled out for me to read. They were titled "Outside" and "Inside", and Barten's note said I'd probably find Johnny's case history in Chapter Five interesting.

Interesting was putting it mildly. After reading Chapter Five I was so moved my heart ached with longing for the impossible: to have been a pupil at that special school, in 1962 – I'd be myself but I'd have Johnny's character – and I'd be one of the troublemakers on whom Barten rested his benevolent gaze the moment he arrived and for whose salvation he'd fought day and night ever since.

Johnny is more imaginative than me, but he's a lot worse off. His mother drinks and his father's never home, so Johnny acts the man in the house. He's so good with his little brother and sister it's heart-rending. Barten claims Johnny gets bored in class not only because he's cleverer than the rest but also because he misses the challenge he always feels at home.

None of this applies to me. I can reel off the names of at least four people in my class who are ten times cleverer than me, and we never quarrel in our house either. My mother doesn't drink except for a glass of liqueur on New Year's Eve and I see my father every day, even if it's not for very long.

What Johnny and I do have in common is that we both like writing. Johnny spends all his time writing and Barten persuades him to let him read his diaries. How horrid, I think to myself, to have someone else read your diary. I'd die of shame.

I must tell Barten I can see what he means about inside and outside and that I can follow the jargon, like interior and exterior motivation. He's absolutely right. Like Johnny I never do a thing I don't see the point of. And I must also ask him how you go about writing a dissertation, because his is really brilliant, and it would be great to write something like that myself. But I can guess what he'll say. Something about exterior motivation, I shouldn't wonder.

It was a long time before I fell asleep. My final thought before drifting off was that I wouldn't dare tell Barten all the things I wanted to tell him.

3

FIRST IT CAME IRREGULARLY, THEN AFTER ABOUT A year it stopped altogether and in November 1974, a few days after my eighteenth birthday, at eleven o'clock in the morning, I lost my virginity in the city hospital to a speculum wielded by Dr van Dalfsen. The instrument had been warmed up beforehand.

There are girls who have a harder time of it than I had. Given the story of my life up to then something like this was bound to happen, I reckoned. For some reason things never come my way the way they're supposed to.

"Stopped having those tummy-aches, have you?" my mother asked me one day.

"Yes," I said.

"Good."

I didn't mention that the bleeding had stopped too.

I didn't tell her about that until the day she said with a little laugh wasn't it time she got me some more of those pad things and I said there was no need, because it had gone.

"How do you mean, gone?"

"My periods have stopped."

"Since when?"

"I don't know. A while. About a year, I think."

Our family doctor did not put me through an internal examination: he prescribed some pills. They would do the trick, I could be sure.

They didn't do the trick on the inside, but on the outside their effect was unmistakable. In no time I had put on four kilos of extra flesh and was shocked when I caught a glimpse of myself in a shop window. Instead of a slip of a girl there stood a hefty creature who looked like a stranger. In my head I still weighed forty-seven kilos and my plodding reflection did not match that weight.

It was hormones, the doctor said, and he prescribed another course of pills.

"This will get you going all right, there's no girl can withstand the strength of this," he said, handing me the prescription.

After yet another bloodless month I had swollen to fifty-three kilos and the doctor referred me to the hospital. The reaction of people who hadn't seen me for a month filled me with shame.

Had he known I was still a virgin Dr van Dalfsen would no doubt have treated me with a little more solicitude, and he would not have summoned three male interns to come and poke me around. The only person who had any inkling of how I felt was the nurse who stood by my head and wiped my brow from time to time when I was lying on the examining couch. I was flooded with love for her, but if I'd come across her in the street the next day I wouldn't have recognized her.

It's having to lie there in such a ridiculous position that makes you feel a complete idiot. Secretly I tried to enjoy losing my virginity, by dwelling on it and telling myself over and over that this was an important occasion in my life, in spite of the circumstances. By treating me like an ordinary patient, someone who had something wrong with her body, the nurse helped me to conceal the pleasure I took in my singular initiation.

*

When you're in distress and someone shows sympathy and tries to help in some way, you can go all weak inside and feel you'd do anything in the world for that person out of sheer gratitude. But stuck there with your legs in the stirrups there's nothing you can do, and because you're totally helpless, love just sweeps over you.

A good way of feeling really and truly in love is having an accident together or being locked up just the two of you in a cell with standing room only and held hostage by some madman or other, that always works. Being out in a rowing boat together when a storm breaks overhead is pretty good too. In a situation like that you'd even fall in love with someone you wouldn't even have noticed if you were in your right mind and if your life, far from being in danger of ending, was simply jogging along at its usual unconcerned pace.

Love and fear must have something to do with each other, I'm convinced of that. No wonder they talk about the institution of marriage, because, once you're in an institution together that's it, you get to be so dependent that love comes automatically.

The gaping feeling between my legs was not unpleasant, but it made me walk as if I'd spent hours on horseback. Before letting me return to the changing cubicle the doctor told me to sit down because he still had a form to fill in. All I could think of was that I didn't have my knickers on and as I still wanted to be just a tiny bit in love with the man who had taken my virginity, I couldn't think what to say to his questions. They didn't sink in. He felt my hands, muttered "moist", and scribbled on the form. He asked questions, got no reply, growled that everything was just fine down there and that perhaps it might be a good idea to get a doctor to take a look up there, in that little box.

I didn't get it.

They'd already done things with my head, with wires and electricity, which I hadn't felt at all but which did produce a result that my own doctor had found satisfactory.

"Nothing wrong with the cerebral functions, thank goodness," he had said, but he added that I should go for an internal examination. His words had surprised me, for they implied that having your brain examined didn't count as an internal examination. I couldn't conceive of a more fully internal examination than being connected to a device that said something about how my brain was working.

I was putting on my clothes in the cubicle when there was a soft knock on the door and someone pushed it open.

"I expect you'll need this," she said, holding out a sanitary pad. She was right. I hadn't even noticed.

In the yellow-tiled corridor my mother sat on a wooden bench, waiting. She was waiting for me. Never before and never since have I seen my mother look at me so tenderly. She felt compassion for me, I could tell. To my amazement tears welled in my eyes. It was strange, because the last thing I wanted was my mother's pity, but it was much too complicated to make her see that there was no need to feel sorry for me and that my tears had nothing to do with the reason for the tender look in her eyes.

"Come on," she said, offering me her arm, "let's treat ourselves to some of those gorgeous cream cakes."

My throat tight with happiness, I walked at her side, awash with gratitude to the doctor and his speculum and to the nurse and above all to my mother for sitting there on that wooden bench in the hospital and giving me that look. My sole regret at that moment was that I couldn't tell her why I was so elated.

*

She got rather a shock when I mentioned that the doctor had said I should talk to the hospital psychiatrist.

"I expect it's all my fault," she said.

I protested that it was just a routine appointment and part of the whole check-up and that she shouldn't worry about a thing because she was a wonderful mother, we all thought so, and that we were very glad we had parents like her and Papa who did everything for us and that we were all very grateful, even if we didn't always show it, especially the boys, but that didn't mean to say they didn't feel the same way, for they were good boys at heart even if they did wear their hair long, they weren't taking drugs or anything, and didn't they come to see us every week-end, which was more than you could say for most families with children that had left home, that they came back to visit so often.

"Yes," my mother said, "perhaps I was too good for the lot of you."

Returning home from our trip to the city I discovered that Ara had brought me a bunch of wild flowers, which she had put in my bedroom. There was a sealed envelope lying next to the vase. I waited for my mother to leave the room before ripping it open and reading the card inside.

"Dear Kit. I hope the doctor didn't hurt you. I would hate that. It's hard luck you had to have this experience artificially. Naturally is better. I think of you all the time. Ara."

Ara didn't understand either. It didn't matter. Anyway, it was probably something weird about me, not being so sure I'd prefer the natural way to the artificial.

"*She* can be really kind at times," my mother said when I came downstairs, but she seemed a bit upset when I put my coat on and made for the door to go to Ara. I suppose it was because we'd spent the afternoon so intimately and now she might be thinking she wasn't good enough for me.

"Ara this and Ara that, Ara from morning till night," she said plaintively. "You're at her beck and call. She takes advantage of you, Kit. You shouldn't get so involved."

I remembered how my mother had sat and waited for me at the hospital and decided she was right. And so she was, but it made no difference. Ara just happened to be better at controlling her feelings than I was, and a prouder and more independent sort of person.

It seems to me I'm completely dependent on Ara.

My mother says it's because I'm too one-track minded, too obsessed with Ara, it's all very well pretending the other girls can be my friends if they like but they know they'll always take second place anyway, because of Ara.

On occasion, coming home early from college, I'd know Ara was home too and then I'd wait an hour to give her a chance to take the initiative for once, simply because she longed for my company as much as I longed for hers and couldn't bear the thought of her being in her house and me in mine all this time we could have been together. It never worked. Ara never came. When the hour was up I'd go to her house, a bit put out.

"Why didn't you come to my house?" I'd ask.

"How d'you mean?"

"I've been home an hour already."

"I know."

"So why didn't you come?"

"I knew you'd come here," she'd say, with a secretive, superior smile.

"But don't you want to see me right away?"

"No," she'd say, her expression blank. "I don't have to have you around me all the time. You're with me all the time anyway."

That's one of the things I admire so much about Ara. Without batting an eyelid she'll say things you think can't be said, be they home truths or super-romantic confidences.

"Oh well, might as well stay here I suppose," I said to my mother and took my coat off again. Suddenly I felt very tired and faintly sick. I feel like that sometimes when I can't decide what to do because I want two things at once.

"Very sensible, dear," said my mother. "There's no need for you to go running after anyone. Let them come to you. Yes, you just stay here and I'll make the two of us a nice cup of coffee. Or would you prefer some hot chocolate? There's one of those low-fat desserts in the fridge, for my diet you know, you can have it if you like."

Since I've been dieting I think of nothing but food and since I've been thinking about food I've got fatter and fatter. Of every biscuit, every slice of bread and sliver of cheese, every morsel of braised or roasted meat, every spoonful of vegetables and potatoes and of every single fruit, piece of chocolate or pie I know the exact number of calories.

I can't put anything in my mouth nowadays without thinking of the numeral I'm swallowing.

If I don't know the numeral that goes with a particular food I don't dare eat it until I've found out what it'll cost me in calories.

The moment I started to wonder why our Chris could down three platefuls of chips with mayonnaise and a giant fricandel (at least 1600 calories) without getting the least bit fat while I allowed myself just one handful of chips, while I had exchanged mayonnaise for pickles and frankfurters for a gherkin – which ruined the whole idea of chips anyway – I began to see the light.

Especially when, an hour later, I gobbled up all the cold fricandels that were left over from supper, because my mother couldn't get used to cooking less food now that the boys had left home.

You don't get fat from eating unless you're fat already.

It's not the eating that does it, but the forbidding, even if you're the one doing it.

I simply had to stop myself from thinking constantly about forbidden foods.

But by then it was too late.

For another year I couldn't eat without thinking of the food itself. And I don't mean thinking about whether I liked the taste, I mean thinking about the connection between how good certain foods tasted and what that signified in terms of calories.

I have stopped making mental notes of calories because I have stopped blaming the food.

Food is blameless.

Only people can be blameworthy.

What I didn't know yet was that I also had to stop thinking about food when I wasn't eating. It was all right to think about cooking, buying ingredients and how you'd mix them together and look forward to the delicious flavours awaiting you, but it was wrong to think about eating itself. Thinking about eating when you're not eating is one of the mainstays of the addiction and the obsession, but I didn't know that at the time any more than I knew I'd go on to become an academic whose obsession would be addiction.

Ara was taken aback when I explained my idea that thinking about food and dieting made you fat.

"Didn't you think of food before, then?" she asked.

"Not that I can remember," I said.

She said that ever since she was five she had thought of nothing but food all day and that it was almost impossible for her to believe that everyone else wasn't constantly thinking of food same as her.

"Waking up in the morning, the first thing that comes into my head is will I be able to control myself today, will I succeed in not eating too much. Then at breakfast I have an extra piece of toast and from that moment on that day is ruined. It starts with toast and after that food wins hands down."

It began to sink in that there was a difference between Ara and me, a difference I'd sensed for years, in the form of a whirlpool in my head or a knot in my stomach, each time Ara said something I couldn't imagine anyone saying although I had never figured out why. Now that Ara was telling me about her daily struggle with eating, it hit me that her explanation contradicted all my ideas about the whys and wherefores of overeating and that most of the time we actually thought the exact opposite in matters of cause and effect.

I was hesitant about telling her what had just occurred to me, whether I should give my idea away off the cuff, so to speak, and keep her happy, or whether I should keep it to myself for a bit, so as to ponder it and then secretly get to know and understand her better. The advantages of telling Ara about an idea worked out at about the same as the advantages of not telling her, because she was quick to sense when I had uncovered a fresh insight into her character, and the fact that I was thinking about her filled her with pride and affection, even if she didn't know quite what I was thinking.

"Food is your most beloved enemy, Ara," I wrote in my exercise book that night. "You treat it like something weird and unpredictable which stalks and commandeers you, it's seductive and makes you dependent. Instead of seeing food as something you decide about and you control, as something you can take or leave, of your own volition, you see it as having a hold over you, as controlling you. You fight it as if it's something external, which has nothing to do with you. Perhaps that's it. Perhaps eating is a way of keeping out something that needs keeping in.

"(This sounds ridiculous I know.)

"Fighting means either losing or winning, and you think food always wins. I think it's something inside yourself, an enemy within, which keeps winning day after day. But who the enemy is, I don't know. Nor do you, I expect."

"I never used to think about food until recently," I told her that afternoon.

"It must be great not to have to think about food," she said.

"Yes, it was rather nice," I said.

4

I WAS PRETTY NERVOUS ABOUT SEEING THE PSYCHIATRIST. I'm not really used to people asking me personal questions, because even Ara doesn't do that often. Ara and I usually think we know all about each other, even if we don't discuss it. Whenever Ara does question me about something private I get so shy I can't think straight and have a hard time giving an honest answer. Which is so daft, because in the end I'm always very glad that she dared speak out when things got a bit strained between us so we could clear the air. Besides, saying what's on your mind always ends in assurances of how much you care about each other and then I can tell her our friendship is the best thing that has ever happened to me, and sometimes I feel so blissfully relieved that I tell her life wouldn't be worth living if I didn't have her. And I'm not so sure I'm exaggerating when I say that, although it's also true that bliss tends to make you lay it on a bit thick.

Ara's a lot calmer than me. She has no qualms about saying we're meant for each other and nothing will ever change that. She knows this for a fact.

"We are each other's fate," Ara says.

And I don't contradict her when she says that, mainly because I don't want to discourage her and also because the way she says it sounds exactly right for our kind of friendship, but neither can I bring myself to agree wholeheartedly, because the giddy feeling in my head tells me I think differently deep down.

"Yes," I say, "I suppose we are each other's fate, but there's a logical side to our fate."

"How do you mean, Kit?" Ara asks.

"It's a chosen fate," I say.

The only people who are your fate are the members of your family.

All the other people you become allied with later in life, not counting blood relations, are not your fate, they're your choice. Each choice has a history and a logic of its own, however deeply personal, elusive and sometimes impossible to reconstruct it may be.

The sort of fate that has no logic can be kept out of your life until you begin everything all over again by having a family of your own.

And that was precisely what I didn't want.

Which was what I told the psychiatrist in so many words.

He asked me whether anything had happened a year ago, anything that might have caused the deregulation of the menstrual cycle.

I told him I was afraid I myself had caused the bleeding to stop, because I had willed it to, and that the power of the mind, when you want something so desperately, is probably strong enough to overrule the body.

It was over a year since I'd seen our family doctor. Not having told my mother about the appointment, I was terrified someone might come into the waiting room who'd mention having seen me there to my mother. I didn't think my parents would be too pleased about my wish to be sterilized.

Our doctor gave a chuckle when I asked him to refer me to the hospital because I wanted to have my womb taken out as it was of no use to me. I was absolutely certain, I told him, that I would never want children, and as I was so certain there could be no point in suffering all that pain every month, it wasn't so bad to suffer pain if you knew what it was all in aid of, but if you were so positive that your womb wasn't going to be of any use to you, not later either, then you might as well get rid of it, and besides, that would make it clear where you stood, for your own good, because it would end all that muddle about the mind going in one direction and the body in another. As it was, one week out of four was sheer misery and it meant being an invalid for two days at least because it hurt too much to sit, walk or ride a bicycle, and all that purely on account of my body blindly complying with some law of nature dictating interminable preparations for an event I would never ever allow to happen. Ever. It was totally pointless, I said. Bleeding in my case was a farce.

"And I delivered you with my own hands," the doctor said.

It wasn't fair of him I thought, to play the sentimental card. To show him how strong my resolve was, how serious I was about this, I said coolly that I didn't remember that occasion but that I'd been told about it and that I hadn't come to him with any intention of ending my own life but merely to be relieved of my superfluous and painful womb.

His demand to know how I could be so sure about never wanting children came as no surprise, and I reeled off my arguments as if I were being tested in class. In the middle of my explanation that should I ever decide to have a family after all there were plenty of unfortunate children around who'd be glad to be adopted, he interrupted me.

"When you're a little older you'll understand that having children is not like that. You want to produce your own children because they're part of you, because you can live on in your offspring."

"But that's so selfish!" I burst out, and went on to say that was exactly what put me off about all those couples having one child after another without even being really glad to have them, simply because they were obeying a natural instinct that told them to reproduce, while those poor kids were saddled with a life which they'd never asked for and which would be terribly difficult, life being almost too tough as it was, for children as well as parents, it was well-nigh impossible for people to make each other happy, especially if they really loved each other a lot, and what with everybody causing suffering to everybody else while they worried themselves sick about it – how selfish and self-centred could you get.

"Human nature is selfish," the doctor said calmly. "Blood follows its own course."

I said you could rebel against nature and that you didn't have to obey the laws of blood, that surely it was more worthwhile to lavish your affection on a child that was already there, unwanted by its parents, that at least you yourself weren't accountable for its existence and that from then on you would only be making the life of that child better, and that, speaking of living on after your death, there were other ways of making your mark.

"Which, may I ask?" the doctor asked calmly.

"Art, for one thing," I replied.

"Books and paintings aren't quite the same as people of flesh and blood."

"Exactly. So you can't make them unhappy either."

"How old are you now?"

"Eighteen."

The doctor shuffled the papers lying in front of him. A feeling of having lost my case came over me and I could barely muster the concentration to listen to his closing argument. There was no doctor in the country, he said, who would agree to sterilizing a perfectly healthy eighteen-year-old without there being the slightest medical indication. I'd take a different view in a few years' time, as he had no doubt I'd have cause to rethink the matter in the course of my future life.

A few hours later a sense of relief came over me – at least there was no operation to be dreaded – and by the end of the afternoon my rage had dwindled to nothing as I sat hunched over my exercise book and found consolation in turning a fine phrase: my womb was renamed *the organ of my doubt*.

It was the same afternoon I had that trouble with Karel and I wondered whether I ought to tell the psychiatrist about that too.

Karel was our Makkie's friend. Before Makkie went off to live in town he and Karel used to play in a band together and spent hours listening to records in the boys' bedroom. They had the blues on a permanent basis, they read Jack Kerouac and hitch-hiked across Europe in the summer. I'd never noticed any sign of Karel being in love with me. I was convinced my brothers' friends were unable to fall in love with me because I was a daughter and a sister within the walls of our house and not just a girl. It wasn't easy to see my brothers' friends as ordinary boys either, because in my eyes they were friends first and foremost, and that ruled them out as boyfriends.

A few months ago Karel asked me to be his girlfriend, he'd been in love with me for years, he said.

This puts me in mind of the time I discovered a fat spider behind the wardrobe in my bedroom. What I found really infuriating and disgusting was not so much that I was terror-struck by the spider, but that I kept thinking how it might have been there for months, spying on me without me knowing.

I was equally infuriated and disgusted by Karel's request. Instead of feeling flattered I got very angry. I felt betrayed, spied on in my own home. He'd looked at me not only as a girl, but also as a girl who was available. His misery at my refusal left me cold.

For the next couple of months I saw to it that I wasn't at home when he came to see Makkie at the weekends. The times he turned up without warning I got out of the house as quickly as I could. Makkie took it very well.

Back home after my visit to the doctor's surgery I went up to my room to write in my exercise book. There was a knock on the door. Thinking there was no one in the house except my mother and little Chris, I shut my exercise book quickly, slipped it under a textbook and said: "Come in."

Karel's face gave me quite a shock. He was as white as a sheet, his eyes were wild and staring and his forehead glistened with perspiration. He had grown a beard and a moustache and though moustaches aren't too bad sometimes, full beards give me the creeps. Karel's lips trembled as he blurted that he was giving it a last try, that he wanted no one but me and that he'd been depressed for months, he was being treated by a doctor, he was taking sedatives and sleeping tablets, and might do something crazy if I turned him down again.

"I've got the stuff with me," he said, his hands shaking as he brought out an assortment of little boxes and a medicine bottle.

Since I was seated I was at a disadvantage and I had no cover from the back either, so I sprang to my feet and spun round to get the window behind me. Before I knew it Karel had clasped me in his arms and thrust his head against my neck. He was sobbing. The hairs of his beard tickled my cheek and the wetness of his tears and saliva around my ear filled me with loathing. He wept and begged me to touch him and be nice to him, because I was good at that, because he knew that I was the sweetest girl in the world, that he couldn't go on living without me and that I'd come to love him too once I got to know him better, after all

I also had it in me to love a difficult person like Ara, he could see that.

I couldn't speak.

I couldn't move either.

I hated him.

My mother had knocked on the door out of habit and, without awaiting a response, burst into the room. She took stock of the situation at a glance, gave me a look of concern and took hold of Karel by the shoulders to pull him away from me.

My mother is not the type of woman who likes to cuddle or be cuddled, and even less someone you'd throw your arms around, so I was deeply shocked when Karel clung to my mother and begged her to hold him. She nodded at me over his shoulder and mouthed something telling me to make myself scarce, she'd sort him out.

I was scared Karel would do something to hurt my mother and didn't dare leave them until my mother waved her arm impatiently for me to go away. As I left the room I heard her telling him there were more fish in the sea, a whole ocean full of fish as a matter of fact. She'd made the same remark to me a thousand times and it always drove me spare, but now it moved me.

I waited in the living room for them to come downstairs. It took ten minutes. Ten minutes during which I chewed my nails down to the quick. Biting your nails is a bad habit, in our family we all did it except my mother, while Makkie had cut his habit by fifty per cent since he started taking guitar lessons. Makkie had proper nails on his right hand and my mother didn't bite hers. Never had done.

"I don't know if this has anything to do with anything," I told the psychiatrist, "but I'm telling you anyway."

"Well, it's bound to be important," the psychiatrist said, glancing at my hands. "Wouldn't you say you find it very disagreeable to be desired as a woman?"

It took a while for me to understand what he meant.

"D'you suppose I don't like being desired as a woman?" I asked Ara later that afternoon.

Ara has a lot more sense than me about a lot of things, specially when it's to do with being a woman, with what's natural because every woman has it and because it's a physical thing, according to her. She decorates her body, too. She uses perfume and lashings of make-up, especially on her eyes. She draws a thick black line across her eyelid which ends in a point on her temple and which she then connects to a thin line under the eye. She got the eyeliner trick from Cleopatra, she says, but pinned up over the mirror in her bedroom there's also a postcard of Sophia Loren, and her eyes are like that too. Actually I suspect her of thinking she looks a lot like Sophia Loren, but she doesn't look anything like her, although I'm not going to tell her that.

Putting on make-up is one of those things Ara says is natural for a woman. She has taught me to apply mascara to my eyelashes and I put it on when I think of it, but I don't enjoy fiddling about with cosmetics as much as Ara. The first time I did my eyes under her supervision she guffawed, because when Ara does it it looks good enough for the movies whereas I always make a mess putting make-up on. Elegance is not in my nature.

Ever since Ara's been wearing all that black eyeliner I've been in two minds about her make-up and when you're in two minds it's difficult to express your opinion in words. If you're trying to say two different things at the same time you might as well keep your mouth shut, otherwise you only get the other person confused while you're the one who's in a muddle and who ought to do some more thinking before expressing an opinion.

As soon as people talk about there being two sides to every-thing I switch off, it's so inane, it turns my stomach every time and goodness knows you hear it often enough these days. Usually people say there are two sides to something when they're trying to make you believe they've thought long and hard about it and that years of fretting and pondering have resulted in a considered opinion, while the truth is that they simply refuse to think and don't have an opinion at all, because even a child knows there are two sides to everything, that's not the point, the point is which side you're looking at and how it strikes you, whether you think the front more attractive, better, more worthy than the back and which of the two you ought to give priority to.

And so, as long as I'm in the sort of quandary where on the one hand I like Ara wearing lashings of make-up and on the other I hate it, I know I have some more thinking to do as there's obvi-ously something I haven't fully grasped yet.

You think things are bad enough but they can always get worse, because although I really loathe all that waffle about things having two sides, what I find even more sickening is when it goes on under the surface, when someone maintains two different things at once but in such a subtle way you hardly notice, so you have no idea why you're suddenly left feeling a nervous wreck and going round in circles because you can't tell whether you're supposed to take a step forwards or backwards.

Since starting college I've begun to understand that it's a ques-tion of someone telling you in one breath to walk forwards and backwards at the same time. Which you can't.

From my very first day at teachers' training I've known I don't want to be a schoolteacher, and yet for the first time in my life I'm learning things I find interesting. The theory and science of education aren't particularly fascinating subjects as such, but parts of them are. Development psychology, for instance, that's great and I keep getting books about it from the library. It was in one of those books that I came across that wonderful expression which says exactly what I mean when I say I get all flustered and nervy when someone makes a remark I can't cope with, because there are two sides to it.

Finding that expression excited me so much I had to stop reading, so overjoyed was I at the fact that it existed. I got up and ran round and round the book like a puppy, and didn't dare open it again until the turmoil in my head had abated somewhat. It was almost too much to bear, having to take in so much in one go. As if there was too much of it to fit inside me, that's how it felt.

It was the first time in months that I wasn't racked by hunger.

The first person I told was Ara.

I wanted to tell her I'd found an expression which had suddenly made me understand a whole lot of things, but I was especially eager to tell her about the thrill of discovery, that I'd almost suffocated from joy and that I'd felt it in the pit of my stomach and in my head, which suddenly made me realize it's true: you can burst with happiness.

Ara's the only one who really understands what I mean and I don't know anyone I'd rather talk to about the stuff I've been learning and about my ideas, than her. Ara looks her best when she's listening and you'd wish you could go on talking for hours, just for the sake of that soft and grateful look she turns on you without ever glancing away, and you get the feeling you can actually make people happy with a bit of understanding and that it's a sort of gift, even though it's only words and not a present you can hold.

Ara herself is really eager to learn, but reading a book takes her five times as long as anyone else, so she likes me to explain to her what it says in the books I read. The funny thing about Ara is that she seems to take a lot of new stuff for granted which to me comes dropping out of the sky.

I reckon she's wise by nature and I'm not. Ara takes a good look at the world and at people, while I'm always finding coins on the pavement and never notice what's going on around me. I still can't manage to walk this earth without staring at the ground, even though I've left the Not-Stepping-On-Cracks phase behind me. She knows a lot about animals too. I can confront her with the most spectacular theories, how children master the principles of mathematics, say, or something even more outlandish, and Ara will have something to say about some Balinese piglet or other and how it finds its mother's teats, that being comparable to learning mathematics. This habit of hers gets on my nerves at times, although I realize Ara understands things better if she's seen them with her own eyes or if she can connect them with something she knows a lot about.

As I'm not too keen on animals myself, I'm always glad to learn things that are not even remotely connected with the eel, rat or chimpanzee, because they're things that concern exclusively humans and human behaviour.

Basically, that's all I'm really interested in.

The "double bind" is a condition too human for words, it doesn't occur among animals, I was certain about that, and that made me relish the idea even more of telling Ara all about what it meant and why I thought this had been my problem all my life, and that she was part of it.

"I think you quite enjoy being desired as a woman," Ara said calmly, "but you want to be desired more for your mind than for your body, and with most women it's the other way round."

That's typical of Ara. She's opinionated and says exactly what she thinks, even if psychiatrists say the opposite. But what really gets me is that her opinions sound so considered, as if she's been pondering my character at length and has reached certain conclusions as to how I feel about my body and about being desired. She says so herself, that she's always thinking about me, and that I'm her favourite subject of study. She says I'm the only person in the world to think she has considered opinions, in fact she clashes with people all the time, because she's grouchy and says things that make them angry, without her being aware of having said anything wrong.

"And I asked very politely," she'll say, amazed when people in a café turn their backs on her abruptly, while all she did was ask for a little more space. She doesn't realize that all that coal-black eyeliner gives her the look of a rapacious predator, and looking like that you can be as polite as you please but your eyes'll still be the eyes of a killer.

Now that I'd found out about the double bind I'd be able to find a better way of explaining to her why she offended people unknowingly.

Ara wasn't as impressed by the double-bind theory as I was, I could see that, and if I'd had any sense I wouldn't have told her that some remark she'd made had given me the perfect example of how you can tear someone apart by admiring and disapproving at the same time, and that that was exactly what she did.

She didn't speak to me again for a week.

5

A MOTHER COMES HOME WITH A SURPRISE FOR HER little girl. She's bought her two jumpers, a red one and a green one. The little girl is delighted, runs up to her room, puts on the red jumper and races downstairs to show her mother how it looks. Her mother says: "Don't you like the green one, then?"

The example chilled my spine, and I couldn't help shuddering when I told it to Ara.

"Pretty gruesome, don't you think?" I said, seeing that she wasn't particularly impressed.

"So devastating for the poor kid," I offered in a last attempt to convince her.

"She could have told her mother she liked the green one too, but that the red one was on top," Ara commented, with a hint of irritation in her voice.

"But by then the harm's done," I said wearily.

They tell me I'm a bit of a yo-yo sometimes, because of my mood swings, roaring with laughter one moment and in floods of tears the next, and they're right. It's the things people do to each other that gets me. I'm not soft, but a chance remark can floor me at times, and on the other hand I'm a sucker for the unexpected show of kindness.

Ara hates it when she feels she doesn't understand something the way I understand it, she worries about losing me in case some new enthusiasm of mine should outclass my love for her. Mostly I make allowances for her anxiety, but I felt let down by her cool reaction to the example and had no intention of sparing her now.

"You don't understand a thing," I told her, and also that I'd have to think up a better example to convince her.

"What don't I understand, Catherina?"

"The drama of it all. The drama of being torn apart."

Ara had probably seen how mad I was at my failure to convince her, and sometimes she'll pretend not to notice but usually she'll say she can't stand to see me upset. Like this time: she decided to put aside her own bad temper and set me off talking again by saying she'd grasped the theory itself all right, and that what she really likes about me is that I enjoyed thinking things over, it was written all over my face.

This always has the desired effect on me.

Out of sheer gratitude I told her how excited I'd been to read about the double bind, how a word can suddenly take on meaning and trigger all sorts of ideas and insights, and that I'd felt as if I could go without food for days because I was so sated with ideas. I said I'd realized in a flash that a single word, a phrase, a chance remark, can actually change your life.

"That's what I envy about you," said Ara, "being happy just thinking and not needing another soul."

Then I told her there she was doing it right now, so this was a good example.

She gave me an icy stare, plunged her hand into the bag of peanuts in front of her and stirred the contents furiously, then crammed a fistful into her mouth.

"Ninety calories," I said.

She gave me the silent treatment for a week.

We made up when I got drunk for the first time in my life.

Ara and I seldom went to the same places when we went out, because she knew a different set of people. She didn't like my friends and I didn't know what to talk about with hers. She said my friends were poncy show-offs, phoney, arty-farty. I thought her friends were wimps, dumb, feeble and boring and they all had one thing in common and that was that they thought Ara was perfect and worshipped the ground she walked on.

I worship her too, but I don't think she's perfect.

What I absolutely loathe, for instance, is when she acts the femme fatale and goes out all tarted up, twisting the men round her little finger and stringing them along for months on end simply by bestowing the odd favour on them and luring them to her side, only to send them off again not having a clue whether they might stand a better chance next time, or indeed whether there will be a next time at all.

That's why it's better for us not to go clubbing together. It drives me spare to see her making eyes at some fathead who'd be just as happy being drooled over by a slag with an IQ of 60. She doesn't deign to look at what she's trawling for. It's not the catch she's interested in.

If a man so much as glances at her she fixes him with her special stare, even if he's a gnarly ginger-haired creep the wrong side of forty, the kind of lech who'd trail after anything in a skirt. She's even proud that it works, too.

In fact once Ara's given some man her special look he's her captive for the rest of the evening, can't take his eyes off her but doesn't dare approach her either because her look also tells him to keep his distance.

I can do without witnessing this kind of scene, because it always makes me hate her a bit.

"I communicate with looks," Ara says, when the subject crops up. She says other people chat each other up with words, but that she has to say everything with her looks, that she happens to be more liberated in her body than in her speech.

"You've got language," she says, "I haven't."

And then she'll go on and on about how scared she always is of the wires getting crossed in her head, of certain words getting stuck in the wrong places and of forgetting the connection although she knew it once, and that it can happen that she needs a particular word, like "cultural", for instance, for what she wants to say, but that she's lost it somewhere and so she just says the next thing that comes into her head, like "criminal" or "natural" and before I know it I'm oozing sympathy all over again. And I'll regret having criticized her, as she's bound to have good reason to behave the way she does, even if it strikes me as wrong and silly.

I have to remind myself of that more and more often these days, because we've been getting into a lot more arguments lately.

She winds me up when she says I make an Orphan Annie impression on people and that she finds that hard to take, too.

"As soon as you open your mouth people want to feed you and take care of you."

I didn't know that.

I thought I was quite capable of taking care of myself.

"Why d'you think that is?"

"It's so obvious that you're eternally hungry, that you yearn for something: attention, contact, love. You've got a sad look in your eyes and that's pathetic. No one will ever think I'm sad, Kit. I don't look sad. If you look like me people always think you're self-sufficient. And that suits me just fine."

Ara says all this very evenly, so as not to give me the impression she's being nasty or thinking things up just to confuse me, but I can't get rid of the feeling that she hates me every bit as much for what she calls my Orphan-Annie look as I hate her for her come-hither look.

Ara reckons it's better if we don't go out together and don't spend too much time together in the company of other people.

"I want us to be unique," Ara says. "What *we*'ve got, I wouldn't like you to have with anyone else."

I'd hate it too if she had what we've got with anyone else, but I can't see how she can be afraid of that happening. It's true that I've made a couple of new friends at college, and also that Marga and I see a lot of each other, but all the world knows that Ara is my only true friend and always will be. Even Marga, by no means one to play second fiddle under normal circumstances, accepts this as her lot because there's no doubt in her mind about how close Ara and me are. The only one with any doubts is Ara herself.

Sometimes I get sick and tired of having to prove to the people I love that I really love them.

With some people you have to go on proving it ad infinitum because somehow they always make you feel as if you don't care enough about them, or that you don't really love them, or that you love them in the wrong way.

It's probably got to do with insecurity, because my mother tends to do this and she's a bottomless pit, she's as bad as Ara: no matter how much love you pour in, the effect never lasts. My mother says she used to have an inferiority complex and it so happens my mother is the only person I can take such a remark from, because coming from an ordinary person like my mother fancy words like that sound rather sweet, you can tell exactly which topics her woman's weekly has been discussing lately and then it's not hard for me to imagine my mother being just as delighted with a new word as I am, if it suddenly reveals something to her about her life and so on, but apart from that, "inferiority complex" is an expression I loathe, because you'll never find anyone who doesn't think he or she has an inferiority complex, and if everyone's got one then it's nothing special, just a condition that has come into fashion.

I feel sorry for my mother, because I can't stand it when the people I love are unhappy or have a low opinion of themselves, but sometimes I'm hurt and offended when my mother and Ara express doubts about the depth of my love for them.

Those child-psychology textbooks put far too much emphasis on the child's need for its parents' love, if you ask me. They never say that the reverse might be of like or even greater importance, that the potential for huge, unreserved and helpless love on the part of the child for its parents also clamours to be noted and acknowledged.

The first time I got drunk was in the local disco.

After putting up with Ara's stony silences for three days I rang her up to ask if she would come to the pub by the river.

This pub was in another town, but not far from where we lived. It was the only place Ara and I went to together on occasion. None of our friends knew it, nor would they have gone there if they had. It was frequented by old barge folk, ruddy-faced skippers and their wives who danced to accordion music and weren't in the least interested in Ara's get-up or my Orphan-Annie look. It smelled of stale beer, the tables were covered with red rug-like cloths and it was a place Ara and I cherished the way we had cherished the Land of Fen in the old days, as a secret hideaway where we could pour our hearts out and say things we'd never say anywhere else.

It's funny the way certain places have the capacity to make you behave in a way you'd never behave normally. You know it as soon as you step over the threshold, that it's a place where you can talk about things you wouldn't talk about anywhere else. In the kitchen my mother and I have different conversations than in the living room, with my father it's his car and the garage that elicit confidences, and Ara and I have now got this pub as a special place.

She replied that she had other plans for the evening, said goodbye and rung off.

I can't remember since when I'd been totting up all the hurt, but Ara's snub was the limit. She knew that asking her to go to the pub by the river with me meant more than accompanying me to any old place. By turning me down she was taking something away from me. She was denying me reassurance, clarification, and the trusted sight of her face lighting up with her fond, teasing smile when she read the anxiety in my eyes, knowing perfectly well that she could make everything all right again with a single gesture. That's the kind of power she had. She deliberately wanted to undermine my confidence.

I can't stand my confidence being undermined.

It makes me throw up.

Insult added to injury in my head, and began to raise its own cry. In the bedlam of reproach and complaint, pleading and derision I could make out Karel's creepy whingeing and my mother's frustrated lamentations, but above all I heard Ara's gratuitous, chilly arrogance. To silence all these voices I launched into a long, rambling monologue, in the course of which I manifested a degree of rage I had not dared acknowledge before and confessed aloud to the weakness in me that I had always wished to conceal.

I concluded with: "Sod it!", threw up, brushed my teeth, climbed into my freshly pressed black trousers, wheeled my moped out of the garage and rode off to town, in search of Marga and of deafening soul music to numb my brain, to make me stop thinking about the meaning of love, about my lack of confidence and the hateful realization that other people had control over my emotions.

The funny thing about music is that ever since the late sixties it has divided young people into two main camps. There's soul music and there's rock 'n' roll. You're not supposed to like soul if you like blues and rock as well. Jazz, country or classical music don't come into it at all really, because jazz is for intellectuals and freaks, country for rednecks, and classical music for the parents of rich friends.

Ara plays all kinds of albums, from Johnny Cash to Waylon Jennings, she dances to the latest hits of the local yokels and listens to Mahalia Jackson at Christmas. I don't know if she's aware that country music is considered naff and old hat and I haven't told her either, because I like it much better that she sticks to her own taste without taking any notice of whether country music is hip or not.

Marga's a soul sister. Soul sisters can't wear jeans to the disco, because Levis go with the blues. Tamla Motown fans wear knife-pleated black terylene trousers, slinky twill blouses instead of red or blue checked flannel workmen's shirts, and pointy shoes of soft leather instead of suede ankle boots or cowboy boots with slanting heels.

I don't belong to any group in particular.

I even like Tom Jones.

My older brothers say I have no taste in music at all, because you can't possibly be a fan of James Brown and Elvis Presley at the same time. Tom Jones is just as un-hip as Engelbert Humperdinck or Edith Piaf, and anyone who warbles *San Quentin I hate every inch of you* in the shower deserves to be shot. They reckon.

I can see what they mean, but I couldn't care less. I think it's just my nature to have no taste in music. Once you're stuck with their taste you can't go to half the discos and pubs in the area, you can't wear anything but faded jeans and that would mean I could never go to the places Marga and Ara go dancing on Saturdays and Sundays.

I'd rather have my freedom than good taste.

I knew I'd find Marga in the local disco.

Marga always looks wonderful, she knows exactly what suits her and what doesn't. You can tell with girls whether they grew up with sisters or not. Like Ara, Marga knows all about make-up, cosmetic ranges and ways to capture boys' hearts.

With Marga I'm not so sure what she likes about me, because Marga and I talk about completely different things and if I go off at a tangent about some book I've been reading or an idea I've had, she's likely to sigh and say all that's beyond her and she hasn't a clue. She does want to be a schoolteacher, though, because her mother runs one of the primary schools in town and several of her sisters have been teaching for years.

Most of the literature we're supposed to read for school is utterly boring according to her, except some of the children's classics like *Treasure Island* or *Winnie the Pooh*. That's about as much as she can take, she says with a grin, but what she really likes is romances, she's romantic herself and likes to daydream. She tells me this with a straight face. That's quite extraordinary of her, I think.

Marga does the Tarot for me, she reads my palms, tells my future and calls me "sweetie". So Marga is roughly everything I'm not nor ever will be and all the things that fascinate her are sort of off limits for me because they're petty, vulgar and superstitious, as my brothers keep reminding me.

If you're a soul fan you have to know an awful lot about

clothing labels and also about the Moluccas. As I know nothing about either I always feel a bit insecure when I'm at the local disco, because a lot of Moluccans go there and everyone can tell at a glance if you're wearing the right labels.

Marga was standing by the bar and made a big fuss of me when she saw me, kissing me on both cheeks and then rubbing the lipstick off with a practised gesture.

Unlike Ara, Marga talks non-stop and she told me over and over how great it was to see me. She put her arm around my waist and rocked me to the music. She was surrounded by boys called Mas, Sly or Annis, and told everyone I was a mate of hers and how glad she was that I'd come.

She'd read in my palms once that I was the type to become addicted, never mind the substance, and that I should watch out. I thought I'd reached that point long ago – like my brothers and my father I'd smoked since the age of twelve and had no intention of giving up. Marga threw me a worried look and said it wasn't cigarettes at all, but that she could tell from the lines in my palms that it would be a very bad kind of addiction.

"You must never ever try that nasty white stuff, sweetie," she admonished affectionately, "I've seen too many boys come to no good with that shit."

Her show of concern made me go all soft inside, not that there was any need for her to warn me about drugs, as I've always hated them. Once I dragged Willem out of a pub where he was smoking a strong-smelling cigarette and I stood there in the street and gave him such hell he'll never try anything like that again. And it was easy for me to make fun of the people he was with, as Willem's touchy about that kind of thing. I told him if you go around with people who all talk exactly the same and whose sole topic is how great and groovy and how far out it is to get stoned, then you need your head examining, or will do if you spend more than an hour in the company of those phoney hippies.

Marga offered a round of drinks and they all ordered a Cuba Libre.

"What's a Cuba Libre?" I asked.

She said it was a delicious mix, mainly Coca-Cola, and that it made you a bit tipsy. She ordered one for me too.

Until then I had always drunk tomato juice alternated with mineral water when I went out.

Marga wasn't to know, but it was she who introduced me to my most beloved enemy that very evening. It was drink she'd seen written in my palms.

I started to feel the effect after my first Cuba Libre. It made me light-headed and talkative, mellow and brazen, unashamed, indifferent and impulsive. Every sense of decorum vanished after that first glass. I danced with Marga to James Brown, let myself be kissed by Sly and have my boobs fondled by Annis, while all I could think of was my next Cuba Libre.

Just as I hadn't much liked the taste of my first packs of cigarettes, so I didn't enjoy the taste of my first alcoholic drinks.

It's not the taste that counts, it's the effect.

I wanted to go on drinking so as to get even more carried away, so as to be utterly shameless and oblivious to everything around me. The only feeling I had left was that there was no one in the whole world who could stop me now, no one with the authority to forbid me to drink as much as I pleased, no one to set limits to my behaviour.

I felt inviolable and independent. I felt sovereign, free and divinely solitary.

The monologue in my head petered out and I heard only the strong beat of four words: The hell with it!

Marga had called a couple of boys to kick in the door of the lavatory. I had fallen into a sort of stupor from which I couldn't wake even though I could hear Marga frantically calling my name and banging on the door.

Later Marga said it hadn't been a pretty sight, me sprawled there like that, but I didn't want to hear the details. All I remembered was confronting the problem of which orifice to give priority to, whether I should sit on the toilet or hang my head over the bowl first. And that I couldn't make up my mind.

I have a clear memory of Ara coming into the disco.

Marga had lifted me to my feet with the help of Mas, Sly and Annis, they had sat me down on one of the plush benches standing against the wall of the dance floor and had phoned Ara.

Ara had a car.

Dreams came true for Ara. We had both dreamed of having our own car, but dreams that cost money came true for Ara and not for me.

"My dreams cost money and yours cost you your soul," Ara once said.

In the gloom of the disco I could make out Ara's shape from afar. She kept her eyes fixed on me as she elbowed her way through the crowd. She looked resolute and this time the wave of nausea that came over me was caused by her sudden appearance, by a sensation of love that overwhelmed me.

I groped for such words as were still in working order so that I might utter a suitable greeting.

"Ara" was all I could bring out.

I couldn't seem to find any other whole words and so I said "Ara" over and over again.

Ara, Ara, Ara.

She got down on her knees, leaned forward and, using the flat of her hands, tenderly brushed the hair out of my face. She smiled and looked concerned.

"Kit, what have you been up to?" she said, half shocked and half laughing.

"Ara," I said.

6

THINGS DIDN'T WORK OUT WITH MATTHIAS AND THAT was my fault.

There are people who make a habit of blaming themselves for everything and beating their breasts for being failures, but I'm not like that at all, I don't trust people like that one bit. Lying down on the ground before you've even been hit is sheer cowardice, you haven't even taken the chance of losing and before you can lose you've got to take a risk and it takes courage to take risks. That's exactly what's the matter with those people, although you'll never hear it from them.

I was to blame for the mess-up with Matthias, and I'm not saying that to suck up to anyone either.

I simply couldn't stand him wanting to touch me all the time, that's what it was.

Matthias didn't trust me, because he could see that I didn't mind when people touched me in the pub or the disco, and I didn't know how to get it across to him that there was a world of difference between being held in public and having him hold me.

It's when I'm in a disco or a pub that I don't mind people touching me.

So long as it's playful and casual I enjoy being hugged, but when I'm alone with someone and that someone holds me really tight and caresses me I panic and go rigid with fear. It's because I think something is expected of me, that the closeness is not just affection but that it has a purpose, that it's got to lead somewhere, to something I'm supposed to feel or do. But all it does is make me panicky, and that's not how Matthias wanted me to feel.

He's a nice enough guy, but I've decided it's not such a good idea after all to start an affair with someone just to please your parents. It's too much like hard work for that. And anyway, the guys can sense that's how you feel.

There's only one person in the world who can touch me without giving me cramps and that's Ara. She often remarks that I'm funny about touching and that I behave like an animal that's been maltreated, always cowering and expecting the worst.

"I can't imagine why," I said to Ara, "I've never been beaten in my whole life."

"And you haven't been touched very much either," Ara said quietly. "Not being touched is another kind of abuse."

Ara pronounced the word abuse wrong. She said A-buse, which somehow sounded much better. She'd discovered this about me early on, she said, soon after we first met, it was at primary school and she'd startled me by laying her hand on my stomach. She had felt it contract and knot and had seen that it was half an hour at least before the shuddering stopped, so slow was the skin of my stomach to recover from the shock.

Ara also says cows give more milk if you stroke them and that if you leave kittens alone and don't pick them up in the first six weeks they'll stay shy and shrink from contact with humans for the rest of their lives.

"Perhaps you shouldn't have refused your mother's milk," she joked.

She was referring to the story I so often begged my mother to recount, not that she was eager to. How she fell seriously ill after I was born and couldn't breastfeed me. How she tried again later, but that I wouldn't suckle at her breast.

"You'd be ravenous," she said, "and yet as soon as my breast came anywhere near you'd stop howling and press your little lips together. Tiny as you were you knew it was too painful for me to nurse you. But there was a heavy price to pay. I thought I wasn't taking care of you properly. Things were different in those days. Nowadays it's modern for women not to breastfeed, but then, if you didn't breastfeed your baby you were a bad mother, simple as that."

To bring myself to tell Ara what it was like with Matthias, in bed I mean, I had to fight down so much embarrassment that by the time I was ready I was almost too exhausted to speak.

I'm ashamed of feeling ashamed.

All I told her in the end was that being naked, and his naked-ness too, makes me horribly shy, that it doesn't feel natural and that I can't stand it when things are expected of me, deep emotions, tenderness or excitement, say.

"But you're excited such a lot of the time anyway," Ara said airily.

"How would you know?" I cried, with a nervous giggle.

"I just know, that's all," Ara countered, "I can always tell, Kit, especially if it's someone I know very well."

"Yes," I admitted, blushing, "I suppose I do get awfully wound up in my head."

Ara finds it hard to believe I'm ashamed of my body. She says she'd have more reason to be ashamed of hers, as she's big and fat, while my body's nothing to be ashamed about as it's an ordinary shape, nice and small and comfy, she says.

"But it's got nothing to do with shape," I try to explain, "it's the nakedness that feels so odd."

"Being naked is the most natural thing there is."

That's exactly what I don't think.

Of course the body is the most natural thing in the world, but why should it be naked? Ara's world is divided into separate realms of body and mind, nature and nurture. She's got nature and the body, I've got nurture and the mind. I like that sort of clarity, it saves so much dithering about. We never have to ask ourselves which one of us is better at something, as Ara takes care of all the practical things and I'm quite happy being the airy-fairy one.

Since her mother has joined goodness knows how many clubs and follows umpteen courses Ara and I often eat together at her house, just the two of us. She shops, cooks and lays the table. After supper she clears the table and does the dishes while I curl up with a book. At home I sometimes feel bad about not helping more, as our mother does everything herself: cooks the food, lays the table, clears the dishes and does the washing up, but each time the boys and I offer to help she says no, just you enjoy your telly or do your studying for tomorrow.

At Ara's I never feel bad or uneasy when she's doing the dishes while I'm lounging in an armchair, daydreaming, reading, or writing in my exercise book. I have a great time acting the twit when I'm with her. She reckons she's best at cooking proper meals and is quite happy for me to contribute some spiritual nourishment, as she puts it.

It's just that, lately, I've been finding Ara's way of dividing things up a bit irksome. There's no room in it for my own insights, into myself, into her, into other people.

Sometimes I try telling Ara I can't see why I should be considered frustrated just because she thinks I am, purely on the basis that you aren't frustrated if you feel natural when you're naked, natural suddenly being synonymous with self-evidence and normality, it seemed.

"Frustrations come from the mind," Ara says and I think she may be right, but that doesn't mean inhibitions are unnatural or useless, why shouldn't the mind be part of nature too? If they aren't nature, then what are they?

Breathless and desperate to make my point I tell Ara it would be more sensible in my opinion to consider clothes, for instance, as belonging to nature, as second nature if you like, but still as part of nature in a general sense. Then the changes in styles, fashion trends and so on can be seen as nurture, as expressions of culture.

Ara is still listening attentively, but a frown has appeared on her forehead. I've got stuck. Every time the subject crops up I start stammering, which I loathe, as I really enjoy explaining things and putting them in perspective.

What's wrong, I think, is that my idea isn't quite finished yet, I've obviously not thought about it hard enough. Talking without thinking about what you want to say is so dumb, I find, and that only makes me even more furious with myself.

"And as I'm not frustrated, you can't be right about the division between nature and nurture," I conclude stubbornly. Ara roars with laughter, because she knows I've lost and because she thinks I'm funny when I'm stubborn.

"Come here," she grins.

It's quite easy to sulk and yet to snuggle closer to her with pretend-reluctance, because I'm the offended party and I find there are certain advantages to being the offended party as it lets you off the hook, you don't have to do a thing. Suddenly I feel like the kind of child I never was, stroppy, difficult, cross, like our Makkie I suppose, the kind of child that takes a whole lot of coaxing to make up after a falling-out.

She pushes my head down and strokes my neck. Before I know it I'm lying flat on my stomach, then she pulls up my jumper and strokes my naked back until I doze off.

Ara can do anything with me, she really can.

Talking was often less effective than being stroked like this, I noticed. Ara could say my body was fine a hundred times over, but it didn't make me feel any less shy.

Actually I think her body is fine too, it's big but I like it. That doesn't mean a thing, though. It's love and history that make you see beauty. Beauty is man-made, the outcome of a human relationship, such as between her and me. That's why, when Ara flirts and I can't help disliking her, I think she's unattractive, ugly even.

Nature isn't beautiful or ugly, good or bad.

Considering a willow to be more beautiful than a beech tree, a pig uglier than a cow, a vulture less endearing than a squirrel is only a question of human history, of the way our perceptions have been influenced by books, paintings, films, by words and images, by what people have claimed about nature and how nature has been portrayed down the centuries.

I think Ara's the most beautiful woman I know.

Now she's getting older her face is more angular, it's sharper and even prettier than before. Since she turned twenty-one the first silvery threads have started appearing at her temples, which looks wonderful because they make her jet-black hair even blacker. She's worn her hair a bit longer the past couple of years, it comes half-way down her long neck, and as it's so thick and wavy she can simply comb it back and let it fall around her face like a picture frame.

You wouldn't say Ara's face was ordinary. Her features are striking. Even if she's put on ten kilos you can't tell from her face, because the plane between her high cheekbones and jawline stays the same: as flat and taut as it has been since she was eighteen and the plumpness left her cheeks. Usually when she announces that she must shed a few kilos I have no idea she's put on any weight.

I'm not very observant, it seems. Ara says I've got X-ray eyes, and what she means is that although I don't see what's going on around me, or what people look like, I can see what they're thinking.

Which is not true.

I can't see what people are thinking.

No, really.

I quite like it that Ara takes that view of me, so I don't go out of my way to contradict her. Besides it's not such a bad thing for her to see me as a perceptive sort of person, because I can tell that she's none too pleased about me not noticing if she's gained weight: on the one hand it's a relief but on the other she worries that I don't pay attention to what she does, how she behaves and the clothes she wears, because I don't care enough.

That isn't true either. I do notice a lot, but they're different things. I'm more likely to register a slight change in the tone of her voice, or if she says goodbye with a "Bye!" instead of a "See you!", and I'm more likely to see how the lower lid of her left eye flutters at the slightest mention of her father than to notice she's got wider in the hips.

Ara's father has been living in a flat in town about three years now, with a girlfriend who's much younger.

"She was his overtime," she says sharply, although she doesn't talk about it much. Her parents haven't got divorced, but Ara doesn't want to see her father ever again. She now lives alone with her mother, for whom she feels sorry because she tried so hard to be the perfect wife for the man who is her father and because she failed. Ara's mother was always one for tidying and polishing, but now she's got a mania about scrubbing her own skin to be cleaner still.

"Even the windows get cleaned every day," Ara says, "the glass must be wearing dangerously thin."

It's just as well Ara can joke about it, as it's pretty miserable for her at home.

What I enjoyed most was sitting next to Ara in her car, wrapped up in her scent, and with her big body looming in the corner of my eye. After the first few minutes I would slump back comfortably and then she would be in sight without me even having to look sideways. Whenever I turned my head to study the straight-backed figure at the wheel I couldn't help thinking how happy I was when we were together, how little it took to be happy and how gorgeous she was. She always noticed when I looked at her like that. She always responded by taking her eyes off the road and flashing me a smile.

She felt happy then, too, I know.

Ara's onto something, with this touching business. I reckon she's so good at it because she's used to handling animals. Ara could bring a wild bull to its knees.

We started going on trips abroad in 1976. Ara was twenty-two at the time and had never been on holiday to another country without her family, although she often accompanied her mother on outings. No matter what country we went to, we could never pitch our tent without waking up surrounded by a pack of skinny stray dogs sniffing at the canvas and whining and barking until she crawled outside and patted them on the head or the side.

She does the same with me.

That's probably why I got so sick and tired of all those hungry grovelling dogs trailing after us wherever we went.

*

They were always there. Never mind whether we were camping in Spain, France or Greece, the first morning we would always be woken by dogs slinking and yapping around our tent.

The first time it happened I thought it was rather miraculous and imagined that the local strays had picked up the scent of her magic and had spent all night searching and howling for Ara, the lady of the beasts. It wasn't until our second camping trip that I found out she had already fed and stroked the strays by the time she put up our tent.

Putting up tents is not what I'm good at.

Ara would set about fitting all the bits and pieces together and I'd go off somewhere and read a book.

It wasn't until I had seen how hard it was for Ara to say good-bye to her mother – the first time we left for Spain in the packed Volvo – that it occurred to me that she might not be quite as strong-willed and independent as I had always believed. It took some time getting used to this idea, and I kept pushing it away so as to focus on the far more acceptable notion that the lump in her throat and tears in her eyes when we left were caused by something completely different. She was worried about her mother, that was all, and sorry about leaving her all on her own.

It was unthinkable that Ara should be afraid, afraid of travelling on her own, or that she should cling to her mother.

Ara wasn't like that. Ara didn't need anyone.

She wasn't the nervous, insecure, incompetent one.

The nervous, clingy one, that was me.

7

I TURNED TWENTY-ONE IN THE AUTUMN OF 1977 AND that birthday led to the most violent quarrel Ara and I had ever had.

I had always tried to avoid getting into arguments, but after reading *Who's Afraid of Virginia Woolf* I believed it might not be such a bad idea. If the bond between Ara and me was truly indestructible then surely we were close enough to get into passionate arguments, like George and Martha, complete with screaming matches and even a slap in the face if things got out of hand. In bed at night and even during the day I thrilled to the idea of mutual, raw outrage, the anguish of recrimination, the aching intimacy of all-out war.

We had such a fight a few days after my birthday and it left me feeling utterly wretched.

It's odd, come to think of it, how you have no doubts about a person's intentions if it's someone you love.

It had never occurred to me that Ara's reason for not coming to my birthday parties could be anything other than perfectly sound. I was convinced her decision was inspired by goodness and a special insight into my character, and that it was bad of me to wish so desperately for her to change her mind and come anyway.

I only wanted to show her off. I wanted to show her to my friends, so they could see for themselves that Ara was special and that I was this wonderful person's best and dearest friend. Her aloofness, her silence and her inscrutable look would work in my favour, because everyone would see she was quite different when she was with me, not sullen at all, and that there was evidently a different side to her personality that she kept for me alone because I was special to her. I wanted to bask in reflected glory.

For all my nagging and supplication, she never gave in. Ara saw straight through me. Not that she actually accused me of having ulterior motives, she simply would not sink to my level of deviousness. And I couldn't blame her either, deep down, which only made me feel I ought to thank her for knowing me so well, warts and all, and for not bearing a grudge against me.

"I except you the way you are," Ara used to say, and it always made me laugh.

She knows she's made some kind of mistake, but then I think it's a shame to correct her as the word she's trying to side-step isn't half as expressive as the one she's used. Ara herself wants to say the right words, of course, so usually I help her out, but I suppose "accept" is one of the words that don't agree with her, which is why she has trouble saying it. I've known her to say "I exist you the way you are" and even "I excite you the way you are." It makes her laugh, too, and sometimes I suspect her of making mistakes deliberately, for my amusement.

This time she had promised, cross her heart, to celebrate my birthday in my house with the few friends I had invited. A twenty-first birthday was an important occasion, she conceded, although she thought it a pity they'd picked on twenty-one as an important age as she didn't like odd numbers. They were sharp.

"Take a look," she said, "all the odd numbers look as if they can spike you; the even numbers are different, they're soft and round."

The number Ara hated most of all was seven, it cut you all over the place. The three was a sliced eight, in her opinion. When I reminded her that there are numbers made up of an even and an odd number, she said pairs didn't bother her, they made each other soft.

In keeping with her view of numbers, she liked every form of pairing. She said that was how she saw the human body, it was symmetrical and everything you had in your left half corresponded with what you had in the right half.

"So where's your other heart?" I asked.

It was very early, that day in November 1977, when I was woken up by a noise at the window. I got out of bed and peered outside. There stood Ara, wreathed in autumn mist, beaming up at me. She was holding a big bunch of flowers. She had thrown bits of gravel up at my window. It was six in the morning.

"Congratulations, little thing," she whispered, but I understood her anyway.

That evening everyone was there except Ara. She rang up around ten to say she wasn't feeling well.

For the first time in my life I didn't believe her.

She was lying.

As casually as possible I told my friends that Ara was ill and had just rung off. Most of them had never seen her, although they'd heard plenty, as I used to sit in the canteen at college and hold forth about her at any given moment. I had this uncontrollable urge to talk about her, about how special she was. The evening had been ruined now, and that made me flushed and agitated.

"Never mind," my mother said, following me into the cellar where I'd gone to fetch a plate of snacks. "Why d'you want to go bothering with Ara anyway, you know what she's like."

"I'm sure she has her reasons," I said gruffly.

"What you call reasons," scoffed my mother. "She's jealous, that's all."

That night in my bedroom I took another look at the present Ara had given me earlier in the day, a small ornamental owl, and suddenly I realized I didn't even like it, it was kitschy, sentimental, naff. I opened the window and tossed the owl into the neighbours' orchard.

Sod it! I thought.

I didn't get in touch with her for three days: a record. I filled a whole exercise book with rage and resentment.

During a lull in my anger I made a list of all the grievances I could think of, so that when we next saw each other I'd be able to tell her once and for all what I resented about her. I reached a total of seventeen.

She phoned on the morning of the fourth day. Would I come and have supper at her house. I said yes, trying to sound severe, but her chuckle at my half-hearted attempt made me livid and I smashed the receiver down without saying goodbye.

Quarrels as in *Virginia Woolf* are horrendous and they serve no purpose whatsoever. The day after I was over at her house I had a confused memory of all the things I'd said, of jumping up when she'd put the food on the table and standing face to face with her, fists clenched, of punching her shoulders and storming out of the house without my coat. I didn't get past number three of my list of seventeen grudges.

What I did get round to telling her was that I was sick of her bullying, that she'd lied to me, that she treated me like a dog that needed training and that she was obviously trying to teach me all sorts of tricks I had no idea about, that she was always testing me, rewarding me one day and punishing me the next, and that

I never understood why, what on earth I could have done to deserve punishment anyway, and she could bloody well forget about teaching me tricks as if I were one of her stupid dogs and how could she think she'd ever get me to sit up and beg.

That was about it.

At home in bed I could picture Ara cooking, then coming in from the kitchen bearing her fancy dish, which had obviously taken her all afternoon to prepare, and finally setting it on the table with a flourish. It was my favourite dish, braised rabbit with prunes. She had even tied green paper ribbon round the legs.

She had just finished piling food onto my plate when I flared up and launched into my tirade. I hadn't swallowed a mouthful, my full plate was untouched.

In the end all I could see was the plate piled high with food, the green paper ribbons, and how forlorn it looked. I felt mean, it was wicked and heartless of me to turn down the offer of a plateful of lovingly prepared food. Despite my empty stomach I was sick three times that night. In the end I was throwing up yellow acid.

When I crawled back into bed and shut my eyes, my mind reeled with pathetic and mortifying memories, all of which had to do with food and pain.

I have a lot of them.

Makkie and I are playing in the shed at my grandparents' house. The shed is on a slope, about twenty metres from the house. My grandmother is small and old. She comes up the hill wearing her slippers. She's bringing us white bread spread with butter and treacle. She hands Makkie and me a slice each, but Makkie says he doesn't want his, he doesn't fancy bread with treacle. I tell my grandmother that I'll eat both slices as I'm crazy about bread with treacle. Ten minutes later I pull so hard at Makkie's hair that, to my surprise, I'm left holding a tuft of it in my hand.

One weekend Willem tells us about eating the most delicious food ever in the student canteen the other day. It's Indonesian, he says, and it's called *rijsttafel*. When Willem comes home again the next weekend my mother has a surprise for him: a proper Indonesian meal. She's bought herself a hardback recipe book and collected spices and ingredients from all over, she's left three different kinds of meat in a marinade for days, she's chopped, sliced and simmered. She can't imagine it'll taste very nice, she says, what with all those funny-smelling spices: some reek of mould, or of fish even. The table is crammed with saucers, bowls and dishes. The display is impressive, very like the pictures in her recipe book. She says now we can spend the whole evening having dinner, that's what you're supposed to do. Half an hour later the dishes are empty. The boys ask can they watch the sports news.

When I eat one of my father's sandwiches, he thinks I prefer his to mine. Now he saves half a sandwich for me every day, which he brings back home after work. I don't know how to tell him he's got it all wrong. And it goes on until my mother scolds him for being too generous for his own good as usual and I quickly say she's right: he should eat all his sandwiches himself and not save any for me.

The woman next door has made pancakes with cherry filling. She knocks on the door and offers my mother a thick pancake on a plate. I can't wait to take a bite, but my mother signals to me with her eyes that I mustn't. No sooner has the woman turned her back than my mother snatches up the plate, slides the pancake into the pedal bin and washes the plate under the tap. She says our neighbour is unhygienic. She tells me to return the clean plate. Face to face with our neighbour I can't help saying that her pancake was absolutely delicious, almost better than Mama's.

For the first time I decide to skip Communion. When I get home I tell my father and mother about not taking the Host. I ask them if they'd mind very much if I didn't go to Mass for a bit. My mother says they'd be very sad, but that it's up to us to decide about this kind of thing, that they couldn't force us to be religious.

My father says I'm bound to be desperately lonely one day, that he's quite sure about that, and that I'll have no one to turn to. He says he can't bear the idea. I try explaining that it's not such a big deal, that it isn't so much the religion I find hard to take but the ceremonials. I want to say I can't bring myself to swallow the wafer that's supposed to be God, but it's all so complicated I give up. I simply tell them there's no need to worry.

It was on the night after our quarrel that I resolved to leave Ara, home and the village. I would take Verkruysse's advice and go to university. I would move to the city. Not to the place where my brothers were living, though, the main thing was to get as far away as possible.

I just want to be without people I love for a change.

Before going to sleep I worked out that I had another six months to prepare Ara, my parents and my brothers for my departure. That seemed plenty.

I am firmly resolved.

There's no one can stop me now.

Not even Ara.

No one can.

In the weeks after I made up my mind to leave I slept badly, suffered dizzy spells, and had to get up several times to vomit a few minutes after getting into bed.

Although all I wanted was for this useless upheaval to stop, for the heartache at leaving the nest to go away, I continued to be racked by fear and guilt. I felt like a traitor abandoning ship. It made me ill to think I was taking the easy way out, that I wouldn't see Chrissie grow up, and that I had failed in every-thing: showing gratitude to my parents and making my mother happy, convincing Ara of my loyalty, being Matthias' girlfriend, choosing a profession, showing the boys how to live their lives.

As soon as I detect a flush of excitement in my mind, a desire to break out, to get away, a longing for detachment, discovery, study, for life in the city and for being on my own and not having to love anyone, I am overcome with shame, and torment myself with immense regret at abandoning all these people who won't know how to cope on their own.

I keep having pictures of our fridge, how spotless it is and how neatly my mother stores everything away on the shelves. Visualizing the stacked boxes of clear plastic is the worst. Zeroing in on my father's smoked ham, Willem's salami, Makkie's boiled ham and the finely sliced smoked beef which is our Chris's favourite makes we wonder all over again if I oughtn't to stay with her for ever.

The morning I decide to start telling her about my plans I find her in the kitchen. She's in tears, as she so often is, sitting at the kitchen table hiding her face in a tea towel. A tiny vein in her right eye has burst, her lids are red and swollen and there are deep purple rings under her eyes. She always worries so. She doesn't get more than three hours' sleep at night. She scrubs her face with the tea towel and gives a couple of strangled sobs when I come in.

"What's wrong, Mama?"

"Oh nothing, everything, it's this dreadful headache," my mother says. Her mouth sags. She's set to cry for hours, I can tell.

"Go on, have a good cry," I say.

And cry she does. I sit down facing her, as usual. I can't just go up to her and put my arm around her or rub her back, because I know she doesn't like me pawing her.

"When will it ever be my turn?" my mother asks no one in particular.

We must do something about this accursed language business, flashes across my mind. It's the language that's to blame, it causes misunderstandings and those misunderstandings make people profoundly miserable, they make my mother miserable. Happiness is not something you get a turn at, nor something you find.

People who sit and wait for happiness to come their way will never get it. Happiness is not there for the taking. It isn't one of life's wonderful secret gifts which everyone will receive in due course, which life keeps hidden away until the right moment comes to bestow it on you, as is your right. No one has a right to happiness.

Within a quarter of an hour my mother has calmed down. I'm pretty good at soothing her. My mother is the sort of person to whom you can say that she shouldn't have unrealistic expectations of life and that happiness is not out there waiting for her, she can handle that much, but all my speechifying doesn't take away her unhappiness. Quite often I trot out the boys and me in support of my campaign to talk her round: after all she's got us, her children who love her and Papa so dearly, none of us is taking drugs. She's got good kids hasn't she?

"But I can see you're unhappy, all of you," my mother says with typical, repellent bluntness. "You can't fool me, you know."

I decide this is not the right moment to make my announcement after all. Besides, maybe I'll change my mind about leaving home after the exams, maybe I'll hang around here. I could find a job as a primary-school teacher somewhere or other. That way she'd have at least one child properly settled. I think that would do her good.

Ara was the first person I told about my plans. We were at the pub by the river. She didn't mind me flying into a rage about her not coming to my birthday party, she said, but she did mind me running off like that.

"That's no way to treat me," she said. "When something's up between us you don't run away, you're supposed to stay put and face things."

I said she was right.

"How d'you know about all this," I asked, "about how people are supposed to get along with each other?"

"It's instinct," she said, "I trust my instincts."

Our quarrel was still too fresh in my memory for me to disagree with her, even though I would have done so in the past. It was always about the head and the heart, and she would conclude triumphantly that where she had intuition and instinct I went on about analysing things and being rational, as though there were less merit in that, as though I had no heart.

The heart is the most kneaded, mangled, exploited muscle we possess. If any organ in the human body has been at the receiving end of deception and infiltration during this century, it is this blood-filled pump. I can't see how women can flaunt their sensitivity and intuition if all it means is that they're excused from trying to understand or explain things. What's the use of knowledge if you can't communicate it to other people? How can you have an understanding of something if you can't make it clear to someone else what you've understood?

The heart and the brain must be connected, given that knowledge can cause hurt and emotion, and loving someone can be the start of deep understanding. But they've severed the link between that muscle and the head, and not only is a degree of autonomy now attributed to the heart which it doesn't possess, they've also romanticized and glamorized it and have now bestowed it, with a lot of phoney ballyhoo, on women. I don't like that one bit.

You can't fool me.

I don't take it as a compliment when people tell me I'm sensitive.

Regarding the heart as essentially autonomous and self-willed means turning a blind eye to the strong, sometimes highly personal logic lurking behind a so-called passion or overwhelming emotion. Heart and brains belong together. Feelings make sense and thinking is sensitive.

As long as Ara refused to see this and went on taking her heart to be her most reliable advisor, she would be unable to intervene in the incontrovertible logic of her own drama and her own happiness.

I kept silent and nodded. She could tell I wanted to be friends again and didn't want to get bogged down in a difference of opinion, but she wasn't having it. Her eyebrow turned into a circumflex accent. I pretended not to notice. I wanted to tell her I was going away and that I wouldn't be going to study in a town nearby either but much further away, in a city where I didn't know a soul.

Feeling challenged and defiant I felt an urge to dramatize my announcement, I wanted her to think it was her fault I was going to live far away, and even wanted to tell her my departure signified a clean break with the past, complete with the termination of our friendship, which like all my other relationships was too complicated for me, too impossible, too hurtful, there was too much incomprehension, strain and inadequacy.

I didn't say any of these things.

For the first time since my introduction to my dearest enemy I ordered a Cuba Libre. After three glasses I declared my love to her, told her I would never have another best friend and also that I had to go away.

"Yes," she said, "you must go, I always knew you would."

Ever since the day I told my parents I was leaving my father has been fixing up tables and cupboards for me and my mother has been buying household necessities: pots and pans, towels, sheets, crockery – expensive goods.

"I don't like cheap things," she says. "You should always get the best," she advises me, "that's what I've always done. You get more out of them in the end."

She chuckles as she packs her purchases into boxes.

"You're not going to get married, are you," she says, "so this might as well be your dowry."

At the word dowry she laughs. The word doesn't sound right for me somehow, she says.

I like it when she laughs. I tell her I'm grateful for the trouble she's taking.

"Yes," says my mother, "as well you might be. I wish I'd had someone to make a fuss over me when I was your age."

Now and then she can't resist trying to make me change my mind. I'd make a good primary-school teacher, she'll say, look at all those letters I've received from pupils at the schools where I spent trainee periods, and did I know the headmaster of our local school has been inquiring when I'll graduate as there'll be a job on offer soon, that she can't see why I should want to do even more courses, surely teaching is a wonderful job for a girl, why weren't simple ordinary things good enough for us and why go off to the city now to do more studying, she says it's all beyond her, it's a mystery to people like her and Papa, all right she can see that studying is what I really enjoy doing but why insist on going all the way up north, it's a dangerous place, it's two hundred kilometres away, it would be so much nicer to stay closer to home, to find somewhere in town near the boys, why not, then we could keep an eye on each other, but she can talk till the cows come home, it won't get her anywhere, we never listen to her once our minds are set, do we.

On the morning of my departure Ara wakes me up once more with a patter of gravel against my window-pane.

"You're leaving," she whispers, but I understand anyway. I go downstairs to let her in by the back door and we hug each other for minutes on end.

"It's all right," she says.

There's an unfamiliar edge to her voice. Raising my head I see tears welling in her eyes. It has never occurred to me before that I've never actually seen Ara cry. It makes me fearful and proud.

"We'll always be together anyhow," I say.

"Yes," she says, "I know."

She takes a deep breath and quickly recomposes herself.

She says: "You take care, little thing, out there in the jungle."

"Have no fear," I say, "I'm one of the predators."

III
WORK AND LOVE

I

I'M THIRTY YEARS OLD AND NO ONE HAS BROKEN MY heart as yet. That's because I've never been in love with anyone I can't live without. Since the age of ten I have been secure in the knowledge, every moment of the day, that there is one person who will always be mine: Ara.

I am no longer used to an eventful life, with things happening in rapid succession. I prefer a steadier pace anyway.

For the past ten years I have spent most of my time in the seclusion of my small second-floor bedsit. Screened windows, no phone, no newspaper, just books. Every change, every adventure I've had has taken place within these four walls. This is where I see the occasional friend or acquaintance, where I had a few flings, and where I had a lover for ten years.

Not any more.

He left me a week ago. He wants us to be just friends. He's got a new woman, one he wants to marry and who's made him promise he won't sleep with me any more. I thought I'd be properly heartbroken at last but instead I was quite aroused and curious to see what it felt like to be given the push.

Outside, I told everyone that Bruno had finished it. Inside my bedsitter, I waited for the pain to hit me, the tragic anguish of lost love which, so I had noticed, left some people looking nice and thin.

Not until Ara pointed out that I talked about the break-up with Bruno as if I'd won the lottery did I realize that suffering was not on the cards for me.

I didn't suffer from love.

With Bruno I'd known love and I'd lost, but was it the sort of love I could not live without? No it wasn't.

Bruno became my lover under Ara's nose. Ten years ago, right after I'd moved out of my parents' house, Ara and I decided to go to Paris for a week. It was the autumn of 1978, and we drove straight to the Bois de Boulogne in a rented VW van.

For the first time in years Ara had lost ten kilos. In the months before I left home we had spent more time together than ever. She said she wasn't hungry when she was with me, that the idea of eating turned her off, and that as soon as her thoughts strayed to food it was enough to look at me and listen for her to control herself.

"I'd be as light as a feather if we were together all the time," Ara said.

Since Ara had started losing weight she often irritated me. At first I wasn't bothered, but as time went on I'd catch myself more and more often thinking how awful she looked. Especially her face, neck and shoulders had become thin.

Ara had got into the habit of touching herself constantly.

As soon as we were in company she would stretch her neck and clench the muscles in her jaws which made the sinews stand out like thick cords on either side of her throat, she would flare her nostrils and push her shoulders forward so that there were deep hollows and shadows all over the place and her face looked thinner than ever, and then she would put both her hands in the hollows or run her fingers along her jutting jawline.

She seemed to be greeting the sinews and bones that had been hidden by the fleshiness of former years, and at first I could quite imagine it being a pleasant sensation. But you can't go on greeting for ever, and Ara never stopped.

She couldn't have a normal conversation when she was pulling these faces, she had to relax the muscles first. Craning her neck like that dragged the corners of her mouth down which gave her a grisly expression, which I hated. Increasingly I found I couldn't bear watching all this crazy stretching and fingering of muscles, but I didn't dare say anything. She looked like a bad-tempered crow with its body-feathers fluffed up from the cold, but I knew she felt more attractive and more normal than she had ever felt, that she felt the time had come to take revenge for the humiliations she had always denied, and I thought her illusion too fragile for me to tackle head-on. She was also stretching her neck when we first saw Bruno under the trees in the Bois de Boulogne.

The older I got the less often I was bowled over by a man's looks, but both Ara I thought Bruno was irresistible the moment we set eyes on him.

It's not so easy to make out what attracts you in people.

Years later Ara told me that all the men I have loved had something in common with one or other of my brothers. Honest-looking, a bit gruff, that sort of thing. And there was something about their appearance, too, which was even more difficult to put your finger on. It could be the look in their eye, the jawline, or the way they walked. Ara always noticed these things, I never did.

There are certain facts your brain simply will not acknowledge. You won't get to know everything about yourself in the course of your life, I'm afraid.

He and his friend had put up their tent ten metres away from our van. Next morning Ara and I went past them on our way to the campsite store to buy fresh baguettes. We heard Dutch being spoken and saw two men sitting on folding chairs facing each other. They were fortyish and wore heavy-knit sweaters. The taller one had flaxen hair and a thick beard and moustache; he was talking animatedly while the other one listened.

On our way back the taller one waved cheerily at us and addressed us in a French that couldn't have sounded more Dutch. Ara and I couldn't help laughing. He offered us coffee and we shared our first baguette with them. The tall one was called Pim and the other one was Bruno.

Two days later I crawled into their tent when Pim and Ara had gone for a walk in the wood. I lay down in the hollow of his shoulder, he put his arm around me, rubbed my back a few times and fell asleep again. I was surprised at the mix of excitement and peace that came over me and suddenly I knew it would be Bruno, he would be the man with whom I would make a serious attempt to shake off my irksome legacy of fear, shame and guilt.

It was Bruno.

It was an attempt.

He was forty-one, married with two children, and he played the trombone in a professional orchestra. He lived in a town not far from where I was living and he came to see me for the first time six months later, because, he explained, he hadn't been able to get me out of his mind. I was glad. Since our goodbye in Paris I had thought of him constantly and I longed for him with the nervous hankering of one who is in love. I didn't dare write or phone, because he was married.

He stayed with me that night and we became lovers. He couldn't lie, so he told his wife. For three years she tried to live with it, found she couldn't, then took another two years to divorce him.

That wasn't my intention at all.

After his divorce Bruno came to see me more and more often. All the years I had known him my longing had only increased. As soon as I saw him I felt a slight tremor in the knees which didn't stop until I was off my feet, for how long didn't matter, nor where we ended up.

Each time I swelled with pride at having become someone who felt desire and who could bear someone else touching her. For the rest I didn't feel there was much to be proud of.

One year after his wife had left, Bruno broached the subject: he hated living on his own. I found this very hard to imagine, because all I wanted was to be on my own as much as possible.

He was thinking of moving, why not find a flat big enough for the two of us. I told him I didn't want to live together, that it was inconceivable that I should ever share a space with anyone else, I was not capable of it and had no intention of trying. I told him I didn't want to be someone's wife, not his either, but that I would be his lover for ever, his second-hand rose, and that I would never want it otherwise.

"Your second woman – for ever," I said.

I said I always longed to be with him but also wanted him to leave again, so that he could come back to me whenever he wanted.

He said he loved me.

I said I loved him too.

If he couldn't stand living on his own he'd have to find himself a proper wife, I told him, for in the house.

He found her last year.

It was only last week that I realized that I had always taken it for granted that he would not love the woman he wanted to live with. As if love and living together were mutually exclusive.

Where love was concerned Ara and I went more or less parallel ways, because one month after I told her I would be leaving home she picked Bing from among the boys who had been dancing attendance on her. Ara and Bing were together as long as Bruno and I were, but in a different way.

Bing is a stocky Chinese with a stammer. He was born in Holland. He's a head shorter than Ara, he's got a crewcut and a strange little laugh. His father is a surgeon in the city down south and Ara met him at the animal refuge.

Bing wanted to become a vet, but he was taking a very long time over it and didn't seem to pass any of his exams.

Ara thinks he's a genius, but I'm not that impressed by the superiority of Bing's intelligence. In my opinion Bing is more of a shrewd, scared rabbit, whose sole stroke of genius was falling in love with Ara. I loved him the moment I got to know him for the way he loved Ara, and I still do. But that's as far as it goes, I can't see the talents Ara says he is so generously endowed with.

"He's simmering with talent," Ara says, and I realize it's reasonable to admire the person you're going with, but to say a person's talented when they've got absolutely nothing to show for it I find exasperating. Simmering talents don't exist any more than failed geniuses.

Talent is the manifestation of talent.

Before talent comes the desire for manifestation, expression, revelation, for the affirmation of an ability. Simmering isn't enough.

Ara keeps telling me that Bing hasn't had the kind of luck in life I've had.

"What d'you mean, luck?" I ask irritably.

"With everything, surely, Kit," Ara says in a questioning sort of tone.

She looks at me darkly, as if surprised at my incredulity.

"You'll have a go at anything, and everything you undertake seems to work out."

But the suggestion that I've just been lucky rankles. Rather than tell her for the umpteenth time it's not true I opt for a more crushing argument by pointing out that it isn't Bing and I who resemble each other, but Bing and Ara.

Bing and she, I explain, recognize each other's fear of failing.

"That's true," she says.

Then I continue. As calmly as possible I explain that her fear of failing might well have more to with her pride and arrogance than with her insecurity, which is generally rated a far more sympathetic and pardonable feeling.

"Possibly," she says.

Her forbearance having dimmed my anger, I lower my voice and go over the same ground again, trying to win her over to my idea that fear of failure and arrogance belong together, that neither she nor Bing want to risk a challenge to their sense of superiority, that they manage to sustain each other's inflated egos all right so long as they're at home in their farmhouse, but that they haven't the guts to take on the outside world. It makes Ara sad to hear me talking like this. She doesn't put up much of a fight.

"Still, I can't see why people always think you're so special and not me," she says in a final effort to defend herself. "I'm special too, but no one seems to think so except you."

"What other people think about me," I say, "is the very least of my concerns."

It was an old bone of contention between us and I had never succeeded in convincing her that I was right. Her silences made me acerbic and indifferent. Less and less often did I take the trouble to contradict her and explain yet again that a lot of what she regarded as talent, as a gift you could take or leave, was in my opinion something of your own making, something inside yourself that was connected with your personal history.

Underlying the wish for happiness, talent and excellence are motives, grounds and causes, and those you can discover if you set your mind to it. Talent is a prerequisite.

"Lucky dog" was an expression I couldn't stand any more.

Winning the pools makes you a lucky dog.

I had yet to discover why, but in my most exasperated moments I would hold my peace and think to myself: all right then, don't understand, don't bother to think, just stay fat.

Bing and I don't last longer than an hour in each other's company unless Ara is there. With me his stammer is much worse than with Ara and I'd be quite willing to do what she does, but I don't dare. Bing tends to get stuck at the beginning of words, and in flagrant contravention of all the rules about how to deal with people who stammer, Ara gets impatient and starts groaning and sighing when he can't get past the first letter. If he gets stuck at the p of problem Ara will say it for him within half a second, so that Bing can skip the word and ramble on until the next hitch.

It might be because he's Chinese, but Bing always laughs at Ara's impatience. They've got so used to each other you never hear Bing talking on his own, at least one third of his conversation is filled in by Ara. When I'm at their house and I take it upon myself to correct Ara when she speaks for Bing, it can happen that we get so tangled up in correcting each other that we can't remember what the conversation was about in the first place.

Bing doesn't bother me. He can move about in a room in such a way that you don't notice him. The three of us often take trips together and that always works out fine. Bing hovers around and surprises us at the beach with drinks, fruit and snacks. He brings them within our reach without becoming visible and then goes off again, to take a walk by himself or just to disappear. We all sleep together in a tent, which is a tight fit. Ara lies in the middle and not only takes up the most space because she's bigger than we are, she also sleeps on her back and flings her arms and legs wide. Bing and I lie left and right of her, on our sides. We make ourselves as small as possible.

Ara says Bing is different from other men and I believe her, because whenever I'm with Ara Bing just smiles and leaves us alone. He'll sit happily in a corner, watching us. Ara says he knows how much she cares and how much I mean to her, and he likes us being friends. I agree with Ara it's quite extraordinary of him to feel that way.

I have never been jealous of Bing, not for a second.

Over the past ten years I have done the things I considered important in such measure as I could cope with. Plenty of work, not much love and a growing familiarity with my most beloved enemy.

It is my work to understand that there is some relation between the small measure of loving that I can tolerate and the amount of drink it takes to stop me from seeing this all too clearly the whole time.

Four years ago I completed my degree in psychology, two years later in philosophy and for the past year and a half I've been working at the Department of Psychology. Eighty per cent of my time is taken up by research and the rest is lecturing.

Teaching didn't appeal to me right from the start. Not only did I dislike having to show up at a fixed time, I soon discovered how exhausting it was having to talk for hours, and also that I was repelled by the attention the students fixed on me.

One of the main advantages of being a student myself was not having to deal with people unless I felt like it.

I didn't feel like it very often.

One morning at the lectern was enough to make me pine for the seclusion and diffuse light of my own room.

The same day I received confirmation from the Telephone Company that they would connect me on such and such a date, I received notice from the council that the house I had been living in for ten years was to be renovated. They offered me the choice between substitute accommodation for a period of six months in the same part of town, and moving directly into another, bigger flat. They couldn't guarantee it would be in the same neighbourhood, though.

I had to move out in three months' time.

I opened a bottle of wine.

The only move I had made until then had been from my native village to this cubby-hole in the city. For several weeks before leaving home my excitement and desire for change had battled with the most sentimental fancies. I looked at my village and realized I had never seen how pretty it was, I felt a surge of love for the wood I had never loved, I saw my parents and brothers as the only people who would love me for ever and at one point I was convinced I could never make a fresh start, anywhere, unless Ara was around. I reflected with horror that the duration of our friendship would never be equalled, that everyone I met in the city would only know me from the age of twenty-two and that I could never share the history of my childhood with them. But then I didn't have that much longer to live: finding it so hard to picture a future for myself I gave myself another three years at the most, by which time I would be twenty-five and doomed to die the liberating death I had so vividly imagined ever since I was a little girl.

I resented my own sentimentality, but I couldn't stop myself.

I was young, inexperienced and to some extent romantic, and it was too early then for me to know that my death fantasy signified nothing but the wish to rid myself of my dreams and of the terrifying obligation to make them come true.

Once people's dreams come true they cease to be romantic, but I didn't know that yet. I was unaware, then, of the strength of my determination to make short shrift of everything resembling a burden.

As the day of my departure neared I got more and more anxious that it was a hair-brained scheme after all and that I was about to exile myself voluntarily from paradise.

And so I was, of course.

Paradise doesn't exist unless it's either behind you or ahead of you. Paradise, like hell, is never the actual place you're in. Paradise has always been on the far side and so it will remain for ever, I have no doubt. It's the same with perfection. Perfection and reality are rarely if ever seen in each other's company and if they are it is never for long. They cancel each other out.

Having an ideal, even an ideal about space, will always be the stimulus for action, for the effort to realize your ideal. Once an ideal becomes reality it ceases to be ideal.

After two glasses of wine I took a pair of scissors and snipped off my long fair hair. That night I wrote Ara a letter telling her I had just cut off my hair and now looked like a complete idiot, that I was upset because I sensed that great changes were afoot and that she knew how scared I was of new surroundings.

This was not entirely true.

Ara had told me on several occasions that one of her greatest fears was that I would become a different person and would make choices that she could not fathom, that one day I would stand on her doorstep with the announcement that I was emigrating, or that I had joined a philosophical movement in which there was no room for her. In any case that I would depart to some place, a spiritual place maybe, where she would be unable to follow me.

I made allowances for these fears of hers when I wrote that I dreaded a change of environment, leaving unsaid that it was not such a bad idea at this point in my life for me to emerge from my shell and follow a call that had been getting ever stronger over the years and that was best described, perhaps, as a desire for more reality.

2

ARA AND BING HELPED ME MOVE HOUSE. THEY WERE used to it. Ara had already moved three times and the last time Bing had moved in with her. For the past six years or so they had been living in a small farmhouse in the country, not far from Ara's mother. Four hundred metres away was the animal refuge, of which Ara was now the owner. If she took the car and drove fast she could be at my new flat within two hours.

Bing was in her employ and took care of the practical side, leaving Ara to concentrate on training police dogs and guide dogs for the blind.

She's good at it. I've seen so myself.

Some weekends she gives training courses too, and now and then I accompany her. With the men and women of the police she's as bossy and domineering as any officer in the Force, but with the blind she's gentle and easy-going. I always like watching Ara, but when she's busy with blind people it's extra enjoyable. I reckon it's because of the envy, but you can't seriously envy a blind person, so it's a funny sort of envy, the kind that makes me smile as soon as it rears its head. I suppose it's because the only enviable thing about being blind I can think of is that you get to spend time with Ara.

On one of those Saturdays when I was with her she went as

usual to collect her group from the institution for the blind and drove them in her car to the field by the kennels, where she instructed them in how to handle their guide dogs. That time there were two men and one woman. They were sitting around a table in the canteen, waiting. I had gone on ahead and stood waiting by the door, as I was hesitant to go in. Long before I heard Ara's footsteps I could see on their faces that they had recognized her heavy tread. They raised their heads in unison and all three faces lit up with irrepressible joy. By the time Ara actually arrived, they were sitting with their heads atilt waiting for her to touch them in greeting. She did so, and flitting across Ara's face I could see the expression that she so rarely has but that makes you go all soft inside when you get to see it. Every trace of sullenness had vanished and she was all gentleness and sympathy.

"I wish I were blind," I told her that evening.

"How d'you mean?" she asked with a laugh.

"Because then you've got to trust people, whether you like it or not."

There was a growing demand for her training programmes, also among private dog owners. There had been some talk lately about writing a book. She rather fancied the idea, she said: she had learned such a lot about dog-training why not try and make some money out of it, with a little book.

She had been careful about telling me because she knew she was encroaching on my territory, but she went on and on about it, presumably to convince me that she was serious.

The first time she mentioned it I flew into a rage. I said that since I had left home she had hardly ever bothered to reply to my weekly letters even when I begged for some reaction, and that I was supposed to take all this lying down just because she always had the excuse of her phobia about writing. Had she suddenly been cured, I asked with a sneer.

A book was totally different from a letter, Ara retorted. When you wrote a letter you had no editor to check your grammar and spelling, and so any letter she wrote meant sending out something that was shoddy and flawed and there was nothing more private than showing your flaws.

"That's the whole point," I said.

"I hate my own shortcomings," said Ara.

She had written one proper letter in all her life. It was to her father, when he was out of the country for a week to attend a conference. She was fourteen at the time. Her father had given her letter back to her when he returned. He had praised her for her originality, but had also corrected all the mistakes in her writing with red ink.

"It looked like a bloodbath," said Ara.

"How awful," I groaned, as I did each time Ara mentioned the letter.

It had always consoled me to think of this incident when I was hoping in vain for a letter from Ara, because how could you expect anyone to run the risk of such humiliation a second time?

However hard I had tried to convince her that I was delighted with the rare, always very brief notes that I had received from her in the space of twenty years, that they were safe with me and that I wouldn't dream of doing anything as hateful and gross as her father, she had just dug in her heels and left most of my letters unanswered.

As if that wasn't hateful and gross of her, I said.

Ara reacted calmly, almost condescendingly. She said she did not have the impression that I wrote all those letters only for her, but that I also enjoyed writing for its own sake.

I could not deny this, but it wasn't the whole truth either.

"So do you reckon they aren't intended specially for you, that they could be for just anyone?"

"No," she said, "they're for me all right, but I don't believe it makes any difference if I write back."

I didn't know what to say.

She never answered my letters, so how could I know if it would have made a difference?

We dropped the subject.

When I was a student I made a habit of sitting in on lectures at any faculty I could get into. As soon as I met people who were studying something else I would ask them which of their lectures was heavily attended and whether it would be noticed if a stranger were to mix with the students, where and when it was held and what the topic was. It was very rare for a topic not to arouse my curiosity.

There were days that I spent eight hours straight attending lectures, listening and making notes and using the intervals to cycle from one building to the next, so I could join the medical students for a neurology class, the anthropologists for hair-raising accounts of initiation rites, and the biology students for an introduction to the theory of evolution, all in the same day.

I was insatiable.

During these years I was afraid that this would turn out to have been the happiest time of my life, that I would never again be as self-absorbed, independent and distanced as during those long days that I was a learner whose sole concern was how to quench an unquenchable thirst.

Ara was surprised by the news that I was taking biology and had even chosen it as my official subsidiary subject.

"You've changed so, Kit," she said, "in the old days you didn't care a hoot about nature."

"I still don't," I said. "I'm a biologist who doesn't love nature. Nature doesn't move me. Birds and bees and trees still bore me, but I get such a kick out of reading about how animals spend all their time hunting, mating, eating, how they reproduce like clock-work and protect their young or make them fend for themselves. I find that sort of predictability very amusing. Don't you worry, I'm only studying animals by default, so to speak, so as to eliminate them in my search for what is purely human, for what is left when you've scraped off all the beastliness. Do you know what I mean?"

"With you I do," she said. "You're an animist, after all."

Ara said the word and as always when she made a mistake, I was touched. I realized that she thought animism was something to do with animals and that it was conceivable that you might be against the animal side of things. I did not correct her, and at the same time I realized that she was right, that I was an animist and that it would never have occurred to me to apply that word to myself.

Knowledge often makes my heart ache with a special ache which is simply delight in a word, or an immense gratitude for its existence. It's a sort of happiness that stays at the back of your mind rather than an understanding you can communicate.

The word was right for me and I could sense that Ara had said something wonderful by accident, something that deepened my understanding. I didn't tell her that animism was not what she thought it was, and I hugged her.

It's not at all difficult to get a degree in two fields of study if you take the relationship between those two disciplines as your subject, which is what I did. Sometimes I would write simultaneously. The left half of my table was for my psychology notes, the right half for philosophy. What I called *hunger* in my left-hand notes I called *longing* on the right.

That was what it was all about.

Hunger and longing were the touchstones for comparing two ways of thinking. By taking hunger and thirst to be the physical complement of longing, of that intangible, elusive spark of the soul or the spirit, at any rate of that other, invisible, powerful body, I hoped to be able to reconcile the two. The history of psychology as well as that of philosophy had shown me how much importance had always been attached to keeping the two separate.

Now and then I thought of myself as crafty more than anything else.

As soon as you develop a passion for a subject you can, if you stick to books, connect everything with everything else and complete as many degrees as you please, because it's nothing but variations on the same theme. All you need to do is vary your perspective.

To make Ara see this and thus to lessen her awe for things like university education, I was flippant about what I was doing. I told her all it took was a couple of changes in vocabulary and there was your dissertation in theology, sociology, biology, history, literature, and goodness knows what else.

She didn't believe me.

But it is true.

I was never satisfied until I succeeded in making it clear to Ara what I was engaged in and what I thought I was getting at. If I was able to explain a theory to her I knew I would be able to get my ideas down on paper. This sort of conversion of what I had distilled with some difficulty from complicated and dull academic studies into something straightforward and interesting, had become such a habit that I couldn't deal with theories other than by translating the text as I went along into simple issues, into stories I could pass on to Ara.

While I was reading I would be talking to her.

Debunking, stripping down and simplifying such ideas as philosophy held in high esteem and psychology regarded as complex – it became second nature to me.

"Try looking at philosophy as a sort of consumer guide," I told Ara. "For ages philosophers have done nothing but promote immaterial goods – beauty and goodness and truth – and they do this exactly the same way as advertising campaigns do: they promise you something, they promise to make you feel better. Love, truth and goodness have been more widely promoted than any commercial product has ever been. Philosophers merely ask a different price. Happiness is not for sale. When push comes to shove the price is always the same: insight and self-knowledge."

Ara asked me how you got insight and self-knowledge.

I told her I believed it was by thinking, by not taking your own view for granted, by asking yourself where your view comes from, why you look at things and people in a certain way, how your thoughts and feelings have been influenced.

"And suppose you know all those things," asked Ara, "does that make you slim and happy?"

That was always clever of Ara, the way she could ask me questions I didn't dare answer.

I told her I hoped that was indeed the way things went, in life, that there was a reward for goodness and punishment for evil, but I had my doubts. I felt a sadness creeping up on me that I did not want and told Ara that at least it made sense to see through the ways in which you get drawn into desire, from grand passion to wanting a candy bar, that seeing how it works makes your freer. The best description of freedom for me would always be: being able to resist temptation.

Although I disparaged the value of university education when I was with Ara, that did not mean I was not wholly absorbed in a profusion of subjects, all of which circled round the most hackneyed problem of all: the link between body and mind.

"So you're studying the two of us, really," Ara would remark from time to time.

If I was feeling generous I would agree with her and say it was true that I was only trying to fathom the depths of our friendship. In a less forthcoming mood I would say she should stop this, that she was dragging herself down as well as me by clinging to the old way of dividing things between the two of us, which had been a lot of fun in the past but which was a nuisance now.

"It's better to focus on the similarities," I told Ara, "then we'll get to understand ourselves better."

It was not until I spent a weekend at her house laid up with a sprained ankle that I managed to make her see what I meant.

The memory of my fall is pin-sharp, I told Ara, and eventually it became my version of what happens when you drink too much, of what it's all about.

I've had a lot to drink and am riding my bike home. I'm not having any trouble cycling, there's little traffic at this hour and I'm sure I'm going in a straight line, but that's what people always think when they're drunk. I manage to find my way home, turn into my own familiar street, head towards the place where I normally park my bike and lift my feet off the pedals. Suddenly I'm dead tired. The bike slows down. I vaguely remember that there's still some important action to be undertaken, but I can't think what it might be, and I don't really care. Once the bike has come to a standstill I topple over, bike and all. A stab of pain brings it all back: the certainty that, once you've got onto a bike there comes a point when you have to get off. I can't stop laughing.

Ara gave me a worried look. I had not expected that. I had tried to pass off my accident as a hilarious joke.

I couldn't remember which conclusion I had intended to draw from the story. In Ara's look there was a hint of compassion, and that confused me. Everything I could put forward by way of explanation for my torn ligament would be a denial of what had aroused her pity, of its truth. And it was a truth I could not bring myself to face. I was curious about it all right, but my curiosity was not as strong as my desire to leave the truth to Ara, where it was safe and would not be taken advantage of.

Ara knew a lot of things about me which I did not know, that was one of the pillars of our friendship. She possessed knowledge about me which I did not possess, and I possessed knowledge about her which she did not possess. And this secret knowledge about the other, this prize that was attainable for no one but ourselves, united us.

What we didn't know also made each of us permanently wary that our friendship might come to an untimely end, that it might be destroyed by the discovery and subsequent condemnation of what the one knew about the other.

"I can't remember exactly what I was trying to tell you, Ara," I said.

"No matter, little thing," she said.

In my opinion addiction always has something to do with trying to restore the balance between body and mind. People who drink a lot blur their minds and that blur is necessary in order to loosen control over the body. You only keep that body upright, feed it, wash it and dress it, because you are conscious of it. You can also become too conscious of your body, which can hinder you in experiencing sensual pleasure.

Besides all the flesh, blood and bones that make up the body it also has a language almost as expressive as words. People who are unable to relate to their own body on a symbolic level, who can't talk with it or who have prohibited themselves from doing so for some reason, start drinking in order to overturn that prohibition, to silence an unreasonable, harsh, too terrifying mind and to give the body a chance to speak at last.

Drunks hate the lies the body tells when sober, they hate its language, the spoken words, the smiles, the thwarted longing of the flesh, the betrayal.

Addiction is the expression of a forbidden language. And as such it is itself a language, a disclosure, a signal that can be decoded.

Getting drunk is not the same as getting fat.

I was the kind of person who had to think things over before taking action and I knew that Ara got in a muddle when pressed to think, and yet she always seemed to know what to do. The first and as yet only postulate I had come up with for my dissertation was: Show me your addiction and I will show you your forbidden language.

I wasn't sure I would actually use it, because in a way I can't stand that kind of sweeping statement, but at the same time I feel that sweeping statements, by virtue of sheer audacity and rhetoric, outclass the more nuanced kind of statement any day.

Ara knew that she was the focus of practically everything I enjoyed thinking about. It had all started with her, with groping to find explanations for her hunger, her eating, her expanding body and for the suffering she caused herself. As long as I myself had been able to keep a distance from my dearest enemy and drank little or not at all, I had been able to reflect on the nature of addiction without having to face up to the fact that all this might have some bearing on me.

Smoking and nail-biting were just bad habits, they gave you ugly hands and killed you, but they weren't addictions.

Ara was addicted.

To food.

I reflected on Ara.

By focusing my attention on her pain I managed for years to keep my own at bay. Unaccountably, I was quite content with my obsessive pondering of the workings of her mind, her motives and her happiness. In this way I was able to distance myself from pain and suffering until the day I met Thomas and Ara gave me the first glimpse of the language of her longing.

3

FROM THE MOMENT I SET EYES ON THOMAS I COULDN'T help thinking of Ara. Not only was he tall, he was also hefty and good-looking like she was, and he made my heart stop exactly as Ara had done twenty years ago when I first spotted her, the new girl, in the school yard, and all I could think of at that moment was that she was my fate and that this encounter would alter the course of my life.

I was no longer a child and my ideas about fate had changed somewhat over the years, but the moment I saw Thomas the word *fatal* starting flashing in my head, and try as I might I was unable to switch the irritating warning signal off.

I regarded the study of psychology as a way of keeping in touch with my personal fate, and the study of philosophy as a way of distancing myself from my fate by sharing it with everyone else. What attracted me most of all in psychology as well as philosophy was, I think, that both disciplines held out the promise that acquiring knowledge of them would actually make it possible to live a life less governed by fate.

There are days that I am overcome by a desire to have done with it, no matter with what, with everything.

It is still the God of my childhood to whom I turn and whom I beg for respite, for permission to take a day or two off from the merry-go-round of life.

"Having to go round and round like that makes me dizzy, once in a while," I tell Him.

Most of all I liked imagining myself as a go-between, as an intermediary between two ways of looking at things, and I busied myself trying to bring them closer together, to marry what philosophy calls ideas to what psychology calls emotions.

It wasn't until I met Thomas that I began to see why I was so keen on understanding all these things. Knowing him gave me the opportunity to read a couple of chapters from the scenario upon which my life is based. It was then that I discovered that vast tracts were completely new to me, as I had not even known of their existence, let alone read them.

Falling in love invariably means falling into the trap of an ancient drama, and it's always a drama of bondage. Suddenly I realized that all these years I had managed to banish love from my life. I had relegated love to the chapter about pain, fear, insecurity, confusion, guilt, powerlessness, shame, and a crushing pity for everyone, except myself.

Memories are swaddled in emotion, they are wrapped and tied up with feeling. Refusing to have anything to do with the one, with the pain and fear, means losing touch with the other, with memory, knowledge and understanding. And those are the very instruments of personal happiness.

It was Ara who made it clear to me that I would never experience love if I didn't give myself to Thomas.

She can only have had the faintest suspicion that by urging me on in this way she was allowing me a glimpse of her forbidden language, and that our friendship might suffer as a result.

Thomas was 1 metre 93, he weighed 115 kilos, was fifty-three and had black hair with a lot of grey in it. He had wonderful luminous eyes and thick dark eyebrows. You could tell right away that he was a moody sort of man. The lines in his face expressed wariness and exasperation rather than sorrow. But not his eyes. His eyes were the strangest thing about Thomas and it took me quite a while to see what the look in them was.

It was fear.

He was involved in design and advertising copy. He worked freelance, at home, alone and in silence. He had that typical shroud of silence about him, that autistic and monastic aura people get if they spend more than five hours a day without speaking.

Hendrik had thrown a party to celebrate the publication of a brochure about the institution he worked for.

Hendrik had become one of my closest friends in those years and he cooked for me nearly every day.

Ten years ago I didn't know how long it took to boil an egg, let alone potatoes. Preparing food was my mother's exclusive domain and I never sought to encroach on it. Nor would that have been possible, I am sure. The meals she cooked were tokens of love, and you don't take that away from anyone.

I soon learned to cook for myself, but didn't fancy having strangers, visitors, intruders in my flat, so I called on Hendrik practically every day. He always got home around six, when he would launch into another of his experiments with stuffed cabbage, unusual stews and wobbly puddings.

Ever since I first knew him I dreaded the day that he would get tired of my company, that he would intimate that he was not in the mood either to shop or to cook for the two of us, that the food would become a painful issue, but the day never came. Hendrik was happy in his kitchen and never failed to greet me with a radiant look in his extraordinary eyes.

It was through Hendrik that I met Thomas.

It was through Ara that I got to know him.

"This is my best friend," Hendrik said, putting his arm around me, "and this is Thomas Herstael."

"And does this best friend have a name, may I ask?" Thomas said gruffly, without extending his hand.

The first thing that struck me was that this sort of stand-offishness was nothing new, that it had held sway over me for the past twenty years, delighting and disappointing me by turn, and still took me by surprise however hard I had tried to get used to it.

"I'm not as fond of people as you are," Ara said without a trace of cynicism, when I asked her why she couldn't simply be friendly to people she knew nothing about and who hadn't done anything to merit so much grouchiness.

"It's got nothing to do with being fond of people," I said, "I don't love just anyone. I hate it when people say they love the whole world and everybody in it. It's got to do with common decency."

"So you reckon I'm rude?"

"Yes," I said, "I suppose you are a bit."

"I'm just straightforward, that's all," said Ara. "I'm no good at pretending. I don't like all that bowing and scraping. If I have nothing to say I keep my mouth shut, and if there's nothing to be friendly about then why be friendly? What you lot have is a little switchboard in your head, all you have to do is press a button for the right signals, and I haven't got one."

The more I felt that Ara was accusing me of posturing, of sham and insincerity, the more I cast around for convincing arguments to support my condemnation of her behaviour, which, for all my criticism, also inspired a sneaky admiration in me.

Sometimes I get into the sort of mood where it doesn't have to be true what I say, so long as it strikes home and hurts a lot.

"You're so eager to make contact," said Ara, "Everyone can tell right off. I prefer keeping a distance."

"But that's exactly what you aren't doing," I said. "The best way of keeping a distance is by being pleasant to everyone, by being civil and not letting on how you feel. Showing your feelings is what I call intimate."

She gave me a surprised look. No doubt it was my expression, which must have been fierce, grim.

"And you're so odd about kissing, too," she said gravely, as if she was mulling this over. "Before you know it you've run off again without having felt a thing."

"Exactly," I said.

"Funny," she said, "that it has taken me until now to realize this."

As soon as I've won I rest my head in her lap. She uncovers my neck and strokes me, because she knows that makes me blissfully happy.

Five minutes after Thomas and I were introduced we found ourselves caught up in a volley of words. I had asked him if his surname was spelled with ae, because if so he had the same name as the owner of the country estate near the village where I was born and could they somehow be related.

"I have no relatives," he said.

"Everyone has relatives," I said, which was just as well, I went on, as the distinction of being the son or daughter of your parents was just about the only thing in life you got for free, that you didn't need to lift a finger for and that couldn't be taken away from you either.

What on earth did I mean, he asked, but by then he had looked into my eyes. He smiled and seemed surprised.

With the eagerness of someone who's spent a year on a desert island going through chestfuls of books and who's now brimming with ideas about what she's read, I launched into an explanation of what I meant, and what I had been trying to get down on paper these past years. The more his features softened and the longer he met my gaze, the deeper I fell in love. Suddenly it was conceivable that I might see him again, that here was a man who might eventually allow me to love him.

In psychology, the theories about behaviour and emotion take you right back to your family background, to the days of early childhood when the cards were dealt for a game that was new to you and you unknowingly began making up the rules for your own life. The kindest thing a psychologist can say is that it's not your fault, that there was a time when you were helpless and innocent, and that the only ones who should have known better were the others, the people playing the game with you.

Guilty parents produce innocent offspring, but if that is true they themselves were once the innocent offspring of guilty parents. And so on ad infinitum. An endless cycle of guilt and innocence. Mankind is made up of a long chain of guilty individuals with valid excuses, and if you go all the way back to the start you find Eve, who forfeited her freedom by giving in to the temptation of food and left the role of super-innocent to the man, since man was never the initiator but became guilty by association with woman.

It must be a pretty good story, seeing as it's been doing the rounds for so long.

The twentieth century is the age of acquittal, of the victim, of the taboo surrounding guilt. The church and the therapist's consulting room are no longer the only places where adults can revert to a blissful state of innocence and unconditional absolution – in the past half century the whole world has become that place.

Even a murderer is a victim. Ask him and he will cite extenuating circumstances.

The second half of this century has seen the transformation of societies sharing faith, morals, laws, norms and rituals, into societies bound together by injustice, sickness, contempt and humiliation – societies of victims.

The perpetrators are the others.

That's the snag in this line of thinking, because there is no room for perpetrators nor for victims in a guiltless world. But victims need perpetrators, they are dependent on them. That new perpetrators keep cropping up is one of the inconsistencies of an age in which everyone is seen as guiltless.

I think this is what makes people ill: the dualism, the ambiguity, the utter lack of logic.

Instead of looking for ways to distinguish themselves by personal achievement, everyone seems to be searching for a collective hurt and humiliation, for the privilege of a public, shared discrimination from which to glean a religion, a bonding with a community. In this century you stand pretty much alone unless you suffer from some group infirmity and are to be pitied or indeed discriminated against. It must be an extraordinary moment in history that finds women frantically racking their brains for suppressed memories of having been abused, sexually or otherwise, by their fathers. It's like a hysterical kind of jealousy, this desire for a shared lot which gives you significance.

And maybe that's what it is.

Maybe the second half of the twentieth century is marked by a terrible jealousy inspired by the only society of victims our century has produced, by the lot of a mass of people, who are thus bound together, inescapably.

It would be awful if that were true.

However that may be, I can't see the celebration of guiltlessness as any more than a low attempt to abdicate responsibility, including responsibility for the way you distinguish yourself from others and consequently give meaning to a unique existence.

Discrimination is a prerequisite for meaning.

If you make no distinction between one person and the next, then they cease to exist in their own right and failure to distinguish leads to indifference.

The opposite of love is not hate, because hate still has to be earned, the opposite is indifference.

The distinction you get by being a victim is a free offer. There's no effort involved, and it's not your responsibility either.

Philosophy is the only domain where guilt has not been dismissed out of hand. To a philosopher, the fact that certain behaviour is understandable does not automatically mean that it cannot be bad.

Nowadays we tend to dodge notions of good and bad when forming opinions.

Philosophy stands for the prosecution. Which is why philosophy is not for innocent children. All the theories about rational thought and self-knowledge are theories for adults. Philosophy has no bearing on you until you are ready to make up your own mind, choose, persevere in your intent, wield power, become slave or master, assume responsibility, accept challenges and judgement by others, and so take the risk of being found guilty.

I love the forbearance of psychology, but I find it impossible to give meaning to life without the gimlet eye of philosophy. If you can't even be guilty of your own life it's not worth living, I think.

The only sort of fate philosophy acknowledges is the existence of God or some entity without a capital letter, like language, spirit, production figures, death or the world of ideas. The teachings of philosophy exonerate only on the grounds that you are human, a creature with a God and with ideas, that you can't think any other way than you think, because God created the world in a certain way or because that's how your mind happens to work. Never because you suffered abuse as a child, because your mother was schizophrenic or your father a collaborator in the war. Philosophy doesn't care about those things.

I told Thomas that the best way for me to try to understand things was to compare mankind with language. In language, words never stand on their own. A word doesn't mean anything unless there are other words around for it to make sense with. It's the same with people. We gain significance through our alliances with things or people, family, friends, lovers, and even with the world, too, by virtue of our work. I guess whether you consider your life to be meaningful or not depends on the kind of personal relations you have. To be a mother you need a child, it's as simple as that. To be a lover you need a lover, to be a friend you need friends, and to be a writer you need readers. It's the drama of dependence and there's nothing you can do about it.

"Funny you talking about such things," he said.
"Meaning what?"
"It sounds so old-fashioned, like a fad of the past, there's a mothbally smell."
That could have been one of Ara's words, I reflected. I told him these ideas might sound old-fashioned to him, but they still offered explanations for a whole lot of things that were susceptible to fashion, like the scourges of the modern age – take addiction, for instance, I was really interested in finding explanations for things like addiction and what it meant to be addicted, and that I was

pretty sure it had a lot to do with the drama of dependence and the desire for meaning.

At that point Hendrik came past with a tray of snacks. Fresh herring, sliced sausage, crackers with shrimps.

Thomas jerked his head back and waved his hand across his face when Hendrik offered him the tray. I took a cracker with shrimps.

"I'm on a diet," Thomas said grudgingly.

"Fat people are always on a diet," I said, stuffing the cracker into my mouth.

As the evening progressed and I drank more, I lost track of what I was doing. There was nothing to stop me from following my own blind intuition which said that all Thomas wanted was to listen to the tales I was bursting to regale him with, about meaning and happiness and love, about food and drink and how that might have something to do with strained relations within a family. I talked my head off and my attention for his eyes slackened so that I did not notice when his gaze, which he had kept fixed on me from the moment I began to speak, became tired and sated.

That's why I was so startled when he suggested we should dance.

We danced and I had nothing to say. He led me with a firm hand, spun me round, lifted me up and laughed. When he put his hands on my hips I suddenly remembered I had hips and the way he moved told me what kind of lover he would be: passionate, rough, a bit off-hand maybe and it occurred to me that this was just what I needed.

His body brushing against mine and the fleeting kisses I felt now and then in my neck excited me and I knew then that it wasn't a question of seeing each other again, but that he would come home with me that very night and that we would enter a relationship for which neither of us was well equipped.

4

IN THE YEAR THAT IT LASTED, THAT IT WAS THERE twenty-four hours a day, the urgency and fierceness between Thomas Herstael and me, in the same year that I was his lover I was to ally myself with my dearest enemy.

The two went together, my drinking and my love, which I'll call love for lack of another word.

From the very first day with Thomas I was conscious of a change in me, I could see that I had turned into the sort of woman who hangs around at home waiting for the phone to ring, and I saw with fearsome clarity that there was no going back. To break the pact I had made with this man and with drink would take violence, and the wounds would be self-inflicted.

It started right away, in the very first week. I am a stranger to myself and I greet this new person with interest, with a little disdain perhaps but also with amusement – because of the cliché, I expect. There is not a shred of difference between me and all those women who used to astound me the moment they had a man, with their witless pursuit of one single aim in life: to hold his attention and keep him happy.

Now I understand.

I am no different.

I am just the same.

This is the first time I have bought a bottle of wine when there isn't someone coming for supper. The wine is for me. It is my first experience of drinking alone. Before the week is out I am sitting at my desk at half past ten in the morning with a glass of wine and a sheet of paper, scrawling desperate messages to Ara. Even my handwriting is unfamiliar to me. All the roundness has gone, leaving words which are tiny and pointed and which Ara will find hard to read from now on.

Ara complains, she frets. She says she spends hours deciphering my letters because she doesn't want to miss a single word, and that it drives her mad to have to face defeat and skip some of my meaning.

On the days when I feel too tired to pay attention to my handwriting, I type my letters to her. My typing is fast and furious. Ara is shocked by the first one, which is full of typing errors. She sounds alarmed on the phone.

"How could you do that," she says, "you've got a nerve!"

I was the kind of person who wrote letters without a single mistake in them, who writes a rough version first and then laboriously copies it out so that not one word is crossed out or misspelt.

That was what I used to be like.

Not any more.

At night in my dreams I witness carnival parades with sliced pigs' carcasses. The grotesque images of the night linger on during the day, looming like huge realistic paintings, uninvited, unpleasant. During the day they scare me.

I don't understand these dreams.

I was born in the season of slaughter. Each year my father's father presented each of his twelve children with half a pig. My father shared a pig with one of his brothers. My memory tells me it was slaughtered each year on my birthday, in our back yard. But my memory must be inaccurate.

From the window I watched as they dragged the pig, squealing horribly, to the middle of the yard, whereupon the butcher killed it with a shot to its head. Everyone stood ready. The main artery in the neck was slit with a long sharp knife. One of the women caught the foaming blood in a pail and went off with it at once. She was going to make black pudding, that much I knew.

I didn't eat black pudding.

Making meat out of blood was not a good idea, I thought. Since God had given his own blood in the form of wine and his body in the form of bread, there had to be something wrong with turning blood into a substance you could chew. I found this idea troubling and preferred to stick to my own trusted set of rules.

I had tried to explain to my mother how I felt, because I knew she was disappointed when I turned my nose up at the fresh black pudding, after all it was a gift from our grandfather and we ought to be grateful. She had said that it wasn't right to compare God with a pig in the first place, that pig's blood was a far cry from the wine the priest drank in church, that you can't make wine from blood, and that I was making a fuss about nothing.

Theological debates always made my mother nervous, so I never mentioned the unspeakable transubstantiation of blood into sausage again and did not eat my first slice of fried black pudding until I was way past twenty and on a very different footing with God than when I was a child.

Before the butcher spliced the pig, pails of boiling water had been poured over the carcass, the skin had been scraped and there had been some ghoulish manipulations with a hook and the legs.

I didn't dare watch when he was actually slitting it down the middle. The next time I looked I saw the pig splayed open on a rack, suddenly transformed into two symmetrical halves.

Oddly enough that made the whole thing look more human than when it was still undivided and so unmistakably an animal.

In my dreams I keep seeing the same procession of floats bearing racks of splayed pigs going round the village.

I don't tell Thomas about any of this. Nor that I spend entire days crying sometimes, and that a sadness has crept into my being which is immense and ancient and leaden. All I know about this sadness is that I cannot blame it on him. That would be unjust.

The sadness is all my own.

My meeting him merely opened a door and let the sadness out of its hiding-place. Falling in love, longing for love, was in my case governed by a desire to know.

It didn't even have anything to do with Thomas, really, which is just about the worst I can say about him.

Looking back, Thomas could have been any other man who wanted me and yet didn't want me. That was the recipe for love and pain, it had to be that kind of person.

The phone is becoming an instrument of torture. Each day I wait for Thomas to call with some proposal for the evening, to come and have supper with him, for example. Thomas likes cooking. He cuts a fine figure at his stove, washing vegetables and chopping them, tearing lettuce leaves, roasting meat. His body looks too big for its surroundings. He reduces the kitchen to toy proportions. When I watch him sketching it is almost impossible to imagine how such big hands can make such delicate drawings, and when he's working with scissors and glue he looks like a little boy.

Each day I strain to make out the tone of his voice, to hear whether he is still there for me, whether he still wants us to be together.

He says he's perfidious by nature. He wants this love more than anything else, he says, but on the other hand he's not so keen. He is still drawn to his other bride, he says, his solitude, his dreams. But when I ask him what he dreams about he says from now on he can dream only of me. All he wants is to be with me, to lie with his body next to mine, to be in me.

"I lose myself when I'm with you," he says, and goes on to tell me this delights him but also repels him.

"Please don't lose yourself," I tell him, "or else I won't have anyone to love."

What both of us like best is lying in bed with our bodies intertwined. The confidence I feel now is new to me. It is as if I can't go wrong with Thomas, as if this immense body holds no secrets for me and I know exactly how to pleasure it.

Sometimes he turns his back on me abruptly. By remaining calm, by not being startled, by asking him why he is behaving in this strange way I discover that he is consumed with jealousy, that he keeps asking himself where and how I learned to give a man pleasure.

I'm naive. I can't imagine anyone being jealous on my behalf.

I tell him I learned these things from a woman.

Ara rings me every day, even during the night sometimes.

She can feel when something is upsetting me, she says. And she's always spot on. Every phone call catches me when I'm weepy and scared.

From the moment I told her about Thomas she could sense that it would be different this time. It had to be.

"We mustn't make the same mistake all over again," she says.

Although I can't put my finger on it, I know what she means. She is saying that she has a very clear mental image of Thomas and that, from the day I met him, she has felt there was a certain kinship between them, that she is like him.

"It's very odd," she says.

I tell her I don't know how to handle this, how to conduct myself in the arena of love.

She says: "You've got to want to live with him."

She says: "You must stop running away, you must stay put and face things."

She says: "He wants you. There's no one in the world like you."

She says: "Fancy you wanting a love like this."

She says: "I know how great it is to be with you."

The things she says sometimes make her cry.

I remember every word she says. During the day her voice goes round and round in my head, and I make notes of her pronouncements in a thick scrawl.

You have to want to live with him.

I am beginning to feel more and more dependent on her to lead me safely through this love, I am afraid that I will be totally lost without her and that this love will be the death of me.

And then there's the drink.

Drink, death and love are knotted together somehow, I don't know how, and perhaps it's just that I don't want to know and so I drink to blot it out, to escape having to untie the knots, because I am afraid if I do that I will lose my love.

*

Since Thomas and I got together there was one thing I knew for sure: that I could never be alone again. At the same time I did not know what the "never" of my new disability entailed. I was drinking too much to notice that I was not so much involved in allying myself with anyone as in severing old ties.

For the time being drinking stops me from seeing that I'm scared witless, that my idea of hell is to have to commit myself all over again.

5

I SPEND THE WHOLE DAY THINKING OF THOMAS, OF Ara and of drink. As long as I am not actually drunk I can still reflect on the effects of drink and attempt to write about them.

There is just one standard that I try hard to uphold against the onslaught of emotions which, although once willed, threaten to overpower me, and that is my work. As soon as I notice a lapse of concentration because I am waiting for the reassurance of Thomas' voice asking me to supper I go wild and have to waste enormous amounts of energy forcing myself to calm down and stay sitting at my desk. I spend hours telling myself to come to my senses so that I can do what I set out to do and not feel spineless and powerless.

Real life and the subjects I am writing about keep getting tangled up. Sometimes I suspect myself of making a rigid distinction between overeating and overdrinking because I am still busy sorting out what separates Ara and me instead of what unites us, and describing our friendship in those terms.

I refuse to countenance the idea that our friendship, her eating, my drinking and Thomas could be related in any way at all.

I am finding it increasingly difficult to write my dissertation without making it too personal. My longing to make my study a one-off, a book which does not fit into a well-worn category, is rivalled only by my longing for Thomas' body and for his constant companionship.

Lately she has taken to ringing me several times a day. She says there's something creepy about our telephone conversations.

"I feel as if I'm letting you in on all these secrets," she says. "I keep thinking it may be more than you can take, that knowing these things might turn you against me."

It is true that I am astounded by what she tells me, but by now I am hooked.

The phone calls all follow the same pattern. First I tell Ara about something Thomas has said or done, which I can't understand but which scares me and makes me feel ill. Then it's Ara's turn to divulge her interpretations and comparisons, and to offer exhaustive advice. I feel weak and powerless and can't get enough of listening to her, although at the back of my mind there is a nagging doubt that there is something scandalous about our exchanges.

Ara talks about Thomas as if she is talking about herself, and I am beginning to have trouble keeping them apart. But there is something else that is even more disconcerting, and it intensifies the feeling of entrapment, of being caught in a web of allegiances.

I try telling myself there is nothing wrong with letting things happen for the time being, that the time for understanding will come later.

The only thing I keep from Ara is that I have this niggly feeling deep down. I can hardly tell her that I feel more and more like her when I'm with Thomas, when I'm giving him such good loving that he can't help getting me under his skin.

It was a month after I started seeing Thomas that I introduced him to Ara. He let himself into my flat and stepped into the room to find Ara waiting for him. She seemed calm, until the way she shot out of her chair gave her away. She went up to him and introduced herself as "Thomas."

"But I thought that was me," Thomas said, laughing.

After she had met Thomas Ara often talked about we this and we that, when she and I were on the phone.

"You're so distant, Kit. We're always scared you're about to disappear. There's something in you that locks everyone out and we can't stand it. We want all of you. We want to know everything about you there is to know. We want to read every word you write, to sit in your briefcase surrounded by all your exercise books, to be the words in your head. Which is a pretty grim state of affairs. And can you imagine living with anyone who gave in to such desires? You wouldn't stand for it, I'm sure. That's why we back off. To keep control. We don't want to get out of our depth.

"You needn't be afraid. He wants you, I'm sure of that. I know you, you can make us so happy. You have a hold on people, whether you like it or not.

"That's the way it was for us, we both knew from the start that this was a once-in-a-lifetime thing. And it's your lifetime. What more could you possibly want? We're in your clutches, why else d'you think we're still around? It's too late now. Too late for Thomas, too, in spite of your stubbornness and your imperious nature. Is disturb the right word? You are a disturbance and being disturbed happens to be good for us. As long as we're with you we let you disturb us because that makes us feel better, more whole. But when you're gone we stop feeling good and whole. That's why we behave the way we do. That's why you think we've changed when we meet again after a short separation.

Thomas thinks a lot about these things, too. Which is hardly surprising, since you're always making us think. But sometimes we just don't have the appetite for it. Sometimes we don't want you in our head so badly that we stuff ourselves with food instead, until we're too fat and contented and lazy to do a thing.

"It's as if I'm giving you away. It's gruesome, but it feels as if it must be done.

"He feels me in you. He can't stand it.

"But you always pick people like us, Kit, people with thick skins. You don't like people who surrender to you lightly. You can't abide them. You want to work on your relationships and we're just the ticket because that's what we want you to do, too. But not all the time. Sometimes it's too much. Sometimes you're too overbearing.

"I knew better than to surprise you with a visit. People were claiming you all the time and you always got sick of them in the end. You came to see me because I never went to see you, because I didn't run after you and left you free. That's how I always felt. That there was no other way of being your friend. Thomas feels the same.

"Quite frankly I never thought you had it in you, Kit, this desire to commit yourself. I thought you'd stay on your own for ever, with only me in your head. Sometimes I'm sorry about that. Maybe we missed out on something, maybe things could have been different between us, better."

Until Thomas and I went to the States for three months I relished our heart-to-heart talks. Not a day went by without her soothing me with talk about what she and Thomas were like and why that made me feel so out of it.

I still haven't a clue.

I was not to know, then, that the memory of these conversations would one day flood me with a terrible rage.

Having shrugged off Thomas' delaying tactics I went ahead and made arrangements with my department so that I could go to the States with him. He had an important assignment from a big advertising agency, there was a studio plus apartment waiting for him in New York, and he was in two minds about taking me with him, so he said. But I listened to Ara, who told me I should follow my instincts and prove to him how dearly I wanted to be with him, because he would never believe me otherwise.

I decided to do exactly as I always did when he was moaning and groaning or sulking without even daring to look in my direction. Then I would know he wanted me out of his house and out of his life, but I would simply go into the bedroom and crawl under the blankets. It could be hours before he came to bed and nestled into me.

It was always the same.

His huge frame looms in the bedroom. He's standing by the bed, looking down. I look up at him. Then his smile tells me that he is moved to see me lying there, waiting for him. Sometimes he says he regrets being the man he is, a man who has no faith in anything, and that he is glad I am stubborn enough to put up with an oddball like himself.

"I suppose I should accept this as manna from heaven," he says.

He says he has never being capable of surrender, of commitment.

I know exactly what he means, I know the pattern of his non-committal and I am already tearing it to shreds.

Actually I can't stand the word surrender any more, I tell him, and that it used to have meaning for me too, that I think people take it to mean something physical, something wonderful and uplifting, and that is an area in which I am maddeningly deficient. I tell him I think there are words which defile love, and that surrender is one of many such polluting words. The word that has been lurking at the back of my mind for the past weeks is intimacy, but I don't dare say it out loud, I hardly dare to admit even to myself what I am discovering.

It is just too disappointing.

I am far too attached to the word to drop it just like that. I would rather drown my brains in drink than face up to the idea that intimacy might be just another twentieth-century advertising slogan and might not exist at all in the way I had imagined, as an exquisitely physical sensation, a blending of two beings, and also a bit like dying.

Facing up to that will not happen until I drink less and stop punishing myself for a deficiency that is not a deficiency but a mistaken perception.

By explaining the absurdity of the word *surrender* to Thomas, I talk myself into confronting that other notion, too.

Surrender goes with cowboys and Indians, and cops and robbers. The enemy surrenders when you hold a knife to his throat or a pistol to his heart, but a lover does things differently. Why do lovers lavish care on their clothes to please one another, if all they want is to shed them at the first opportunity so that they can feast their eyes on a sight that is beyond their control? And since experience tells us there is no greater fulfilment than knowledge, why are we lumbered with fairy tales about total surrender, about abandoning self-control, consciousness and knowledge? What a nightmare to have no idea what is happening to you – where is the fulfilment in that?

Lovers gain something extra from being loved, it is a distinction that does not come your way until you allow yourself to love and be loved in return – if you happen to have a propensity for that sort of thing. There is no other way of gaining that distinction than by loving another person.

It has less to do with surrender than with dependence, control, choice, understanding and trust, I explain, and that all this makes it very dramatic and heavy. The question is whether we will be up to it, I conclude.

One day my eye is caught by a plane ticket to New York lying on the kitchen table. He has obviously left it there intentionally. I lift the corner of a newspaper to check whether there is a second ticket underneath, but I know I will find nothing. I do not wait for him to come home. I go straight to the travel agent and order my own ticket. There are no seats left on his flight. It will do him good to be alone for a bit, I think, so I buy a ticket for a week later. When I get home I tell him I will follow him, that I will fly across the Atlantic Ocean just to be with him.

"What if it turns out to be a drama," he says.

"So what?" I say.

I mean it.

Drama is what I want.

6

A WEEK BEFORE LEAVING FOR AMERICA I GO TO STAY with Ara. Bing is busy in the shed and we hardly see him. He gives me worried looks when our paths cross in the yard and during supper. He says I look wretched, that I'm too thin. Bing has never taken much notice of me before and I'm impressed by his daring to tell me these things to my face. That must mean I'm in a pretty bad state, and I suppose I should take better care of myself.

"So much love scares him off," Ara says.

But for the time being both Ara and I maintain it's just nerves, I'm in a state about going away. Ara does her utmost to calm me down. She strokes me and brews me funny-tasting potions with healing roots and herbs.

She treats me like an invalid.

At night I can't sleep unless I've drunk a bottle of wine.

"Why must you drink all the time, Kit?" she asks.

"Because I don't want to know," I say, "that much I do know."

"What don't you want to know?"

"That's just it," I say, "that's what I have to find out."

It was not until one late afternoon in August, three days before my flight, that it began to dawn on me. I had spent the whole day in the sun, I had drunk some wine and had fallen asleep, and had woken up with a bad case of sunburn. Ara was shocked when she saw my angry red skin. She climbed onto her bicycle and rode to the shop in the village nearby. She came back with a basket full of cucumbers.

In the meantime I was feverish from the sunburn, my teeth were chattering and I was shivering. Ara acted calmly and efficiently, not saying much. She lit a fire in the grate, dragged the sofa up close and fetched a couple of blankets, one of which she wrapped around me. I was still wearing my bikini.

"Lie down," she said.

She tucked the extra blanket around me carefully, pulled up a side table to be within easy reach and poured me a glass of cold white wine.

"I'll be back in a moment, little beast," she said, smiling sweetly.

I followed everything she did with my eyes and had to remind myself that it was Ara who was going through all these motions. There were moments when I lost all sense of who she was, she seemed a complete stranger although there was something vaguely familiar about her, as if she was a person I had never seen before but who reminded me of someone. The weirdness of it all made me feel worse than ever and I screwed up my eyes to make the feeling go away and stop interfering with the picture of Ara I had in my head.

Something was evidently amiss, and I got alarmed. I hoped she would come back into the room quickly and that the weirdness would be over, that I wouldn't lie there marvelling at that outsize body, those swaying hips, the sleek skin and the most beautiful face I had ever seen, that she wouldn't look like a weird and wonderful stranger but would be her old self again, not some person I had never set eyes on.

When she came in it had gone.

I was so relieved that I told her how for a moment I hadn't

recognized her, how I had looked at her and found that she did not match the picture I had in my head.

"It's the sunburn," she said. "You need to take a lot of liquid."

Did I see her as herself now, she asked, or as someone different.

"As you," I said.

"Good," she said, "because otherwise I wouldn't be here making a fuss over you. I'd never allow a stranger to make a fuss over you, even if the stranger was me."

I crumpled up laughing, and discovered how badly I was burnt all down my front.

A plate of cucumber slices stood on the side table. Ara folded down the blanket and undid my bikini top. Touching my skin as lightly as could she slipped the bottom off too.

"We've got to fight the fire," she said.

She made me lie down flat on the sofa and started cooling my skin with a layer of cucumber slices.

Not feeling the slightest embarrassment surprised me, and also that I could not only stand all this attention but actually enjoyed being touched in this way.

She spoke softly and said she was always startled by how small my body was and that she sometimes wondered how anyone could live in a body as small as mine, how anyone could survive in the world with such a wee defenceless body, so light you could knock it down with a feather.

After that she sang a song for me.

She sang *You were always on my mind*.

As she was busy covering the skin of my legs with cucumber slices and had her back to me she didn't see I was crying, but she could sense it.

In the middle of her song she stopped, turned round and sat down on the floor next to the sofa. She said nothing but took my hand in hers and fixed me with her eyes, and a few minutes later I saw there were tears trickling down her cheeks, although her features were composed.

"You're knackered," she said.

I nodded.

After a quarter of an hour Ara broke the silence.

"You're actually crying. I haven't seen you cry for the last ten years. I never thought I would miss it, but I did. In the old days I used to be amazed each time you burst into tears, which you did loudly and often, even in public. But when you stopped doing that I missed it."

"Me too," I said. "I had no control, it was stronger than me. Some sort of body-language, I expect."

"You haven't cried for ten years, Kit," she said.

"Almost ten years. You weren't there," I said. "I was alone. I think I cried twice. When I wasn't home I mean."

"What happened?"

"One time was at this Karl Marx tutorial we had, and they were falling over themselves defining historical materialism in terms of Hegel's master-slave theory. The other time was at Hendrik's. I was leafing through some old newspapers and came across an obituary notice. It was for Michel Foucault. And all that time I hadn't known he was dead."

I felt like weeping all over again.

"So what exactly made you cry?" she asked. She was still holding my hands, massaging my palms.

"I'm not sure," I said. "But maybe it was the cruelty of not knowing," I continued, "feeling cheated, goodness knows. Left out, something like that. I don't know. Ara?"

"Kit."

"I'm too miserable to talk."

"This time it's your own doing," she said jokingly, "you're a right Untouchable now."

"That's just it," I said.

I didn't dare tell her the rest. I was too ashamed. Then I told her anyway.

"You're still the only person I can bear touching me," I said.

"You let Thomas touch you," she said, but she knew.

"No," I said, "it's not the same."

Dusk was falling. We could only distinguish each other's faces in the glow of the fire. We did not eat nor did we talk about what we might have for supper. Ara had spread a towel over the layer of cucumber, and a blanket on top of that. My teeth still chattered occasionally. We heard someone shut the kitchen door, but we didn't see Bing. We knew he would leave us alone for the rest of the evening.

Now and then Ara turned and put a log on the fire. She did this without letting go of my hand.

After saying nothing for a while I told Ara I was flying all the way across the Atlantic in order to finish it, to tell Thomas it was over. I told her I'd found out this afternoon, that I now knew what I was going for.

"Right," said Ara, "you go ahead and do that."

Then her face crumpled. Her upper lip began to tremble.

"He's going to miss you terribly," she said, and then: "You'll be finishing it with me next."

Her voice and her face were distorted with grief.

Her distress was painful to see. I reflected that she was the last person in the world to deserve such misery, and I was to blame, and I wanted desperately to be on her side, to be with her, part of her, so that I would not hurt her any more, so that she would have done with me and yet have me exactly where she wanted: in her heart and at her side. And at that point that was I wanted too, to merge with her, become one with her, vanish from the face of the earth and be in her until her body died and I was dead too. All I wanted to preserve were my own thoughts, and I knew that would be asking too much. That was what made it impossible.

After I had said that I would never ever leave her, that she meant everything in the world to me, that I adored her and that life was not worth living without her, she let go of me and covered her eyes with her hands.

I had never seen Ara cry properly, not with her body convulsed by the kind of spasms which I knew started in the belly and the chest, which cut your breath and drained the blood from your head, they were that powerful. I didn't know she had it in her to break down crying like this, nor that she could ever look so haggard. In a flash I understood what she meant when she used to say that showing her emotions wasn't her thing, that it didn't suit her.

It was true.

People like Ara show their sadness in their weight. Crying for them is superfluous.

Spilling cucumber slices left and right I flung my arms around her, pulled her onto the sofa, hugged her against my burnt skin, held her in my arms and waited with my heart in my throat for the grief to subside. I had the feeling I understood everything, that I knew everything about her and me, and for the first time it occurred to me that the possession of knowledge might offer something besides contentment. While I was thinking that I knew all about Ara and me, that I understood the nature of our friendship over all those years, I felt the stirring of a great, uncontrollable rage, which I would go on to unleash over Ara.

*

239

One remark was enough. She made it the evening before I left. She said: "I have always been amazed at your loyalty. It was incredible that you kept coming to see me."

"You aren't very subtle, are you?" I said trying to sound casual, but with everything I said after that my anger only increased and I wanted to blame her for everything that had ever gone wrong, including my relationship with Thomas. The longer I spoke the more I perspired, in my face and under my arms.

It was so hard.

It was so hard to put our history into a different perspective and to find a way of explaining to her what she had done to me.

Ara had so often complained that I was the sort of person who planned ahead, who liked structure and always knew what she was doing. It made her nervous, she said, to be confronted with the order and discipline in my head. I began my tirade by reminding her of this constant disparagement of my mental make-up, so that I could throw it back in her face by telling her that I had come to realize, during the past months, that all those times when I had felt insecure in our years together, sick with fear and revulsion and self-loathing because I had been made to grovel, it had been because of her, that it had finally sunk in that all this was part of a plan, an instinctive plan if she preferred, but a plan, a strategy, an understanding that was beyond me, a knowledge of how to dominate, how to get a suspicious, wilful animal exactly where she wanted it, which was at her feet, and that I could not describe how humiliating and hurtful it had been to hear her say she loved me so and at the same time that she did not trust me, and that during all those years she had been putting me to the test with provocations, challenges, experiments, with her ridiculous, insane, wounding rebuffals. That I always thought it was a moral tactic of hers, that her sense of morality was too exalted for the likes of me, that I was in effect not as good a person as she was, and that everything she did to me was inspired by lofty emotions and goodness on her part, by her insight into my weaknesses, my sins and my insincerity. That whenever she went into a huff or made fun of me, although I had no idea what I had done to deserve it, I always thought it was because she could see through me and that she was the only person in the world who was not fooled by my behaviour the way all those other morons were – no wonder I looked down on them: they didn't know me the way she did – and that she was therefore a superior sort of person, so highminded as to forgive me my dubious fidelity and to love me more than anyone else in the world. Not only that, her love was also on a higher plane, morally speaking. It was so incredibly stupid of me to have fallen right into her trap, to have believed that there was a logic, a moral, to her strategic cruelty and to regard this extraordinary logic as a sign of her love, as being cruel to be kind. I must have been out of my mind. The endless testing, being booted out of the way first and then patted on the back, being fed and kicked by turns. Go away, dog! Heel, dog! And there she was, doubting my love and my loyalty, as she had done for twenty years, which isn't that illogical when you think how she was always plotting ways of controlling that same love and loyalty. How could she have been so thick, for goodness sake? How could she not see that if you think you have to bully another person into loving you by drilling them you will only get out of it what you yourself put in, something of your own making? Which is the exact opposite of what you wished for. No wonder she didn't trust me. My behaviour was a perfect reflection of her own tactics and had nothing to do with me, but all the more with her, with the outcome of a calculation, a plan.

I did not calm down until I had told her I had realized all this when I was in bed with Thomas, when I had felt as if I was her, Ara, who was capable of such serene, shameless and confident caressing and who knew how to pleasure the body, without fear and reluctance, in such a way that it felt like true love, like something you could give away. I said that being with Thomas had made me realize you need a whole lot of love to be able to make that happen, but that from the moment I felt I was her all that loving had revealed itself as an almighty power that you wielded over someone, it made you feel inviolable seeing the effect of your caresses, sensing how willing the body became under your hands, under your mouth, in your mouth, under your body, knowing that you possessed the other person to the extent that a wiggle of the hips was enough to make him beg for more, for your body, for your touch, for it to go on for ever. I said it was shocking how simple it was, it was a game, a mighty game, that I had asked myself why I had felt as if I was her, and had discovered that it was because it was in my power to make someone hanker after me, and from now on I would refuse to let Thomas or indeed anyone else make me hanker after them, at least not in the same way, with the same tyranny, the same hysterics, the constant doubting of my loyalty, the wanting me and not wanting me year in year out. I was sick to death of this drama and intended to analyse it down to the last detail so that next time I would be prepared and would see to it that this absurd scenario had not the slightest effect on the course of my life.

Ara had not taken her eyes off me the whole time, while the tears ran down her face. Now she squared her shoulders, sniffed a few times and clapped her hands on her thighs.

I wanted to say one more thing. Something nice.

"You know," I said, to hold her attention a little longer, "it's also the first time I realized how much you actually loved me. The worst part is still to come, of course. I've got to find out why you were right, in a sense, why this was the ideal way for you to love me and for me to love you. Up to now it was easy. For us to be six of one and half a dozen of the other – that's hard to take."

She smiled.

"Why couldn't you love me and still trust me?" I asked.

"Because then you wouldn't have loved me, you beast."

7

DEAREST ARA,

I have not decided how to go about it yet, as I must still find the right tone. I want it to be different from the tone of your average academic discourse. My research concerns everyone, I believe, and I've had enough of writing articles that my mother can't read even though they deal with all sorts of things she's interested in. All those dull, plodding texts nobody reads but a bunch of dull, plodding ladies and gentlemen have come to repel me.

Writing is giving your mind another body.

Obviously I am not keen on displaying the body I am lumbered with, my own real blood-filled body, to the eyes of the world, and so I will make me a body of words, of paper.

That will be the body I send out into the world, and that is what other people may judge me by. I can handle that kind of criticism. I like being challenged, but not to my face. By exposing myself in this way I am only guarding against too much fear, shame, insecurity and betrayal.

There is nothing that strikes me as more deceitful, false and make-believe than the human body, and that includes mine. In my case the exterior is worse than the interior. Just asking for a loaf of bread at the baker's is enough to bring out the actress in me, the pretence, insincerity and betrayal. I find it difficult to describe what I mean and also to define how that feeling works, what brings it on and whether it is pathological, but it is a feeling I have often. I am also aware of the times that I don't have the feeling at all, that I am delivered from this fundamental unease, and that is what I have come to call intimacy.

I am intimate with you.

I feel right when I am with you. I would rather have you looking at me than anyone else, it makes me happy. The way you look at me, with your head full of knowledge about me, is reassuring and gratifying.

I try hard not to feel like a coward for having chosen to lead the life I lead. God, after all, also comes to us in the shape of a piece of bread, a gulp of wine and some words. We call them the tokens of His love for us and our token of love for Him is that we receive and consume those things.

I just don't feel at ease with people, really. It's ridiculous I know but I still find it hard to believe that film stars actually dare to be with their mouths so close together for such a long time, that they talk to each other, and can therefore smell each other's breath. And this is only a job they are doing, it is make-believe intimacy.

Until now I have been a dutiful student and have reconciled myself to the fact that scholarship more or less forces its disciples to produce a body of work that is not only dreary but that will dwell for ever in the pages of drab academic journals.

But it doesn't have to be that way. I am determined that the body I make will be attractive and will dwell in a welcoming home.

There was a time when beauty, goodness and truth, really went together.

*

Until now I have given only two styles of writing serious consideration. One of them is the rambling style of a women's magazine feature tackling a serious subject, the other is the epistolary style of a letter written to you. What they call a genre in literature and science is roughly the same as the gender of a text. Which means that there are particular expectations concerning the behaviour of a text, as if it has a body and a fate of its own and is destined to obey certain natural laws.

Not necessarily.

Genres can be modified by writing different texts for a change.

To write an essay in the form of a letter is going to be very difficult, it seems to me, but each time I succeed in explaining to you what my research is about and I can tell from your expression that you have understood everything I have been saying, I also feel a slight pang of regret, as if I have squandered all my precious material in talking to you and will never be able to write down all the things I said to you in the same way, the way I told them to you. All I have to show for my effort is your happiness. And that is not enough.

Maybe that is why you were indignant. If I write the way I want to write, it amounts to saying your happiness is not enough and that I want to make other people happy in the same way.

"You make me inclusive," you said.

So sweet.

I can understand your anxiety about what you call my sudden change of heart, but it is not as sudden as you make out. You told me once that your only rival was my notebook, and in a way you were right.

You have always been scared to death of any change in me, but change I must. There is no other way.

Thinking means changing your ideas.

That is all.

It is like cooking. You take raw ingredients and turn them into something digestible, and you try to make it taste good while you are at it.

I remember you used to talk about me contributing some spiritual nourishment, and I thought that was well put. Ideas are nourishment, and they serve the same purpose as real food. Thinking is necessary in order to survive, to arm yourself against suffering and to increase your happiness. It really makes a difference if you can bring yourself to change your idea of something and to acknowledge that your feelings have changed as a result.

It does complicate matters if you persist in admiring me for my ideas and yet forbid me to think them.

You say you don't want me to write about you, about us, that that is not what our friendship is for, you don't want to be researched nor do you fancy being directly addressed in a letter written for publication.

I know it hurts when I say that, as far as addiction is concerned, you are no different from anyone else. I dare to be so outspoken because I do not treat myself as unique in any respect neither do I make undeserved claims to being an exception.

When I have too much to drink I am like anyone else who has too much to drink, and the same goes for you when you eat too much.

Addiction has to do with boundaries. People who never stop thinking are probably more afraid of life than most other people. The protection provided by spiritual nourishment becomes a basic necessity.

Your eating has no bounds. You have made yourself a disproportionate body the better to guard yourself against the world.

You think the world is a scary place, too, scarier than I ever suspected.

I am sorry I never realized this before, sweetie. Now that I have left Thomas I can see the three of us for what we were: three sick, scared people. It seems we always underestimate the fear of others because we want them to be less afraid than we are.

Do you remember when I was trying to explain what philosophy means and I said there were only two ways in which philosophers view themselves, the world, and everything in it (including God)?

I told you that according to one view the world is in your head and according to the other it is outside.

When I was little I used to get a queasy feeling in my stomach because I lacked the words to turn what was in effect an intuition into a sort of knowledge, and later on I saw that it stood for the difference between you and me: you regarded the world as something that lay outside you and I had the world in my head.

You and I switch cause and effect.

Someone asked me recently why I am so preoccupied with guilt and innocence. I will tell you. In my view I am always partly if not wholly guilty. It is infuriating to discover that other people are less bothered, or indeed not bothered at all, by a guilty conscience.

Unlike you, I am not concerned about putting the world to rights. I don't train dogs and I don't protect their rights, I don't go around with blind people, I don't take action against farmers maltreating their cattle and I have never stuck my neck out for nature conservation.

I don't weed gardens.

I couldn't give you the first bit of advice about how you should love Bing.

But my thoughts change all the time.

You're right about that.

It is not even to my credit that I believe I am the only person who is truly within my power. Because what applies to me applies to everyone else too. I believe each individual is the only person truly within his or her own power. What makes life so heavy is the helplessness, the innocence and the dependence, and those areas interest me just as much as the area of guilt. What I see happening in addiction is that the two areas get mixed up, that guilt blends with innocence. That is the type of complexity that appeals to me.

Addiction is a friendship without a friend.

I want desperately to understand. And I want to explain it all to you properly.

That's the way I am I suppose, I fancy the role of tutor, teaching other people how they can change their thoughts. You can learn to think, to a point, and that is where I would like to exert influence, to provide input, so to speak, but the input would not come from me personally, but from books.

Now that it is over with Thomas I am certain that I do not want to work as a therapist, I do not want a job that obliges me to be with people all the time. I want to spend a lot of time alone, in a room, and I want to send books out into the world in place of me. And despite my powerlessness, I make the usual philosopher's claim to a noble motive: I say I want to do this to make other people happy, among other things.

It is difficult for me to imagine anyone seeing their body as an instrument of happiness. Words, ideas and stories determine what we perceive and how we experience things, I believe, and that goes for the body, too.

You have made your body exceptional, and it distinguishes you from other people. Do you remember how you felt as if there was not enough of you when you had lost weight?

"There's not enough of me left," you said.

Later on I understood that it was not a matter of size, but of distinction. You had become more like other people, you no longer tipped the scales and so you were less special. What there was less of was in fact your language. You always treated your body as an instrument of communication, as something that sent out messages and that was what distinguished you from other people.

That is what fat people do.

Like Thomas you want everyone to see right off that you are different. With your size you are saying you are afraid of being overlooked and unrecognized. The question is what you want recognition for. And it is painful to have to ask yourself that question.

Too much food makes you fat.

Too much drink makes you drunk.

Thinking means reducing things to their most simple components. Addiction can be understood in terms of what you do to yourself by consuming substances. People who eat too much alter their appearance, their exterior, their body. People who drink too much alter the interior, the inside, the words, the mind.

Do you think I am making things too simple, with all this talk of inside and outside?

Sometimes I worry about that.

I can get really mad about having to make such strict divisions in order to understand things, such as fate and choice, mind and body, and so on. What keeps coming back is that you have to combine the two in order to discover what it's all about, why it's so complicated. I didn't really understand this until the physics lectures I attended. About Einstein, they were. What it boils down to is that explaining highly complex phenomena like light, for example, requires combining two concepts that are contradictory and impossible to relate to each other.

Understanding that got me into my usual excited state.

Light is impossible to understand if you insist on one single explanation. You need two.

That's wonderful, isn't it?

You could say that relationships give meaning to our lives and also that relationships are burdens.

Roughly speaking I think it's like this: people distinguish themselves from animals by their relationships. People have more relationships than animals and the extra relationships are what makes human existence difficult. What people have extra is abstract, it consists in language, in meaning.

No animal relates to God, to a self, to death, to the name of the Father. People do. People are conscious of themselves and of death, and coming to terms with this is not easy.

Like family, death is fate.

There's nothing you can do about that. Neither can be avoided. They create the conditions for life. Each birth engenders another death.

Hardly a day goes by without my searching happily for the words that make up complex notions, savouring each in turn and promising myself that I will link them together handsomely, so that they will have meaning.

Family, the body, death and fate belong together, and their mirror image is friendship, the mind, life and choice. They appear to cancel each other out, but to find what I am looking for you must bring them together, a bit like the outside and inside in philosophy.

I will try to explain this properly.

I know you will enjoy that.

The words of literature and philosophy hold more attraction for me than the words of psychology. The difficulty I have with terms like frustration, denial, transference, suppression and projection is so enormous that I sometimes wonder how I ever managed to finish my degree.

Emotion is different.

Emotion is a word I have always liked. I like the motion: *e* plus *movere* means to move something outside.

Probably what I did from the start was nothing but translate what I had been reading into a language and a story I could lay at your feet.

I am glad you were my first reader, long before I started writing.

"I get my reading through you," you said.

You consider yourself verbally handicapped, but I always found that you expressed your thoughts very clearly. Even on the verbal level I ascribed a purity to you that I myself did not possess. You had natural wisdom, instinctive knowledge, an animal mind uncorrupted by theories, a vocabulary of your own making. You had no plan, no blueprint, no fear, no intentions but the best.

But I don't believe that any more, as you know.

Sometimes I think it is a shame, but mostly I don't. The change in me is too far-reaching for me to want to turn the clock back.

If you don't leave me I won't leave you, but I will never allow you to have so much power over me again. Power is the word.

There are days when I wonder why I am feeling so well, so strong, and then I suddenly remember I have effected a coup.

I can only forgive you your loving trespasses by reminding myself that I am no better than you.

Ever since I was a child I wondered why I seemed to be the only person in the world that was so desperately eager to bond with someone. Now I can see that the desire for bonding does not necessarily mean you have the ability to bond, nor does it mean that if someone rebuffs you and keeps you at a distance that person is necessarily more independent, more confident, more self-disciplined than you, and does not dream of a bond, but that the person concerned is simply finding it all very difficult too.

You can't get things the way you want them either, not the way you would like them to be in your dreams.

Our dreams were vivid. You and I wanted something special. And we got it, but it is never enough. Emotions are ideals, too.

Since I started thinking about emotions being ideals I have stopped thinking my own desires might be outmoded.

I often think it takes me too long to understand things.

What it is that makes me so angry at times I have yet to discover, but my anger is considerable. As usual it is not aimed directly at you, Thomas, my family or God, but I am furious at another impostor, a nameless drifter who is nowhere and everywhere, for having surreptitiously drawn me into the kind of dream that makes me long for something that does not exist. Not like in the dream.

I can't stand being cheated.

You used to call me a kamikaze queen, but all I want to kill off are certain dreams, myths, words, images and a couple of under-mining, sickening, overly promising stories.

If it is true that addiction brings about an inner or outer distortion, then there must be some connection with all those ideals and stories and probably even with the telling of them or, more generally speaking, with the way of expression, the means of communication, with what I will call language.

We crave meaning because we are born with language.

I think we inflict damage on ourselves because we want to make ourselves immune to a desire, an ideal, a story. We deny ourselves the right and even the chance of future happiness. We do not expect it to come our way. By damaging ourselves we are giving our fate a little jolt, which is something at least. We would rather make ourselves unattractive than have others pass judgement on our looks, our worth and our meaning. We would rather be fat, drunk, unfaithful or unhappy, than take on the important, scary issues and work towards an ideal which we cherish and for which we seek recognition from others.

I think you yourself demand recognition by means of your body, because you don't dare to demand it on an intellectual level.

Seen in that perspective the reason I drink is that I am beset with dreams about physical desires which I don't dare realize. Being visible makes me uncomfortable.

Addictions bind you to your own shortcomings, and there lies the tragedy. It is a friendship with your own weakness.

Being in love with Thomas I expected a great eruption of nature, an overwhelming passion that would leave both him and me defenceless, but loving is a matter of power, art, culture, a delicate task at which you either become proficient or not. The myth of intimacy being equal to nature and sex was what I had to demolish now. Nothing is more widely lied about than sex and sensuality, by women as well as men. I know that now.

Yet addiction is also anarchy, rebellion against this ideal, against the powerlessness, and the dependence on the judgement of others.

The first glasses of wine invariably give me a delicious sense of independence, a refreshing, almost gleeful destructiveness, a sense of being free to take my life in my own hands, to destroy it or do anything I please without anyone stopping me.

But it is a mistaken sort of anarchy. It is also possible to demolish the story that the longing has kindled in you, instead of doing damage to yourself. Since I tracked down the myth about intimacy and the lie about gender I have got better at controlling my drinking.

I have turned the searching, analysing, and interpreting of roving stories into my profession, Ara.

Thomas was heavy and so are you. I like that. I admire you for daring to expose so much body to view and taking up all that space, as I am incapable of those things.

In order to understand things you have to reduce them to simple components. In my book I want to reduce the different types of addiction to a form of behaviour, an object and an effect. What all addictions have in common I call hunger.

All obsessive and addictive behaviour is a form of boundless consumption. Consuming is taking in from the outside, absorbing and using. The part you use I call food.

Never mind whether it is consumption of alcohol, drugs, money, tobacco or women, I call them all food.

Otherwise it is impossible to grasp.

I am particularly intrigued by the inward movement, the passage from exterior to interior. This is contrary to emotion, expression, bringing out what is inside. Addiction is contrary to those things too. It is aimed at the destruction of emotion, understanding and fulfilment.

What I call hunger is the longing for expression and what can go wrong is when the expression is successful on the wrong level.

Your body speaks the language of the flesh, the forbidden language of your sadness or other emotions. What could have become more words has become more flesh.

Drinking is the same, but the other way round. Drunks have trouble expressing themselves with their bodies and rob themselves of their prime means of expression: speech.

Their speech gets slurred. They are unable to combine body and words in a straightforward manner, just like fat people. My forbidden language is the language of the body. I don't want anything about me to show. In fact I would rather not be seen at all.

Addicts feel they are two-faced and that they are always betraying part of themselves, that they are hiding part of the story, the true story, from the rest of the world.

Alas.

If only we were true to our own one-faced selves. No body no mind, no mind no body.

I cherish the friendship between mind and body. I wish you and I could be together always, for as long as we live.

The story that tormented me and that I took for my ideal is the story of an intellectual bond, of an intimacy so great that you sacrifice your body willingly.

Your addiction tells you which sacrifice you are prepared to make, for it is precisely that part of you that you will be betraying.

You betray the hunger of your mind and I betray the hunger of my body.

It always revolves around the same thing: a hankering after meaning, after the truth if you like. Compare it with a good sentence and the pleasure that can give. A good sentence is true. You have succeeded in establishing the correct link between the individual words and their abstract, intellectual meaning. You have succeeded in expressing yourself. No betrayal, no shame.

I know how happy this can make you.

Just a small dose of the truth is enough to make you happy, Ara. So never mind if it doesn't go very far. There will always be more to come.

I have divided the effects of an addiction into expenses and gains, although the two do overlap in the oddest way, as when the cost of addiction is seen as gain.

It is not going to be too difficult for me to lift addiction onto a philosophical plane and to regard it as a problem connected with paradox, free choice and other mental gymnastics which some people are better at than others.

If thinking can give joy, it can also cause grief and pain. I like to think in animal terms. I want to be absolutely sure that it can make you ill and unhappy if you stop thinking and choosing and making up your own mind.

Family and death are what I call Fate, as they stand for relationships and consequently for distinctions that you get for free. They are not distinctions you have to work at. You are born, you are the daughter of your father and mother, the sister of your sisters and brothers and you are mortal. All that is certain and it is all distinctive. They are distinctions that cannot be shaken off.

Family lasts for ever.

Not everyone would agree, but the way I see it, that is precisely what gives it the greatest beauty and the most lasting value. You can never not be daughter, sister, mortal.

To some extent this is a comfortable and easy fate, as easy as being a victim. You are not accountable. You did not choose to be born nor did you choose to spend your early years being loved in a particular way. Love can take the form of chips with frankfurters and also of a good hiding: children take things in their stride.

When I was little my father would tiptoe upstairs when he got in late from work and my brothers and me had been in bed for hours. His sound on the stairs would wake me, as I was only dozing until he came home. He would put his head round my door and whisper urgently that it was very late, that I should have been fast asleep long ago.

"All right then," he would say, "I'll make a nice little house for you."

Without touching my face he would take the sides of my pillow and pull them up tight against my ears.

"There you are, you can go to sleep now," he would say.

But how could I sleep now, terrified as I was of spoiling the little house he had so lovingly built, and I would stay wide awake for the next hour, not daring to move my head until I got a cramp in my neck.

I believe addictions can arise on the side of fate as well as in that other area, that of free will, and I believe that is what differentiates them.

What I call writing with your body belongs to the side of family and death. This is a conservative addiction. It holds the promise of physical, sensual gratification: food, sex, smell, touch. Becoming fat or thin, tattooing the body, hairdos and dress, seduction, sex, they all mean tinkering with fate, family and death. Conservative addictions are, I believe, always a message to the family.

Friendship, spiritual nourishment, the way you give shape to your life are all located on the other side. They are chosen commitments and consequently chosen distinctions. They don't make you any less dependent, but the dangers this dependence brings are not the same as those on the side of fate and family and death.

The addictions that arise on the free-will side are destructive, psychological and hold the promise of altering the mind. Destructive addictions are a message to chosen loved ones.

Parents can abuse their children or neglect them, but that doesn't leave them without the distinction of being the son or daughter of that father and mother.

The terrifying danger in the free-will type of addiction is: if you leave me, I will lose distinction, I will no longer be Ara Callenbach's friend.

That is why I call relationships the drama of dependence.

No one wants it to be like that.

We all have an animalistic desire for autonomy, but if you want a human existence you must deal with the desire for bonding and distinction. It is your desire to be human.

Only animals are autonomous beings, people aren't.

Now I am afraid you will lose interest, that my letter is too long and does not warrant your attention, that it does not engage you enough for you to stay with me. Shall I spoil you with a story all about you, for you alone?

That night when I came to you after getting back from New York and leaving Thomas, I crawled into bed with you.

I could not cry.

Very slowly a feeling which I can only describe as a sense of death crept up on me. It was as if he curled his body around mine and made love to me. The sensation was strongest in my skin, which tingled with an increasing, scary intensity.

The other feeling was in my head, as if my brain was ice-cold. Not unpleasant, actually, but a bit like the tingling, almost too intense.

I suddenly looked hollow-eyed, as if I was going authentistic – that's what you said. I didn't even notice that you had given the word your own little twist. I believe I said I thought I was dying.

And that I couldn't move. You put your arms around me. I remember perfectly. Then you hugged me and dragged me onto your lap, and I felt my body go limp, as if it had already been transported to another place and was no longer mine. You rocked me for hours, you said my name over and over again, Catherina, Kit, and you also called me darling, sweetie, little thing, and little beast. You said stay here, don't leave me, don't ever die.

I did not realize it then, Ara, but that has become one of my most cherished memories.

I finished it with Thomas in a restaurant on 24th Street. We were having steak and French fries. Thomas stared at his plate and avoided my eyes. He ate greedily, as if he was famished. Soon his plate was almost empty and I saw his mounting panic at the emptiness, his fear of not having anything left on his plate, of having nothing to do. I could see how scared he was of the inevitable moment when all the food would be gone, when there would be nothing for it but to face me.

Without glancing in my direction he drew himself up, called the waiter and ordered another portion of the same. By the time his second plate arrived I had told him that I did not want this relationship, that I no longer wanted to live with him.

All addictions are attempts to satisfy the longing for friendship without being dependent on another living soul. Addiction is hunger for the distinction of being a friend without having to go through the drama of dependence with real people and without living in constant fear of that friendship ending.

People who eat or drink too much make themselves dependent on something that is always available and that will never let them down. It is a chosen companionship, with the promise of an everlasting bond. To be addicted is to long for the ties of the family, for escape from the demands made by a life of self-determination.

Addicts want the impossible, they want bondage and they want their independence at the same time, and the odd thing is that they get it, too.

But the cost is heavy.

And there is no gain, not in the way of truth, distinction, or love. Worse than that, it is those things that you expose to that most dreaded loss: death.

The day I left my village I had only one aim: to get as far away as possible from the point I had reached in my life. To be gone, to leave everything behind and never return. It was probably on the same day that a different longing stirred in me, a longing to throw caution to the wind and plunge into this dizzying warm tangle of goodness and craziness again, to ally myself anew – by choice this time – with someone and to share that person's fate and to care about them as desperately and love them as helplessly as I love my parents and my brothers.

The bond of friendship, of marriage, means becoming family of your own free will, and for that you must give your word.

Growing up was a painful business: I prefer adulthood. The only certainty I have in the boundless domain of liberty is that bonds are forged by giving your word. Keeping your word is the only way of preserving your humanity.

The chapter about the cost of addiction will be the most controversial of my dissertation.

There is a price to be paid for addiction. I don't mean the money, not the literal expense. The heaviest price of all is, as usual, the lightest, the most elusive. How am I going to prove that it's all about losing something as elusive as meaning, value, fulfilment and happiness?

How am I to prove that addiction is, in a manner of speaking, the same as the desire for truth, for the solution of a paradox or duality, and that the way in which this desire is satisfied is what gives rise to the paradox, the duality, the lies and the grief?

And how am I to explain that the damage done by addiction lies in the very sphere of the greatest dreams, and that each addict damages his own means of temptation, merely by giving in to it?

Food is gone once you have eaten it. It is no longer there to control you and tempt you, but you can't love it either.

All this is not getting any easier to put down on paper.

Addicts have the wrong idea. They crave a dose of something that cannot be self-administered. You can't have a relationship with yourself, nor can you have love, respect or admiration unless there is someone there with you. Some of the most fundamentally human experiences take place only between and among people, they are never confined to a solitary individual. Love, respect and admiration can only exist in an in-between space, in the rarefied atmosphere of a mutual bond. Nowhere else.

The most human part of you can only be given and received.

Your rating on the market, like that of currency, will be fixed by others.

The most terrible cost of addiction is that you betray this meaningful bond each time you vanish into the illusion of autonomy.

I have a long way to go yet, but I am sure there is nothing better for me to do in the next few years than to write it all down and see if the academic worthies will swallow it. I do not even care much if they do. So long as you approve of what I have done.

As for my book, I wish you would change your mind. I cannot rob you of anything that is not yours. My own history of our friendship is not your private property. It is like the letters I sent you: all those sheets of paper are yours, but the contents are mine. It is these extraordinary bonds that I want to write about, that's all.

It has got late again.

Now I am going to bed, Ara.

I love you.

Without you I am a lesser being.

If I stick up my index finger in the air for you here, will you do the same for me where you are?